# GL TCH
## Time

*Saving dystopia book one*

Brona Mills

# Copyright

Copyright © 2022 Brona Mills

Edited by: Fen Raven.

Edited by: Emily A. Lawrence of Lawrence Editing.

Cover Design: Brona Mills with canva.com

Formatted: Brona Mills

This is a work of fiction. Names, characters, businesses, places, events, and incidents are either products of the author's imagination or used in a fictitious manner. Any resemblance to actual persons, living or dead, or actual events is purely coincidental.          First published 2022

Brona Mills

# Contents

Brona Mills

# Acknowledgements

To everyone who has given me kind words and support on this author journey—who has been excited with each milestone. Thank you! You made it easier to keep typing out the words!

# Chapter
## one

Dystopian lands, UK

13th December 2042

### Erin

Some people are nervous when they leave a camp to hunt. The only thing that scares me right now is riding in this petrol bomb of a car. Like actual flammable petrol you use in weapons. Basically, we're sitting in a bomb, hoping it will get us where we need to go.

No wonder the government only took electric vehicles to the resource centres. Everything else is a ticking, rusting health hazard.

Mum says cars aren't the dangers I should worry about, but this far from London, Apostle patrols are few.

The adults in the group are the most cautious. The most nervous about the missions. The most depressed. At twenty years old, I am technically an adult. I just don't remember life like they do.

This is my normal life.

'Pull off the road and into those trees.' Garvey points left, and Mark turns. We don't use vehicles much because black-market petrol is scarce, and we keep that resource for defence weapons. London had the sense to keep innovating electric

7

vehicles. Petrol cars are loud. People can hear us coming for miles, so we have to ditch them often.

Garvey and Mark, in front, are in their late forties and old enough to remember what driving was like before the world changed. The four of us in the back are happy to let them drive most of the time.

Originally built for only five people, it's hot with the six of us squeezed in. Ollie volunteered to ride in the boot, which is risky considering he can't open it from inside for a quick escape.

My brother, Blake, asks, 'What are we looking for when we get there?'

He's nervous. His girlfriend, Lara, is two years younger than us and usually only scavenges on food hunts, not intel. She's been pushing for more responsibility, and Blake insisted on tagging along for her first gig.

'Mark's with me at the main house,' Garvey tells him. 'You and the others will go to the outhouses and barns, see what you can find that you can carry and note things we might come back to collect in the Jeep if we have time.'

There's a breeze when we step out of the car, but it's warmer than we're used to up north. Three days of travel to our temporary camp and now this drive, and we are all sweaty and dirty, but the adrenaline of a mission keeps us on our toes. Mark turns the red Jeep around and slowly reverses it into shrubs to keep it out of sight. Would have been better if we could have found a vehicle in working order with a more neutral colour, but we take what we can get.

After checking our weapons, we form a circle and wait for the go-ahead. Sweat is rolling down my back. Winters are usually colder than this. Even this little bit south, you can feel the temperature change. Nothing like London, though. London is like hell on fire. Which is a pretty accurate description all round. I check the knife strapped to my left leg and tap the gun on my right. Ammo is in my back pocket, pushing through my ass since we've been riding for an hour. Off-road driving is a bitch. Hell, driving is a bitch. All the roads at this end of the country are broken and uneven, and you have to watch out for fallen branches or the forest growing out of the ground. Plus, riding in a car bomb.

No wonder the world came crashing down. People did stupid shit, like each owning a car. What must it have been like, living with millions of people? Sixty million used to live in the UK, Mum told us. Now it's just under eight, and the majority are in London.

We often come across stragglers who managed to escape the tyranny of living in the capital. Friend or foe—it's hard to tell. We need to be careful wherever we go, especially since the UK government—NewGov, as the unelected dictators call themselves—has no problem adding to the mass graves around the country.

Crossing the border at Gretna Green into England was the quickest route to take for this mission, but instead of the historical wedding town Mum told us it used to be, it's a landmark of bodies. Fourteen years after the general public were killed and dumped at the border, their bodies are still decomposing. You can smell them for miles. It's a reminder that NewGov values resources more than people. They filled mass graves with the bodies of those they poisoned so they could save resources. Oh yeah, and keep the earth from overheating and the core spilling out volcanic ash to melt everyone and everything on it.

Everybody is silent when we pass the graves. It's a reminder of how lucky we are that we get to pass them and weren't tossed in.

A large section of our group is based in Scotland. Gretna Green is the farthest north mass grave we've come across. It was almost like the English couldn't be bothered to trek any farther over the border to look for runaways. You'd think they would, with the weather being milder there. And the land more habitual. If they got out of their egos a little, they would have realised the whole country of Scotland was a place where people could easily survive, even thrive, in hiding. The Welsh mountains too.

Garvey was a special services soldier before the world changed. He spent time training in both places. The elements could be tough when he was a young soldier in training, and he figured the politicians in London had no clue how determined some people were to stay alive, so he taught us. Scotland, Wales, and the northern parts of England became our usual hiding spots. He helped many people. He thinks it's time to start Plan B. He wants to put the shitty world back together.

Daylight shines through the trees, and we're close enough to the road that I can see the grass between the craters big enough to crack a tyre open if you're not careful.

The only good thing about London and its perimeter is that the Apostle soldiers maintain those roads.

I smell last night's rain in the trees and the ground is damp under my boots. It's a wet winter. These are better than the cold ones, but only when we have decent shelter and provisions.

We might be five miles north of Darlington town and three from our destination, but with the Apostle training grounds nearby, it would be stupid if we didn't consider they might be nearby.

We're on the outskirts of the town where Garvey used to live. A large army garrison is close. NewGov has taken control of it as their Apostle's soldier training base. Training and torture, as Ollie tells it.

We're going to a nearby property to see if there is any truth to a tip we got last month. The old guy who runs the clothing dispatch in Manchester is a rebel at heart and tries to pass information to Garvey when he can. You would think the person running the mechanical town in Northampton, or the weapons storage facilities in Swindon, would have more intel, but the soldiers there are on high alert. The ones who collect the clothes orders, however, are loose-lipped. They're not supposed to take any resources that aren't on their list, but no one stops an Apostle soldier or reports them. They dig around the warehouses and homes for anything they can get to impress people in London. Shooting the shit and giving away information that our assets piece together and hand over to the rebels willingly. Garvey trades for information, offering things the compounds might need, but some of the old guys just want the rebels to win. They don't need any bribes.

Our group freezes and drops to the ground when we hear a vehicle. Lara is a second behind us, but Blake yanks her down in decent time. It's easy to hear cars and trucks moving around since there are no other sounds. She needs to learn to focus better.

Garvey said it was hard to hear specific things in the past. Everyone drove places, kids screamed, the farms were full of animals. Radios and TVs could be heard down the street. The world has gone quiet, which means we hear better. But they can also hear us. We crouch and quickly move deeper into the woods.

Mark stays near the road, but after a few minutes, he joins us. 'All clear. One van, with at least two soldiers, moving south. They didn't slow down.'

Garvey stays low and whispers his instructions, 'High-value NewGov officials rumoured to be here. Gather info only. No capture, no kill until we know more. There is power running through the barn, so, Ollie, you need to check out what they're hiding there.'

'I want to come up to the house,' I say.

Garvey shakes his head. 'I don't enjoy changing a plan last minute.'

11

'You need someone else to watch your rear. Two of you heading into the main house while four of us scavenge is a waste of resources. Let's split into three and three.'

'She knows what she's doing,' Mark says.

Garvey and I turn to Mark, but I beat him to the punch.

'I don't need you sticking up for me. I'm more than capable of explaining myself.'

Blake scoffs at Mark, and Garvey kills the argument before it even begins. 'Enough. I need you to work together on this. Leave the personal shit and do as you're told. Erin, you want to do something more? Then you take the lead on the outhouses with Ollie behind you. Mark can hold up the rear with Lara and teach her what she should be looking for. Blake and I are at the house.' Garvey looks at us, and we nod in understanding.

Blake hesitated with his confirmation.

'If you didn't think she was capable, she shouldn't be here,' Garvey tells Blake.

Lara snorts.

Blake nods. 'She is. I'm having trouble not being her backup.'

'Get used to it. We all had to let our loved ones fly the nest at one point,' Garvey says. 'Silence from here on out. Let's move.'

The three-mile route is planned to be done in twenty-five minutes, which means a brisk pace. Mostly farmland is between us and the property we are aiming for, which gives us cover through the trees and in the grass but also leaves a trail.

I pick out markers along the way, like Garvey taught me when I was a kid.

Mark hangs back, pointing out landmarks to Lara. He's the most capable of backing her up in this environment.

Mark's natural scowl, his big build, tattoos, and dirt scare off a lot of the people we come across. He looks exactly like what the Apostle soldiers say we are: savages, killers, terrorists. He's also my mum's new husband. Since our world is small, and our numbers are dwindling, Dad has no problem keeping Mark around, no matter how much Blake and I bitch about him. Guess that's what he had to do when his best friend married his ex-wife. Suck it up and keep on fighting.

The sun tells me it's about midday. A good time for surveillance, since workers wind down for lunch and may even leave things unlocked or unguarded. It's rare to have any rebels this close to a heavily guarded compound. I'm sure we'll live. We mostly do. But anyone we take down in the fight will be used against us in propaganda. Keep the population scared enough of us that they will stay in London and under NewGov control. Better the devil you know and all that.

Garvey slows and drinks water, and I do the same. I learned a while ago that your best chance of survival is to do what Garvey does. Rest when he does, eat when he does, and always run when Garvey runs.

Back at camp, two escape routes were planned from what Garvey remembered of the nearby town. He signals to the left, showing a route that will lead us to the north end of Darlington. With no people in town that are trustworthy, if we're compromised, it will be a hundred-mile trek home. Possibly alone.

I nod at Blake, assuring him I won't leave Lara alone if anything goes wrong. It's the perk of being a twin. Blake and I hardly need to speak. We know each other's looks and movements so well, we can communicate in silence.

Mum was less than pleased when Blake and I got called up to the fighting units at fifteen. It's her fault, really. She made sure we could protect ourselves. Guess she didn't realise how good we would get. That's what Garvey does. He takes people in and teaches them how to survive and fend for themselves. He doesn't want people blindly falling in line behind him. He wants

13

people to branch out, be able to lead a camp. Rebuild a community that can flourish.

NewGov would kill us all to stop that from happening.

We've lost countless people along the way, but I'm lucky. My parents and brother are still alive. I don't know what it's like to lose people, except through divorce. Because even after the world ended, people still broke up.

I used to like Mark—he's been with us for as long as I can remember—but now he's a reminder of a broken family. And a reminder that I'm not a kid anymore. I'm an adult who should be falling in love, then getting married. Instead, there's only time for survival. I'm sometimes jealous of the older ones, who remember when love was enough. Being alive and free is hard work. It comes at a price. We have to put up with the dwindling resources left on the abandoned island of what was once the UK. It's mostly a dystopian land.

London is where everyone lives. Where the supplies, power, technology, and food are. And the soldiers.

People ran there at the start of the war, looking for salvation, responding to rumours of safe water and medical care. What they didn't realize was that their government was culling the population. London was safe, but they were never allowed to leave.

Twenty minutes into the run, and the only sounds are tree leaves moving in the wind and the birds. We take care not to disturb too many of them, or their sudden flight might alert an observant soldier that something is moving through the woods.

At least there are no homes out here for us to pass. It's always slower as we sweep them and make sure no one is watching from a window.

The six of us cover a lot of ground swiftly. We're used to moving as an efficient unit. Normally we go out in pairs to hunt for animals. Two pairs, if we're sneaking into a city to steal supplies from the warehouses. A unit of six is big for us. I think it's why Garvey insisted Mark come along. Despite their differences, Mark is one of the best the rebels have. Garvey sent the rest of the camp to our friends in the Scottish Islands' houses. We've only retreated there a few times over the years, when things gave Garvey cause to fall back or we needed to heal.

We spot the home easily enough. The flowers in the window boxes are the rub-your-face-in-it sign NewGov agents use to show the rest of their work compound they can afford such luxuries and water to keep them fresh. The pristine roof, without a crack or a hole in it, is a dead giveaway.

The farmhouse sits on high ground, with a road out front and a driveway circling the property. We come in from the rear, after crossing fields and fallow land. The house has a great three-hundred-and-sixty-degree view of its surroundings. We'll need to move fast if we want to get up there without being spotted.

Garvey and Blake break into a run, keeping low, and veer off to the house on the right. A five-hundred metre dash by the looks of it. The rest of us have a longer run to the barn and outhouses on the left. Six hundred metres maybe. I glance at Ollie, who's behind me. Mark already has his machine gun drawn and is giving Blake and Garvey cover.

'Break into two,' I tell them, and Ollie follows me as I run for the nearest barn.

After we reach the green steel walls of the sheds, we draw our weapons to cover Mark and Lara, who join us shortly.

'We have ten minutes to assess what's here, then make our way to the back of the house. Don't take any animals. We don't need to draw attention to our presence yet.'

Lara and Mark move to the left of the building, checking out the walls and other points of entry.

Ollie checks the barn door, confused. 'There's no lock,' he whispers.

I move over to him, expecting to see a standard lock instead of an electronic one we assumed Ollie would have to hack for us, but there's only a regular bolt and hook.

Mark and Lara are back in less than a minute. He shakes his head at me. There are no other points of entry.

I move the bolt back slowly. It doesn't squeak or squeal with the strain of metal on metal like you'd expect. Someone's been keeping this greased and silent.

Mark places his hand over mine to stop me and shakes his head sternly. He doesn't want us to go in, but fuck it. I'm in charge, not him.

I glance pointedly at his hand and back at his face. He steps back. I raise my weapon. The others follow my lead, and Mark takes up the rear, gun ready like a good soldier, doing what he's told.

The steel door slips open easily, and Ollie and Mark move in with Lara and me behind them.

Inside, we cover all corners, scanning the room. We're alone.

'There's nothing here,' I hiss. Literally nothing. No machinery or animals, and no supplies. It's a ninety-square-foot shed that's completely empty.

A small circle of sparkling electricity is in the centre of the barn. It's small enough to fit in the palm of my hand. When I get closer, I see it has three even lines of electricity coming from the front, left, and right of the circle, all perfectly aligned.

'What the hell is that?' Lara asks.

'Don't touch it,' Mark says.

Ollie puts his backpack on the ground and searches through it.

I crouch for a better view. I have no idea what Ollie might have in his bag that could help us figure out what this device is. It's not connected to anything. It's not a bomb or mine that I've ever seen before. I float my hand over it, and the electricity brightens and sparks out like a slow reaching current. When I look up at the others, we're encased in darkness.

# two

Darlington, UK

13th December 2018

### Erin

Weapons raised, waiting for an attack, we form a circle around the electrical device with our backs to each other. We can see each other clearly, but everything else is pure black. It's as if our surroundings have disappeared and left us in complete nothingness.

'What's going on?' Lara whispers.

'The door is seven paces in front of Lara,' I say.

'I agree,' Mark says. 'Move now.'

We move toward the exit, but once there, Mark says he can't feel the wall.

Turning around, I see Ollie's backpack on the ground where he dropped it. It's ten feet behind us. I can see that but not the floor under my feet.

I nod to Mark and then to the backpack, and we move toward it and the tiny source of electricity.

At the place where the device should have been, my boot connects with something small. I press on it ever so slightly, and the lights come back on in the world.

We all take in the surroundings and make sure we're secure again. Nothing has changed. The barn walls are still intact. The floor is visible again and, more importantly, there's no one there killing us.

As a unit, we go to the exit and listen. There is traffic outside. More than one vehicle is passing the main road or driving up to the house.

'Shit,' Mark says. 'We need to get Garvey and Blake out.' Opening the barn door, we stay low and slip out.

There are animals in the field we just crossed. 'Why the hell are there cattle?' I whisper. 'All livestock are supposed to be in Surrey.'

'Something's wrong.' Mark's looking past the main house at the road.

Every ten seconds or so, a vehicle goes by at high speed. The houses at the bottom of the hill appear well-kept and lived in. All roofs are intact, and there are curtains at the windows.

Homes should have been stripped of all resources. NewGov proudly stated it only took them ten years to gather and categorise everything of use. Ready for the next hundred years if need be.

Mark looks around the fields. Lara stares at the cows and sheep in the farmlands next to us and beyond. 'Are those horses in the distance?'

'Looks like it,' Mark says.

'We were only inside a few minutes,' Ollie says, 'and this place was deserted when we got here.'

I order the group to move two by two towards the house. Staying low, we edge the shrubbery, which used to be a property line. Once we have cover of the gable wall, we take positions at the window.

It looks like no one is living there. Typical for some abandoned houses to be preserved for potential use by NewGov officials. Not every home was stripped. Some key places were left alone, furniture covered by sheets, and this is obviously one of them.

I make a forward hand signal to Mark, and we move to the front of the property. Waiting at the edge of the house, I freeze when I hear the gates at the bottom of the drive open.

Shit. We won't make it to the front door without being seen.

We move back along the side of the house and wait. 'We have to see how many Apostles are coming and then get Garvey and Blake out. We might need to use force, but let's see how it goes.'

Two cars pull into the driveway. The movements of the tyres on the gravel sound like they are close behind each other.

But the footfall is light. Only two doors close shut behind those that exit. One person per car is prolific, even for the high-ranking NewGov officials.

Mark pulls out a small hand-held mirror and hands it to me. When I move forward, he follows at my shoulder with his gun aimed.

One male and one female are looking out to the view of the road. No one else waits in the cars. The woman is pointing to the road and gives directions to locations I'm unfamiliar with. They are both dressed in clean clothes and look immaculate. They can't work at the resource centres—those people have less than we do. These people must have driven directly from London.

Mark taps me on the shoulder to switch places. 'The house is up for sale. There's a sign at the bottom of the driveway. Looks like an estate agent is showing someone around.'

'What the hell does that mean?' I ask.

'No one buys houses anymore, but I'm just telling you what it looks like. Something is very wrong here.'

It takes half an hour for the man and woman to walk around the home and inspect the rooms before they get back in their well-kept cars and leave. We enter the house and look for Garvey and Blake, but there's no sign of them, their entry or exit. Not that there would be. They're good at covering their tracks. With a heavy dread in my bones, we fall back and then we run.

Many vehicles on the road means we take more than double the time on the return trip than it did on the way in. There are animals in the fields and noise, lots of noise, coming from all directions. Noise feels like it's travelling for miles over the hills and fields, and everything gets mashed in together. My ears ring, and the temperature drop, along with fear for Blake and Garvey, have my insides shaking.

'Where are they?' Lara asks.

Our car's gone, and Blake and Garvey are nowhere in sight. Garvey doesn't leave people behind. Even if he had to run, he would have left the car for me. Then he would have circled back. Even against his own advice, he and Blake would come back for me.

Mark inspects the road to the edge of the trees. I breathe in through my nose, slow, controlled breaths out of my mouth to keep from vomiting. The musty smell that's replaced the scent of last night's rain makes me cough.

'Open your tablet and see if you get a signal,' Mark tells Ollie.

'I can't do that. NewGov will see us.'

'Just do it.' Mark wouldn't ask us to take risks lightly.

'What is this?' Ollie asks.

Leaning over his shoulder, we read his toolbar. '"BT Internet 65777. SkyOpen. Harry's Hairy Hair-cuts open Wi-Fi." What the hell is this?' I ask.

'They're Wi-Fi connections,' Mark says. 'Old-fashioned, free to hack or use with a passcode, internet connection.'

'How are we able to see old internet connections?' I ask. 'The only signals available are tightly controlled London connections.'

21

'Because we're in the past.' Mark looks solemnly at me, then turns to Ollie. 'Find us a hotel in Darlington, hack their website, and book us in fully paid. Once we have a base, we can work on IDs and anything else we need.'

'What the hell are you talking about?' Lara shifts from one foot to the other.

'Time control,' Mark says. 'There was some chatter about NewGov working on a method to build a real-life time machine. I heard about this some time ago and passed what I had on to Garvey. Nothing ever came of it, and we stopped chasing leads. Figured it would never be something that would actually work. Just the egos of the men in charge playing at being God in as many ways as they could. Guess we underestimated their egos.' Mark tucks a handgun into the waistband of his jeans and pulls his T-shirt over it. 'After we're at the hotel, we'll work on our cover story. We're going to need one to avoid drawing attention to ourselves. Last thing we need is someone calling the police on us. We should be set up in a day or two.'

'Two days?' I ask. 'This doesn't even make sense. How do you know where we even are?'

'We have to go with what this looks like.' Mark places his hands on my shoulders. 'NewGov was working on time travel, and now we're in the past. We need to act quickly so we're not homeless. Shelter and food first. There's a whole other world of issues in the past.' He turns to Ollie. 'We need IDs, driver's licences, and bank accounts. We can charge meals to the room in the meantime.'

'How is he going to do all that?' I ask.

Ollie has crossed his legs and is scrolling across his screen. 'If this really is a twenty-year-old security system, I won't have much problem.'

Lara kneels next to him. 'Is that version one of the dark web?' She screws up her face. 'Even I know how to hack from there.'

Ollie snorts and looks at me. 'This looks legit, Erin. All of this stuff is years old and is an example of what went wrong with security in the past. It's first-year training stuff. There's no way the Apostles would use any of this.'

'I told you,' Mark says. 'We're not in the same place anymore.'

I look around at the trees, and although there isn't much difference on the surface, it's the little details that stand out. The ground is wetter than earlier, and it hasn't rained. The air is chilly. Normally this far south, even in winter, there is a dryness in the air. The road we drove down less than an hour ago looks new. I take a few steps towards the tarmac and see white painted lines dividing the road into two sides. No cracks or grass sprouts.

Mark whistles at me, and I hurry back to the safety of the forest. 'There's going to be a lot more traffic than you're used to, so you need to take care on the road and not freak out every time you hear a car.'

Lara, Ollie, and I all stop and stare at Mark. We've been hiding when we heard an approaching vehicle our whole lives.

'What if someone spots us?' Lara asks.

'It will be civilians. They won't pay attention.'

Ollie slams his laptop shut and slides it into his backpack. 'I'm done. We have a two-bedroom suite booked in the centre of town. Meals and room service are pre-authorised, and because I already checked us in, we don't need a credit card or ID to collect spare key cards. I can work on store cards, electronic funds, and anything else you need when we get there.'

'You did all that already?' I ask.

'Told you. Rudimentary system.' Ollie points north east. 'Town is that way.'

The walk to Darlington is what convinces me we've landed in the past. Although I wouldn't have put it past the

Apostles to set up such an elaborate prank to pull Garvey out of hiding, but things are too clean and well-cared for to be anything but real. The vehicles seem brand-new, and the sheer number of people and amount of traffic has me jittery.

'You have to stop jumping every time a car speeds past,' Mark says. 'It's bad enough we're dressed like this. We're already drawing attention to ourselves.'

'How are we dressed?' I have to yell to hear myself. I've never seen a road so busy. There is a constant stream of cars and trucks going by, and Mark has to haul me into the grass verge so I'm not run down.

'We're dirty. If anyone asks, we'll say we just finished work. Maybe we have construction jobs or we're landscapers. Let's go with the latter.'

The road eventually winds into a built-up area of shops. There are so many people here, and they're free. There is a lightness about them, and it's bloody beautiful.

The high street not only works as a promenade to the shops, it also hosts market stalls with pop-up shops right there on the street. Christmas colours and decorations are hanging from wooden pillars and stall roofs. Blinking lights and music attract attention to the items for sale, and it's hypnotic.

'How can they operate black markets here in the open?' I whisper to Mark.

He smiles. 'It's not a black market. This stuff is legal to sell here.' He winks at me. 'The government isn't that controlling, yet.' He tilts his head and chuckles. 'Well, not really.'

Ollie is scanning the store names and tells Lara to note the places that could come in useful to us. 'We can create store cards and shop for free. Everything will get billed to an account I can set up.'

I shiver at the thought of being able to shop in a store. The exchanges we usually make are small and are comprised of a pre-ordered list of things we need. Everyone here, walking the street, is dressed like they have London's finest. The good things that were cleaned and pressed for storage for the last twenty years. Not tossed at the back of a warehouse for soldiers to trawl through.

One thing's for sure, we need coats. I've never experienced a December this cold before, even in the islands. The coats and jackets people wear here, with scarfs and hats, are a variety of colours and lengths. Most of our clothes are dark or camo so we can blend into the background.

'Bank.' Mark inclines his head to a building on the left, near a monument, and leans close to Ollie. 'That's where we'll get cash after everything's set up.'

On the steps of the building, the man and woman we saw earlier at the farmhouse are leaving. They stop and shake hands, and I nudge Mark. They were the first people we saw when we arrived, and here they are in the middle of town.

Mark inclines his head to the sign over the building. 'I told you the house was for sale. Looks like the guy is trying to buy it.'

'We'll need access to that house, and if someone else owns it or is moving in, it will be difficult to keep things under wraps while we get back home.'

'While we *try to* get back home, you mean,' Lara says.

'What does that mean?' I don't turn to face her. Instead, I keep my focus on my surroundings. The streets and roads wind towards and away from the centre pavement we are walking on. People pass with shopping bags, talking on their devices, not paying attention to us or others.

'Do you know anything about how to work time travel?' Lara hisses. ''Cause last time I checked, none of us do. It's not the sort of thing you can just have Ollie search for online.'

Mark shrugs. 'Worth a shot, though, right?'

'Did you just make a joke? In the middle of a crisis?' Ollie asks.

'Enough.' I pick up speed, knowing the others will follow. It's harder than I thought to walk fast when there are so many people about. People are walking haphazardly, like they don't seem to care which direction they are going in. Even in London, where people are scared into submission—and NewGov is watching—citizens walk with purpose to get from one place to another. Here, it's like people are outside for the fun of it.

At the end of the market street, on the right, is a real life, retro, functioning hotel. It looks grander than the abandoned hotels we've broken into and slept in, and we've crashed into a lot of grand places.

Mark takes the lead as we enter. The Christmas tree in the middle of the foyer takes my breath away. It smells like outdoors, and it's decorated with lights I've only ever seen in movies.

Mark is a good liar, and he doesn't falter as he circles the tree and talks louder than he usually does. He always knows how much detail to give and when, and started the charade before we'd even crossed the threshold. He knows the staff can hear us, and he's mid-conversation with me about the mess of the working day and how we lost our luggage and need laundry service, as he has to shower and change before he speaks to clients. I'm nodding and sighing in all the right places, trying to stop from looking at the furniture and art just lying around. Ollie leans on the back of an armchair in the reception area while Mark speaks to the woman sitting behind the desk. He's come to collect the spare key cards left by our employer; he tells her.

Our two-bedroom suite is booked for a week. We take a minute to search the rooms and glance out the windows to see how far we'd have to jump to escape. It's a habit. We're on the top floor, but it's only three stories high. Not ideal but doable.

The four of us gather in the main living space, not sure where to settle. It feels small and cluttered with all the excess furniture.

It was a priority for NewGov, after the first wave of the population culling, to take and categorise all the resources left in the country. Killing millions of people gave them the green light to steal all their stuff. Who cares about the beds and curtains in a hotel outside of London, right? Those things were stored for future use. No need to manufacture any more. Just kill people and take their belongings. Few homes were left untouched. Every can opener and speed boat were seized and used, allocated for parts, or stored.

I'm standing in a fully furnished room, and I can see why the world couldn't keep up with its own expectations. How much of this is needed? How many resources were used to make it? Here in this one room, there is a dining table and six chairs near the window, with a rug under it. Why there is the need for a rug on top of a carpet, I have no idea. There are two couches, with a side table at either end, *and* a coffee table piled with books and magazines. A TV the size of the wall faces them, and vases of fresh flowers—they aren't the typical poinsettias of December, but greenhouse roses, lavender, and ferns—make the room look beautiful and smell nice.

Lara is staring at the flowers, and I can tell what she's thinking: It's not safe here. Fresh flowers on display are always a sign used by high-ranking NewGov officials and Apostle soldiers who have a long-term posting in the field.

It's a symbol of wealth and power to source fresh flowers. Flower farms disappeared a long time ago, along with heavy manufacturing. London has access to seeds and a growing station, and they like to remind everyone that only those who are truly loyal to the cause—building a carefully *controlled* world—can have it all.

Wild flowers are scattered and far from the perfectly maintained flowers of London. If you have flowers in the future,

27

you've paid a high price for them. Morality, for one, and possibly your soul.

I take the flowers out of the vase and dump them in the bin. The heavy thud is a reminder of how thick and lush flowers are.

The sound of running water makes me spin around. Ollie is standing in the bathroom, running the tap.

I stare at him, staring at the water, and my insides churn with worry at what might circulate with the water.

Mark drops a boot to the floor and breaks our trance. On the edge of the sofa, he takes off his other boot and wriggles his toes. I don't think I've ever seen that man not ready to make a run for it before. 'The water's safe. It won't be contaminated for years yet.'

'Why did they target the water source?' Ollie asks.

'Because they could.' Is Mark's answer. 'They could isolate the supply into London and keep it clean. But in the end'—Mark sighs—'I think there was just an evilness that wanted to do it.'

'Bullshit,' Lara shouts. 'It was for a reason in the beginning. It all had to be for a reason.'

'There's no reason good enough to murder billions of people.' Ollie dries his hands on a thick towel and returns to the main room. 'Dying planet or not, if you start believing the cullings were for the greater good, then you might as well start walking to London. Find a nice little spot to live, and when NewGov and Apostle soldiers take over, you can sign up for a collaborator's job. See how it really is, living in a suppressed society.'

I can't imagine filling a glass with water from the tap and drinking without fear. We filter every drop we swallow. 'Let's work on our cover story.' Looking at Lara, I wink. 'Then we can figure out the workings of time travel.'

Ollie and Mark have been talking about time travel for two days. They don't know much.

Lara has been using Ollie's laptop to put together a manual about life in 2018 and how to survive here. She's acquired enough electronic funds to put an offer on the farmhouse property that exceeds the offer the other guy made, as well as set up a business account at the same bank. Ollie's been teaching Lara, his prodigy, how to hack everything and anything in this "elementary system", which she is picking up fast, considering he was already teaching her tech from 2042. Hell, I think even I could manipulate the systems here. He can work on survival as our secondary goal, but his time is to be spent getting us the fuck home.

One good thing is we don't have to hide. We can go out and buy clothes we need, pick up a phone and order food, and no one has come to kill us. It gets you thinking maybe time travel isn't such a bad thing after all.

Ollie has got us a supply of cash we can trade for everything we require. It's amazing what money can buy during this time period. Food of any type. Fresh food in a shop, or cooked and handed to you in a container. The hotel brings it to your room on a plate and clears away the mess afterwards. Shoes, phones, laptops, cables, and wires that Ollie swears are the slowest things he's ever seen, but he created bank accounts and IDs on the server so we could withdraw cash while we're waiting for plastic cards. Credit cards, they're called here. Cooper is the family name we use. One weird-ass family with a single dad in his forties and three kids, all with different skin colour. Cooper Bridge was the place where we met and flipped Ollie and where the younger kids in the group ran to for space

29

and freedom from the adults. It's a cute thing to remember. Or maybe I mean ironic. I never figured out how to use that word correctly.

Underwear is magical here. My boobs have never felt so tight and round, pushed up in a black bra, and when I slide the blue cotton and lace dress over my head, the fabric feels smooth and light, and I can't help admire what's looking back in the mirror at me.

It might only have been two days in this time, but I'm lean and have leg muscles that are prominent when I walk. I've already noticed that fitness is rare here. It's no wonder so many people didn't survive.

According to the internet, today is the fifteenth of December. Every piece of technology, including the TV, has the date and time constantly displayed, like people need to account for every minute of their day. They even have an actual printed newspaper. The latest issue has pictures of three dead girls and the sensational headline of Serial Killer Loose right next to the date and weather forecast—like which one is the most important item people need to know? In 2042, all the serial killers are NewGov, but the climate is more stable and not about to kill us either. I'm not sure which one is scarier.

December 15 is a historical day in Garvey rebel history, and we happen to be in Darlington. I want to see for myself what they were like in the beginning, because tomorrow, the younger version of Garvey is going to change forever.

three

FINLEY

The day before deployment is always tense. Cameron, Dylan, and I have a tradition of finding a pub, drinking three pints, then returning to base for an early night. Sometimes the rest of the team joins us, especially if football is on.

The eight of us have taken centre tables in front of the TV to watch the match, but the two hotties who took the table next to us are trying hard to get our attention. Dylan looks like he might bite, and I leave him to it.

'You good?' I nudge Cameron, who's sitting beside me. Something has him agitated.

He casually dismisses me. 'Just hate leaving on short notice with my sister, is all.' There's a partial truth there. He always feels guilty about having a job that means he can't take care of his mum, especially now that she's sick again. But that's not what's under his skin right now.

'I really need to put in for some leave. Help my sister out, you know?'

I nod and down the dregs of my pint. 'I'll come with you after we finish this deployment and see what needs doing. You ready for another?' Cameron's only halfway through his drink, but Dylan hears me and hands me his empty glass. 'You up for a trip to Scotland when we're back?' I ask Dylan.

31

'Sure. I've not invaded either of your folks' couches for at least a year.'

Cameron relaxes back in his chair. It's not the same thing as being in a job with a nine-to-five schedule, but we all pull together when one of our families need something. It comes with the life and death we face in the field. You don't turn off that kind of concern when you're on a deployment break.

There's a woman sitting at the bar with a drink in front of her. How the hell I missed her coming in is a travesty I shall never repeat. She's a total knockout, with killer, tanned legs and long, blond, curly hair. There is a glow around her, like she's emitting fresh air and calmness, and I know if I talk to her, she's going to fit right into my life. Even though that's ridiculous, and I have no life outside of my career. We could get lost together for a while.

She's perched on a barstool with a Coke, staring at a phone that's not even got the screen activated. She's waiting for someone and pretending she's busy. If she were waiting for me, I'd never be late again in my life.

I stand straighter as I approach her and place the two empty glasses on the bar. 'You alone?'

She jumps and pivots on the chair. 'Christ!' Her arm swings out with her hand tightened into a fist, then she pulls it back against her chest. Her bare arms are as toned as her legs, and I want to know how she got in such good shape. Her dark blue dress is short but covers the rest of her nicely—so nicely I'd like to find out what kind of shape the rest of her is in.

'Do you mind?' she drawls.

I chuckle and step back, but it must piss her off, rather than put her at ease, because her jaw tightens.

I put my hand out. 'Sorry, didn't mean to frighten the life out of you. I'm Finley.'

She places the mobile phone on the bar and shakes my hand. Her grasp lingers for a second and her rough hands have a strength I want to keep holding on to.

'Erin Cooper. I'm waiting for someone.'

Erin Cooper is checking me out as much as I am her. Her gaze roams over my arms and chest and there was a slight shudder when she tried to deflect her eyes and introduce herself. It makes me smile.

'Join us if you change your mind.'

She looks past me at our table. 'And interrupt the football? Even I know better than that.' She sips her dwindling Coke.

'I can join you instead. Just say the word.'

'Thank you, but I'm in the middle of something.'

'Fair do's.' I tap the top of the bar and return to the guys.

'Hey, Finley?' Erin calls after me.

'Yeah?'

'It's nice to hear a friendly accent.' She smiles.

Bloody Scottish accent gets them every time. I sit at the table. Cameron and Dylan glare at me in silence. Shit, I forgot the drinks.

When I glance back, Erin's looking in the mirror over the bar. She's trying to be subtle, but she's monitoring the door.

She catches me from the corner of her eye and knows I'm still watching her. Her lips curl up slightly, but she keeps her head held high.

We are both looking at the door in the mirror when a towering menace with a scowl, rolled-up sleeves, and tattoos walks in. He has to be at least fifteen years older that her. Bloody hell. I should have asked if she was waiting for a bloke.

The thug smiles as he approaches her and looks around the bar. His attention lingers on our table. It's not uncommon for the locals to take a dislike to the soldiers who come in on

33

the weekends. They think we're going to knock up all the girls in town and run off, never to be seen again. I let my gaze linger on the TV for a while.

By the time I turn back to the bar, Erin is sitting at a table near the door with a glass of wine in front of her. The guy has his boot resting on a stool opposite her. He's noticed me noticing him and says something to Erin that makes her tense, but she doesn't look at me.

It's almost halftime, and the girls chatting with Dylan go to the toilets for the second time since they got here. They must be bored. They're not watching the match, and Dylan is giving them scant attention, trying to make sure he doesn't lose his bet on this game while keeping Cameron distracted from thinking too much about his life.

Erin Cooper and her possible boyfriend were in a heated discussion until he left a few minutes ago, leaving behind his half-finished beer bottle. Maybe Erin dumped him, and he didn't take it well. She doesn't appear that upset; she stands and adjusts her dress, pulling it down to cover as much of her legs as it will allow. Her heels throw her off balance on her first step away from her table, but she recovers without making it obvious. She picks up her still full glass of wine and takes a small sip before moving again. I can't decide if she's coming over to me or headed to the bathroom.

A man accidentally bumps into her and spills beer on her feet. 'Sorry, love.' His eyes widen when he looks at her, and his voice gets louder. 'Sorry for splashing you, darling.' He winks and chuckles at his attempt to flirt, and I turn around fully to make sure he doesn't harass her. Dylan and Cameron pay attention to the brewing situation too, since I'm only a few seconds away from leaping out of my seat.

Erin shakes the drunk dude off her arm and sits at the table next to us.

I'm about to ask if she's okay, but the two girls return from the toilet and stare at her, sitting at their table.

Erin pulls out her phone and pretends to be engrossed in a dark screen. I smirk at her attempt to fit in. It's obvious a bar isn't her usual hangout.

'Are you going to follow me around the pub all day?' I ask, leaning over the back of my chair.

She flinches at my question but doesn't get a chance to reply as the two girls claim their seats at the table she's hijacked.

Erin must realise that a conversation with me is better than a possible confrontation with them. Her demeanour changes, and she gives me her full attention and puts the phone face down on the table.

'Are you waiting for your boyfriend to come back?'

Her spine shifts, and she tries to hide her annoyance. 'He's not my boyfriend. Maybe I'm waiting for my girlfriend,' she taunts.

'Fair enough.' I turn back to the TV. That's twice she's blown me off. I should really take a hint.

The two girls stop their hushed conversation with each other, and I can't help turning to see what's going on.

'I'm not gay,' Erin shouts. Her face fills with heat as customers at the surrounding tables look at her.

'That's a shame,' one of the guys jeers from the other side of the table.

I give him a look that quiets him down, then scoot my chair over to her table.

Erin hesitates and rubs her hands on her dress. 'I didn't mean to yell that. I'm not used to flirting, and I wanted to give you hell for trying to figure out if I had a boyfriend, and now I'm babbling.' She puts a hand over her mouth to shut herself up but tries to make it appear casual, and I've never seen anything cuter.

'Does the biker know he's not your boyfriend?'

She purses her lips. 'Considering he's my father, yeah, I think he knows.'

I flash a smile, glad I was completely wrong about him, and tap Dylan on the shoulder for him to join us. The other girls introduce themselves as Ashley and Nanda, who perks up when Cameron pulls his chair up next to her.

Dylan says, 'You don't mind if me and my boys join you for a bit, do you?'

'As long as you last longer than fifteen minutes,' Erin says.

Cameron spits beer back into his pint glass, and I chuckle. This girl really can't flirt. I fucking love it.

She points to the TV. 'I'm talking about halftime, Dylan Garvey. You can sit with us as long as it's not just to fill the boredom of your fifteen-minute wait till the match comes back on.'

Dylan looks her straight in the eyes. 'How do you know my name?'

Erin leans forward. 'It's on your jacket. Maybe don't flash your ID everywhere you go.'

Cameron pulls at the name tag on Garvey's army jacket and laughs. 'Dylan only wears that shit out here to pull the ladies.' He winks at Ashley, and she giggles.

Erin holds out her hand to Dylan. 'It's nice to meet you, Garvey.'

She might not be able to flirt, but someone taught her how to pay attention to her surroundings. And damn, I want to know more about the girl who got one over on one of my superiors.

Cameron and Nanda get lost in conversation, and I rest my arm on the back of Erin's chair. She's all about the small talk and asks which parts of Glasgow I'm from compared to Cameron. She can apparently tell the difference in strengths of accents, which is impressive since most people can only ask if we are from Glasgow or Edinburgh.

When I get a round of drinks in, she asks for tea. When it arrives, she spends a lot of time fidgeting with the white ceramic teapot and moves the cup around the saucer like she can't quite fathom what to do with so many pieces of crockery.

'You like tea sets?' When the words are out, I cringe at how lame that question sounds.

Erin flinches and looks like she forgot where she was for a second. 'It's like one I saw in Beatrix Potter's house. You know, *Peter Rabbit*?'

I nod. 'You've been to the Lake District?'

'Not for years.' She looks over the table at Ashely and Dylan, who are chatting, before she answers absentmindedly, 'It's not been safe for a while.'

I don't move my head, but my eyes shoot up to get a good look at whether she is serious. And damn, this girl knows she said too much. She's not even breathing.

# Chapter four

## Erin

I've said the wrong thing. Sitting here with a younger version of Garvey and Ashley has me remembering what life was like with them. I forget they aren't yet the people who keep the whole rebellion safe, but I've spoken like I was sitting in a camp, meeting one of their friends.

And Finley noticed.

He's trying to figure out why I said a local tourist destination wouldn't be safe. Anyone who wasn't taking me seriously would make a joke and move on, but his silence is making me sweat. I keep my attention on the others at the table, pretending to listen to their conversation, but I keep checking on Finley to see if he's going to pass comment on what I said.

My gaze follows the length of his tanned arm. I catch sight of a tattoo peeking out under the sleeve of his shirt that appears again at the base of his collarbone. Black lines lick the curve of his neck. He's pushing boundaries, being a soldier with tattoos that visible. It doesn't escape me that his neck happens to be attached to a pretty face. Handsome? What words do people use in this time to describe someone who's so attractive they give your belly a tight clenching feeling?

Ashley and Nanda stand in unison. 'Come to the toilet with us,' Ashley tells me.

What that's all about, I've no idea, but I follow the girls around the table and down the hallway.

The version of Ashley I know taught us to pee in pairs, but it was so someone could keep watch while the other squatted. I usually paired up with Blake, 'cause we were always together. And it was safe—family was the safest.

The three of us enter the toilet and take a cubicle each. I slide the lock on my door and take a deep breath. The younger version of the woman who stands by our leader's side is so different in this time. Her youth makes her appear easily led. Or maybe it's the next twenty years of her life that change her into the woman I know. She adapted to her environment.

Man, no wonder Garvey loved her so damn much. She's the best student he's ever had. That's how she and Garvey survived when so many of the population fell, and they taught everyone they could how to do it too. Right after they interrogated them. Rule number seven: You can lend a hand to others, but make sure they're not the enemy before you take them in.

Ashley and Nanda talk loudly through the cubicle dividers. 'Erin girl, you should've been here last week. Nanda and I spotted those boys a week ago in the club across town, but we were too late. There was a whole crowd of scantily clad girls around them.'

The more Ashley and Nanda have drunk, the louder they've become. It's probably why we never drink alcohol, apart from the fact it's hard to find. It slows you down. Makes you less aware and apparently giggle more.

At the sinks, Ashley sprays some perfume shit on me and lets me borrow her lipstick. I peer down at the blue dress Lara bought and told me showed off the right amount of leg to keep it classy. 'What's scantily clad mean?'

Nanda snickers. 'Not us, thank god.'

'Honestly,' Ashley continues, turning off the tap. 'When we arrived, we couldn't believe our luck—not a girl in sight. But those boys were all about the bro-code during the footie. Until

39

Finley caught sight of you. He's hot. You need to kiss him right away.'

I meet her eyes in the mirror. 'You want me to kiss him in a bar full of people?'

Ashley and Nanda giggle. 'You can go outside with him, but then he's probably going to think more than kissing will happen. Oh, man, do you think Dylan will take me outside?' Ashley leans over the sinks and applies her lipstick. Again.

'I have to go.' There's no way I'm kissing someone in a pub.

'You're leaving?' Nanda turns to face me. 'Shit, you know what? We should ask if they're going to a club and if we can go along. You're coming, right? We have to find you a place to stay. You can't stay at the Travel Inn any longer. It's going to fleece all of your money.' She pulls her phone out of her bag and types away while we return to the bar. 'I'll find you a room to rent close to us. We're central, which is where you need to be.'

'Shit.' Ashley halts and grabs Nanda's arm. 'Look who's sitting at the bar.' She snickers.

Nanda groans. 'Clinger alert.'

'What's a clinger alert?' I ask.

'She's being overly dramatic,' Ashley says. 'Nanda snogged the local bank manager hottie, Rian, last week, and we've bumped into him a few times.'

Nanda leans close to my ear. 'Stalker,' she sings.

It's the man who spilled beer on me earlier. 'Oh, I saw him the other day.' I remember what it was like to see my first human in 2018, who was looking around a house I had accidentally used as a time machine. 'He was drinking when I got here. He's been watching the match, hasn't even looked over in your direction.'

'How the hell do you know?' Nanda asks and prickles of anxiety run through me.

'If he'd noticed you, he would've tried to say hi, right?'

Nanda squints at me. 'Whatever. He's a stalker, and there's a serial killer on the loose. It wouldn't surprise me if it was him.' She points her finger dramatically.

'Three murders don't make a serial killer,' Ash says.

'Actually, they do,' I correct her.

Ash squints her eyes as she looks at me. 'And that was in Scotland, not here. We're far, far away.'

Nanda swallows her drink faster so she can interrupt. 'First one was in England.' She holds up a finger.

'Whatever. Let's just get out of here.' Nanda sits at the table.

'You want us to leave with two Scottish guys?' I ask her logic about picking out a drunk guy she dated once as a serial killer but feels safe with two random strangers from the same country where the murders were committed?

'Serial killers are never that hot,' she whispers to us, then says more loudly, 'Let's go.'

'Good idea.' Cameron swallows the last mouthful of his pint.

Five of them have already gone, leaving Dylan, Finley, and Cameron behind. You'd think I'd know Garvey's two best friends' surnames, but he never spoke about the people he lost when he was in the army. My heart constricts, knowing they and some of the other men here today, along with a US-based unit, will die on their next tour. I try to keep my face impassive when I glance at Dylan.

It was survivor's guilt that got him. He tried to keep it together, did another year before he took medical discharge for PTSD. After intense physical therapy, psychotherapy, and spending his spare time setting up a charity to help discharged soldiers, he moved back here and reconnected with Ashley.

It's all part of my new contingency plan. In case we're stuck in the past. If I make this friendship with Ashley work, in

41

two years, when she and Dylan hook up, the rest of us will be around to be a part of his life too.

'House party,' Cameron calls and heads for the door. 'Carry-out next door. What we getting?'

'Carry what?' I ask Finley as he walks with me to the door.

'That's Glasgow talk for off-licence.'

Dylan looks relaxed, naïve even—if that's a word you can use to describe a soldier who's already seen the worst side of war. He has no idea what it'll be like to go on the run in eight years with a group of civilians and a bunch of kids.

Dylan slings his arm around Ashley's shoulder when we get out of the taxi. He's handsome in his twenties, without the weight of the world on him. His short hair and stubble look deliberate, like a lot of the men in this time. Not like in 2041, when his beard grew from long weeks and months of being constantly on the move. There's not a hint of the scattered grey he'll have in my time. Hair dye isn't a commodity to risk stealing or bartering for.

I force my attention from the couple I'll know so well in the future and study the imposing building that takes up the full length of the street. Next to each of the ten ground-floor shops is a solid wooden door, like the one we are standing in front of. 'What was this?'

'Used to be a mill, I think,' Ashley says. She points to the salon window. 'That's my work.' Her finger rises. 'And that's our place.'

Ashley slides out of Dylan's arms and takes out her keys to open the door. 'The place we have is only a two-bed, but Nanda is moving at the end of the month. I was going to stay on my own, but having someone else chip in with rent will help. Are you interested?'

'You've just met me. What if we don't get along?' We've lived together before. It shouldn't be much different, but I'm terrified. When she can choose whether or not to like me, she might end up hating me. I need to be at Charlie Papa anyway if we push the sale of the farmhouse through. But thinking about living with Ashley again brings a different sort of comfort.

I take a step back to get another look at the twenty-one-window wide, old, converted sandstone mill. There are seven residential doors between shop fronts and entrances. The building is huge, but it looks like it's separated into smaller units. From the corner of my eye, I see Mark's car pull into the small car park outside a take-away at the mouth of the one-way street.

Finley's the only one hanging back on the road with me, and he hooks his arm through mine. 'I've got a feeling that when we get in the girls' flat, we'll be left on our own. How about I boil the kettle and keep you company while you look around?'

The four others have paired off. Ashley opens the main door with a click. The heavy door swings inwards, and we enter a narrow hallway with only a staircase and what looks like a bin room.

One exit, no back door or windows in the entranceway. My heart speeds up. Not ideal, but I like the heavy front door.

Finley takes my hand as we climb the stairs. When he runs his thumb across my knuckles, I realise I've paired off with him, as much as Dylan and Ashley, and Nanda and Cameron have. Before I've had time to think about it, my stomach is flipping and tingles run through me. Most of which hit me between the legs. What. The. Fuck.

Finley squeezes my hand. A part of me wants to find out what it'd be like to be a twenty-year-old with a hot man in 2018.

This was one of the safest times in history. It's not like the Gestapo wannabes are going to burst through the door at any moment.

The tingling continues through my body. I argue with myself. He's Garvey's friend—he's a no-go area. A totally hot, tattooed, muscled good guy who fights for his country and smells like smooth skin and aftershave, off-limits kind of guy.

Finley's hard jaw and the smooth skin under the stubble make me want to run my fingers over it. My heart constricts. He's only a couple of years older than me right now, and he doesn't know that his life is going to be over in the next few days.

Vomit rises in the back of my throat, and I have to hold my breath, hoping I don't spill my stomach from the callousness of my thoughts. Finley is going to be dead in a few days, and my only thoughts are if screwing him would have a ripple effect. I should warn him. I should save his life.

But I can't save Finley or Cameron or anyone else in the squadron. Dylan Garvey needs to get fucked up so we can all survive in the future. If he doesn't have the pain, he doesn't have the love that drives him to protect everyone in the future.

Hell, if I tell Finley what's about to happen and save him, I might alter the course of events so much that Garvey becomes the casualty instead.

Mark was right. I shouldn't have come here, but I was hell-bent on meeting Dylan and Ashley, and I knew he wouldn't be back in town for another two years after tonight.

Ashley is talking inside the flat when Finley and I reach the top of the stairs. There are two apartments on each floor. We're three floors up. I assume the opposite flats will be a mirror layout of this one: multiple windows and doors to burst through, and opportunities to slow down a pursuer.

Once inside, I get my bearings. To the left is the front of the building. The bedroom door on my right is open, and through the window I see a graveyard adjoining the building grounds. A handy place to hide. I pull up my memory of the town map we studied. I'm on Hope Street. Strand is one street back, with a fork in the road to the right.

'This would be your room.' Ashley pulls me free of Finley. 'It's small, but it has everything you need. Bed, dresser, wardrobe is built in.' She points over my shoulder. 'Don't let the graveyard scare you. Nothing ever jumps out of the dark.'

I roll my eyes and glance at Finley, Cameron, and Dylan in the hallway. *If only she knew.*

The men are smiling, but it doesn't reach their eyes. Soldiers understand the bad stuff in the world. And it all comes from the living.

Dylan pushes his buddies out of the way and makes his way into the room. He ushers me outside. 'If you don't mind, I kind of want the private tour.' He slams the bedroom door on us.

Ashley lets out her new trademark giggle, and Nanda appears from the kitchen. 'I thought we had wine, but we're out.' She looks at Ashley's closed bedroom door. 'That was fast.'

Cameron tilts his head at her. 'I get to see your room, right?' He grins, and Nanda jumps into his arms and wraps her legs around his hips. 'Right behind you, Captain.'

I snigger at her blunder, then realise Finley and I are alone.

He clears his throat and strolls to the kitchen at the end of the hall. He takes two strides to get there, and I follow him while he talks. 'You raid the cupboards for biscuits, and I'll get the tea made.'

If I don't make a move now, I'll never get another chance. I might not be able to save him, but I can have this experience with him. My life will never be about relationships and dates. Even in the moment our eyes met in the pub, when my heart rate was in overdrive and adrenaline pumped, I knew I'd met the man I was going to fall in love with. I always believed

Mum's talk of love at first sight to be bullshit. She divorced my dad and married another man, after all. But maybe you can find love in the strangest places, even if it's temporary.

Finley takes two matching mugs from the cupboard and places them on the counter. When he turns around to ask me something, I move so fast towards him, I'm almost running. I cup his face and stretch on tiptoes to kiss him. After a moment, he opens his mouth and kisses me back. He bends down and scoops my knees out from beneath me and places me onto the counter, knocking over the empty mugs.

I take a deep breath, inhaling him. He smells like soap and beer and sweet and spicy aftershave. I feel the rough edges around his stubble against my palms. I go right back to kissing him. I'm all hands, feeling his arms, his chest. His bicep moves under his T-shirt. The fabric stretches as he manoeuvres his bulk of a body.

There's strength in his arms. He favours his right but only by a fraction. His chest is thick, and he moves with ease as he slips off his jacket. Muscles flex as he drops it to the floor.

He's used to taking—and giving—blows, dodging bullets, running, and chasing. In his line of work, he needs to be, but I was never in a position to assess kissing before. He wants me. His breathing is fast and shallow. He's moving closer to me. Despite our bodies being pressed against each other, he's moving and adjusting us. He's savouring the movements of being pressed together like they mean more to him than touching. When his hands run over my bare legs, I wonder what his skin feels like.

I reach for his belt and tug at the bottom of his shirt. He helps by pulling it off over his head. I stop and stare and run my hands over his body. He's smooth and tattoos cover his chest and the right side of his stomach, which connect to the ones I saw on his arm and collarbone earlier. It looks like bird wings stretching over his chest, shading and flowers, another animal, and some tribal-looking swirly thing. There are so many to take in, overlapping as they are, and smaller ones like a coin and a clock face that seem nonsensical, filling in the gaps between larger pieces. He's taut and ripped with muscles. He's a perfect killing machine, healthy and fit and a survivor. Someone who can take care of himself, and he's letting me look at him.

I bite my lip and raise my eyes to meet his.

'Like what you see?'

'It's all right.' I laugh and feel heat come back to my cheeks. I try to hide it by pulling Finley close for another kiss, but he doesn't give up the teasing.

'What's the matter? First time you've seen a naked guy?'

Garvey always said my lack of reaction *was* a reaction. Finley notices it too.

He straightens. 'Erin, are you a virgin?'

## five

### Erin

Fuck.

I can usually think on my feet, but this is a question I've never anticipated. I'm knocked off-kilter, and for the first time, it's a good thing. Which screws with my head even more. Pain, phasing, loud noise, and fear I'm used to. Tingly feelings and wanting to be naked and tingle some more, I'm not.

I hesitate a second too long.

Finley slides a hand along my leg, around my back, and flicks his wrist. The kettle clicks on behind me. He catches me around the waist and gently tugs me off the counter. 'Make me tea. I'm going to use the bathroom, and when I come back, I want you to tell me all about that new job you got in town.' He kisses me deeply before retreating. I watch him leave the room, muscles flexing as he pulls his shirt back on.

'Fuck.' I take a deep breath and brace myself on the small kitchen table. I run my hand over the painted white surface. I might sit here with Ashley and my new friend, Nanda, chatting about things that aren't important. There's only one chair and a small bench that could fit two of us if we squeezed.

Tears well behind my eyes. I want to live in a time when we're not running. It's what my parents always fought for. I wish Blake were here, too. I've never been without him. I've no idea if he's still alive. Only a few days separated from my friends and family, everyone could be dead—or worse, captured for London.

Finley's arms wrap around my midriff before I've heard him. I smile. 'When do you leave for your next tour?' I know the answer but ask anyway.

'Tomorrow. We're supposed to be in bed early tonight. Well, guess those two bastards are, but we have to be at the base at five a.m. tomorrow. Tell me about your new job. Is it the dream job?'

'In a way, I guess it is.'

He's leaving, and I want to bare my soul to him because my secrets will die with him in a few days. I've never had a friend to spill my guts to and get their advice. And he's friends with Garvey, for Christ's sake. If Dylan can trust him, I guess I can too.

I pour hot water into the mugs over the teabags and watch the water burst into a dark brown as the tea brews.

'Something happened to my family recently. We might be kind of stuck here,' I confess. 'And my brother Blake isn't with us. I don't know if he's okay or even if I'll ever see him again.

'I've an idea of how to send him help, wherever he might be. And we can build a career to keep us in town. It would take everything we have, but I'm not sure it's the right play for us. I'd rather work on getting back home to him, if we can.'

Finley follows me to the counter and opens the fridge, rummaging for milk.

We carry our things to the table, and I sit on the bench. He slides the table out and squeezes in next to me, laying his arm over the back and enveloping me in his space.

'That's why you moved here?'

'There was an incident at a farmhouse outside town. We want to stay close. It's where my brother might find us—our last known location sort of thing. It's why I would rather stay there if my family can buy the place, rather than move into a flat with new friends.' I look up at the ceiling. 'We've family

49

history in the area. It's somewhere Blake might search for me if he can. Everyone is looking to me to decide whether to go or stay, and part of me just wants to curl into a ball and wait for the inevitable.'

'Your family is looking for you to pick up the pieces? What are you, twenty-three or four?'

'I just turned twenty.'

'Ah.' He sighs. 'That explains some things.'

I nudge him. 'Meaning?'

He chuckles. 'I don't mean anything negative. I just thought you were older. You come across as mature, sensible. I get it. After I signed up for the army, my family thought I was a hero.'

'You kind of are. It's why I trust you. I don't normally talk about personal things with people I just met. With anyone, actually. But you know things the average person doesn't. You understand the real horrors in the world.' I peer out the kitchen window into darkness. 'It's not ghosts hiding in graveyards, it's real people doing the worst things to each other. If I were to tell someone about my brother being missing, they'd want to involve the police, but they can't help us. I need someone who isn't involved with all this to listen to me, you know? Someone like you. I have to keep going. I need to make sure everyone survives.'

He nods. 'When I got selected for Special Forces, in my father's eyes, I became invincible. Someone he respected. He was in awe of me.'

'Why do you say that so sadly?'

'Because when I looked at my mum, all I saw was fear. She understood the risk more than my father did. More than I did. Some soldiers don't come home. Special Forces are at greater risk because of what we do.'

I wonder if Finley's dad will still be proud of his son's career choices. If his mother's been preparing herself for the day she buries her son.

Ashley was scared in the beginning too, but she became Garvey's strength. There was fear in her eyes every day, but she stayed strong. There's no other choice for us. We don't get to quit or retire. We're fighting for our lives. We stand with the rebellion or let the promise of utopia steal our free will, imprison us to their ruling, destroy our hopes and dreams for generations to come.

'The greater the risk, the greater the reward, right?' I say.

'Something like that.'

'How old are you, Finley?'

'Twenty-six.' He grins. 'Kind of old for you.'

He's forty-nine where I'm from. 'Not right now. Can I let you in on something? I can run a full-out boot camp training field in under three minutes.'

'No way.'

'Yes way. I can totally beat you. I'm fast.'

'I don't believe you.'

I slap his shoulder. 'You're all muscle and bulk. I'm half your size, but I'm strong. And I've run for my life on more than one occasion. I know how to focus that kind of adrenaline.'

Finley pauses for a beat and studies my face before he dunks his biscuit. 'When I get back from this tour, I'm going to prove I'm faster than you.'

I run my hand over his cheek. 'I'd like that.'

'Tell me about your brother.'

We tell each other everything about ourselves except coming from the future and being part of one of the biggest groups of rebels. We talk about the things we love and hate and places we want to visit and run away to. I tell him all the things I missed out on as a child and only got to hear about through my mother's teachings. I talk about Blake and the things I miss about him, as well as a long list of annoying things I convince myself I don't miss. I speak about how in the days we've been gone, I've had to keep my family from falling apart.

At 1:00 a.m., we move into the living room. I lie on the couch on top of Finley, and he wraps his arms around me to keep me warm.

He talks about having faith that sometimes things work out on their own. 'Every time I go to work, there are risks, but we're trained well, and we have a good team and equipment and intel. We use our strengths and our belief in our skill to come back alive.'

'That's it? You just *believe* you're coming home and don't bother taking a second thought when you walk into an open courtyard, or you know, duck?' I giggle. 'I come from a military family. Intel isn't always what it should be. Sometimes ignoring the bravado your training gives you and doing the sensible things like ducking out of the way of a flying bullet is the best thing to do. Gut instinct is a wonderful thing, but sometimes you get a feeling that shit's not how it should be.'

I close my heavy eyes. I'll wait until he's sleeping before I sneak out.

A shrill noise rings beneath me, and strong arms tense around me in response.

'It's my alarm,' Finley whispers hoarsely in my ear. He shifts on the couch but holds on tight when I try to sit up. 'Don't move, I got it.' Silencing the phone alarm, he yawns. 'We're going to be in so much shit for being tired.'

It's still dark outside. 'What time is it?'

'Oh-four-twenty-five,' he says in a robotic tone. 'We need to get a move on.'

'Can you get to the garrison in half an hour? It's a twenty-minute drive from here. Does Ashley even have a car?'

'Dylan booked a taxi earlier. It should be here in five minutes.'

I take a deep breath. The proximity has me breathing him in. I can taste his leftover aftershave in the back of my throat. I want to be closer to him. I have my mouth on him before he can push me away. He lets me explore. Our tongues stab at each other, and my body heats and melts against his.

A door down the hall opens, and Dylan bangs twice on the wall outside the living room before stepping in. I try to sit up. I don't want Dylan to catch me lying across one of his friends. But Finley keeps his grip on me, and as I pull against him, he relents, and I end up falling off and thumping unceremoniously on the carpet.

'Five minutes.' Dylan chuckles.

Finley sits up and reaches his hand out to pull me up off the floor. 'Do you want to jump in the taxi with us and get home? Or you going to stay here with your new BFFs?' He rips a piece of paper off a leaflet on the coffee table that he wrote on.

'I have no idea what that is, so I'll take the cab please, if there's room for me?' I roll my neck and rub a sore spot on my arse.

'Always.' He kisses me on the nose, stands, and stretches.

'Any chance the car is diesel?' I ask.

'No idea. Why?'

'I have a thing against petrol cars, is all.'

Dylan bangs on Nanda's door and returns to the living room to put his boots on.

Everyone's in motion quickly, and I pull my shoes on. Man, they move fast.

The four of us are at the front door before Finley's phone pings in his pocket. 'Taxi's here. You boys getting numbers?'

Cameron screws his face up. 'Nope. All good.'

53

Dylan opens the front door and gestures for me to leave first, then hangs back to call to Ashley, 'I'm coming back for you one day.'

Ashley appears and pulls Dylan into a snogfest.

Finley chuckles at me.

'Do me a favour,' she tells Garvey. 'Don't come back for me unless you're here to stay.'

I smile as I jog down the stairs. Ashley will never admit it, but she'll be waiting.

The sun is rising as the taxi drops the men outside the command and staff trainer. Garvey gets out first, digs in his pockets, and pulls out some notes to hand to the driver. I never thought I'd be glad to hear him shut up, but he's like a younger, more hyper version of future Garvey.

Finley talks to the driver and then turns to me, the only one left. 'You're all paid up to get you back to your hotel.'

He hands me a slip of paper. 'It's the contact details of a retired soldier. He might be able to help track your brother. I've already texted him to say you'll be in touch, and he owes me a favour, so don't worry about paying him, okay?'

I stare at the ripped scrap of paper and try to say something. Blake will never be found. Not here. But Finley wanting to help breaks my heart. He's someone who could've run with us. He has the willingness to chase after those who are missing. That's who we are.

'My number is there, too. I'll be back in town on my next leave. If you're still here in a few months, I'll look you up.'

*No, you won't.* I close my hand over the paper and nod. A part of my heart freezes, the restriction pulling at my throat.

He gazes at me a long moment. 'Erin Cooper, it was a pleasure.' He jogs off to the gate, where other soldiers have joined Cameron and Dylan.

I don't want this to be the last time I see Finley. I don't want him to die. I want him to come back, like Dylan did for Ashley, but I can't change a damn thing without screwing with everyone's future. I clear my throat and give him the parting every man going off to war should have. Something to come home for.

'Hey, soldier,' I yell at Finley through the window as he's following his squadron in.

'Yeah?'

'You come back alive, okay? I'd really like to see whether you can beat me.'

'Oh, I'll be back to see you alright.' He grins and turns to the rest of the squad. The younger and slightly annoying Dylan Garvey cheers, no doubt giving him shit about flirting with a girl in front of the army barracks.

*You come back alive too, Garvey. We need you more than you know.*

I trace the handwriting on the crumpled piece of paper in my hand and say a silent prayer for Finley, too.

*Maybe in another life.*

# six

## Erin

The taxi driver gets two streets over and there's a car tailing us. I tell the driver to pull over and let me out. I glance at the two men who have pulled up in the car across the street. Mark's tattooed hands on the steering wheel can be seen even at a distance. Mixed with the scowl, the cigarette hanging from his mouth, and long hair that probably suited him more in his youth, he oozes frustration and anger that's clocked up throughout his life.

I move towards their side of the road, heels clicking. Ollie fidgets in the passenger seat next to him. The shaved head and stubble of the black guy makes him more menacing looking than the scowl he copied from Mark. No wonder people have stayed clear of us since we got here. They look like thugs. I open the back door and slide in next to Lara.

Her eyes are red, and her cheeks blotchy. She might have become accustomed to the freedom here, but she's distraught about Blake. We both are. Spending the evening with a younger version of Dylan and Ashley makes it more apparent that my brother is the only member of my family not here.

Lara needs Blake even more than I do. She has no family left, and they were a great couple. *Are* a great couple. I grip her hand in mine. Not that she knows my mind made a blunder, but I feel guilty thinking their relationship might never be, as we might never get home.

Before I've closed the door, Mark pulls the car back onto the road, cigarette still dangling from his lips.

'His friends all die?' Lara glances at the group of men standing outside the barracks as we take a right-hand turn down the street, away from our saviour.

'Are we really going to let an entire unit of soldiers go off to die and not warn them?' Ollie asks. 'If they're Garvey's unit, his friends'—Ollie spins in the seat to face me—'we can use them in the future. This might be why we're here. To level the playing field.'

'Assuming he believes me,' I say. 'He might think I'm crazy or turn me in at the army base for being a potential spy. What soldier would trust a girl he just met with information on a mission that hasn't even been delegated yet?'

'Garvey has to follow the same path he once did. His life can't change. If they survive, he's never discharged early. He'll be on the takeout list in eight years, when the first wave hits,' Mark says.

'Seems a little callous, if you ask me,' Lara says. 'People here deserve a chance to live too.'

Leaning over the front seat, I rest my elbows on the back of their seats and speak to Mark.

'When my dad lost his friends in the army, it broke him. That was before I was born, but his discharge brought him back here, and his whole life changed for the better. He and Mum got married, and when the world fell apart, they were together. His pain and suffering over the next few days saves his life in years to come, so let's leave Garvey alone, like Mark says. I have a plan that involves staying in town, but I need to know you won't interfere if I make friends with Ashley.'

The slack-jawed look of shock, followed by tongue-biting disappointment on Mark's face, makes me drop my gaze.

Looking in the rear-view mirror, he answers, 'Of course I'm not going to interfere, Erin. But we can't stay here with them.'

'He might be right.' Ollie turns in his seat so he can see Lara and me in the back and also Mark. 'Garvey and Ashley are two of the most important people in the insurgent's future. If you do anything to screw with them and their history, it could cause serious problems for everyone, especially you.'

Lara interrupts. 'What if you screw things up, and you and Blake are never born?'

'My parents' relationship was fine in this timeline. Dylan and Ashley met last night, just like they did years ago, and after he comes back from this tour and heals, he'll come looking for her in two years. Trust me.' I take Lara's hand. 'No one would be more worried than me about not being born.'

Lara exhales, like she's been holding herself together since the moment I left the hotel last night. 'Fine then, but our priority needs to be figuring out these damn time holes and getting home.'

'It will be, but we need a strategy in case we're stuck here.'

'We can't be stuck here. There has to be a way back,' Lara yells.

'We don't belong here.' Mark slows the car at a light. 'I can't live this life again.'

'Working in the past means we can be in a stronger position to take out the leaders if we ever get back home,' I tell them. 'We can save the people we've lost on the way. Imagine if those standing up for themselves are higher in number. We can place people in strategic positions. Stash supplies and create safer places to hide. We can overthrow NewGov. We'd have numbers. We can stop this fake utopian bullshit Sanctuary London is exploiting.'

'You were only a kid when the world fell apart the first time, Erin. But a lot of people survived the first waves. There were a lot more of us, and eventually they chose London.'

'They didn't know what they were running towards. It wasn't salvation, it was slavery.'

Mark nods. 'Maybe, but it was a better choice than being on their own.' He looks out the window, to small-town Darlington and the sixty million people in the rest of the UK who didn't make it the first time around.

Mark's silence is my opening to keep going.

'We can bury bunkers for when our friends in the future need them—fill them with food and medical supplies and weapons. Everything we wished we had when we were running. We already know the places we're going to hide. It's an opportunity to save those who didn't make it. We can give them a place to go to ground while the rest of us keep fighting.'

'The more people we save, the more people it is to feed and take care of—the ones that could barely keep themselves alive in the first place. Hell, they *didn't* keep themselves alive.' Mark's throat bobs.

'More people to fall in love and start families. More reasons to keep fighting.' The romantic side I inherited from my mother is always niggling away at me, and I have to stop myself from thinking about Finley. The only hot guy I've ever met who wasn't embedded in our unit, and therefore answered directly to my father. Except here, where he's my father's best friend.

'You're talking about a war that won't start for another eight years, and then fifteen years of being on the run all over the country. That's a lot of bunkers for the four of us to bury,' Ollie says. He's always a step ahead with the practicalities of any plan. Thinking them through, even if he doesn't agree with them.

'We'd have to recruit outsiders to help. A lot of time for people to double-cross us,' Lara says.

'You could hide it as legitimate work. Come up with a cover story that will work,' I tell them.

'How the hell do we hide bunkers from NewGov and anyone who would sell us out, but still leave them visible enough that the right people find them?' Lara shakes her head. 'Eight years to get this operational and complete won't be long enough.'

'Dylan is due back in town in two years. When he and Ashley officially become a couple, we'll be here. And when the world goes to shit, we'll be right here with the leaders of the future rebellion. We can help Garvey and Ashley save more people, Mark.'

'Not everyone is supposed to survive.' Mark shakes his head. 'You don't get to decide who lives and dies in the past. There are some things we cannot change, and if we do, by accident, it'll screw things up forever.'

Things are already screwed up. People need their lives and freedom back. People who were born free and have never had to fight for it are always the ones who take it for granted. Always the ones who bitch about how hard life is and how much they suffer. They have no idea, but unfortunately, they will soon enough.

'Why do our reasons for fighting have to change because we landed twenty-three years in the past?' Lara asks.

'Garvey's protected most of us our whole lives, right? Might as well start before we're even born. It can't be a coincidence that we fell through a portal in Ashley's hometown and are here for the one day he is passing through,' I say.

'So now you think fate is in charge of time travel?' Lara makes a disbelieving face. 'We don't know how this works. Hell, NewGov Apostle soldiers might be the ones who caused this, to push us out of the way for a while. Whether it was an accident or a fated decision for us to stop a world-ending war, Ollie hasn't had enough time to run through all the scenarios of our interference in this timeline. If this works, and we stick around, what the hell is going to happen when our timelines catch up? When we meet ourselves?'

I raise an eyebrow. 'Be damn impressed with how cool our fighting skills are?'

Mark gives me his best father-scolding look of disapproval, and the lines around his eyes become more prominent. At least we've got the bickering family aspect down.

'I don't want to stay here,' Lara says. 'If we're setting up a new operation, I'll help you but from a distance. Staying somewhere for so long doesn't feel right. I can scout out our most used locations in the future. See if any of those would work for your new proposal. See if there is any where I can leave proof of life for those we left in the future. Staying this close to an Apostle base is stupid.'

'We've got at least a decade before that base becomes a problem. Let's just figure out this first hurdle.'

'Which is?'

'Get Ashley to like me.' A lock of my newly dyed blond hair falls over my face, and I push it back. 'I need a hair tie,' I whisper. I look like a different person with blond hair. Every time I catch a glimpse of myself in the mirror, I flinch.

Mark rolls his eyes. 'And if you screw this up?'

'Well, it's not like we can follow Garvey off to Afghanistan, can we? If I screw this up, I'll be the first to know.'

'Any chance we're going to run into a younger version of you in the past?' Lara asks.

Mark shakes his head. 'There's a seventeen-year-old version of myself in Italy right now, working around Europe with the only goal of saving enough money for petrol and tattoos.'

I frown at him. 'I thought you were in jail when you were a kid?'

He snorts in dismissal. 'Just so you know, people here don't need escape-and-evasion plans, and we didn't have to stake out your date all night.'

Lara faces forward. 'What makes you think we're the only ones here?'

Mark's jaw drops, and when he speaks, he stutters. 'I'm h-hoping there's a r-reason for all of this, something b-bigger than all of us. Get on board with the theory that m-maybe this is our opportunity to win. If there are any agents here, it puts us at a disadvantage.'

I nod and smile, trying to reassure him. 'I know, but it'd be damn stupid to let our guard down. When did we ever not plan for the worst-case scenario?'

We're back at the hotel car park, and Mark has reversed the hire car into a space near the exit. 'You're all going to have to get used to driving with other cars on the road,' Mark tells us. 'It's not as bad as London traffic, so you should be okay.'

'All that was in London was electric buses and bikes. Believe me, it's worse.' Ollie is looking out the side window. There are rows and rows of parked cars we pass on the road out, all full of flammable petrol and waiting for their owners to jump in and take them to the places they're free to go.

'Get started with the business funds,' I tell Ollie. 'We need the full works.'

Ollie looks at me in the side mirror. 'What were they like?'

I smile. 'They were a mess. A ridiculously normal twenty-something bunch of people. It was kind of cute, knowing they're going to grow into people with so much importance and skill. Especially Ashley. She's a liability right now.' I lean forward between the two seats. 'If she stumbled into us in the future, our Ashley would lock her up. No runs, no helping. She's a homer.'

Ollie twists in his seat. 'Shut up,' he drawls.

'Swear to god.' I chuckle.

Ollie turns to Mark. 'You're the oldest. Do you remember them like that?'

'Barely. I met them near the beginning. You were, what, Erin? Six or seven? We all got better together.'

'That's the best part about being my age,' Ollie says. 'By the time I remember meeting them, they were both indestructible soldiers.'

Fumbling around in my bag for a hair tie, I find the slip of paper Finley gave me and run my fingers over his handwriting.

*Don't give up. — Finley* is scribbled under the contact details he gave me.

I sink back against the headrest. 'There's no such thing as an indestructible soldier.'

## AFGHANISTAN

### FINLEY

Sweat runs down my back, but my concentration doesn't waver. When the upload hits 100 percent, I unhook the wire and pack away the hardware. My second insertion of this WT software, and it wasn't any more accessible than the one I did in London two years ago. Two of my team are covering the door for me. At my nod, we move out.

Cameron is my lead. We make quick work of navigating the lower level of the building. Stopping at our exit point, Cameron and I assess the street. He steps into the courtyard. The moment my feet hit the dirt, I hear the static surge of an electrical current that wasn't present on our way in.

Erin's face flashes in my mind, and a caution that wasn't there before passes through me. I grab Cameron's collar and pull him down.

Before we make contact with the ground, pain slices through me. Cameron screams, and as we fall, I see it. Static and electricity closing a hole in mid-air behind shooting soldiers in black uniforms who came out of nowhere.

On the ground, I feel my side getting wet—a pool of blood covering me. The pain is so sharp, it steals my breath. Bullets hiss as they ping through the air above my head. I try to raise my gun, but the guttural sound I hear each time I take a breath and the suffocating feeling in my lungs are more concerning than the shaking arm I raise only slightly. The impact of bullets on skin is a hollow silence before there are shouts of pain from the team that was standing behind me. More bodies fall. I should have been standing, taking the shots to protect them.

My vision's blurred, and I'm dizzy even though I'm lying on the ground.

I hear footfalls from the east. Our backup team is arriving. Someone pulls me back into the building. The shock of movement has me coughing for breath, and blood spills from my mouth. My skin is on fire, and my chest feels held together only by the gear attached to my body. Dylan leans over me, shouting words I can't hear. His face comes and goes as my eyelids get heavier.

I try to speak, tell them to leave me, but there's only an echo of the words in my head.

The last thing they need is dragging a body home to slow them down.

They need to get out. They need to run.

#  Chapter eight

## Erin

There's a caravan of cars being driven from our hotel to our new house. Mark is up front, setting the pace, followed by Ollie, who keeps drifting into the middle of the road. Not helpful when there are cars coming in the opposite direction. You would think, growing up in London, he would be the most used to traffic. Lara is next and I'm bringing up the rear. A car each. What a waste of resources, but apparently, we need them. I invited Ashley and Nanda to come see the house, since Nanda keeps going on about how she loves farmland properties, so technically they are the ones at the end of the line.

Ollie not only got us cash in a bank account to purchase a home, mortgage free, but there was enough capital to start the business and get us all cars and clothing and furniture and everything else we might need to help with our cover story here.

The property where Mark, Ollie, and I are going to live is less than ten minutes from town, on the way to the moors and the landing point where we fell through a time portal. Lara, true to her word, isn't sticking around. She's going to make herself useful in other parts of the country, where we have long-term camps set up in the future. I'm not sure what the hell she's hoping to achieve, but she's grieving, and I trust her enough to keep herself safe. She got through Europe and swam from France to England on her own.

The house is in a prime location to see anyone approaching, one reason we targeted it in the future. Set half a mile from the main road and down a battle-axe driveway, with houses on either side, it's a narrow road that can only comfortably accommodate one car at a time. I slow to an almost stop and open the window. The quiet almost takes me back to the time I'm used to, with minimum people and only nature and the wind to hear. Cars pass me, and I turn into the long drive.

The land under the main house is higher than the driveway, and the last hundred yards is a steep incline to the front door. There are views of the neighbouring farms, roads, and the river to the east. The west side of the property is fifty acres of farmland, only six of which we own. We only needed one to take ownership of the sheds. Miles and miles of unoccupied land is something I'm used to, but not something we've time for here.

Despite the bidding war with another local, we convinced the owner that we were the best family to take over his home. Mark is persuasive. We needed that shed, and the house was a bonus. A prime property to know about for the future—especially since someone else thought so too.

There's enough space at the front of the house for all the cars, but Mark and Ollie pulled around back to unload all the tech surveillance equipment into the barn. Our visits here, under the guise of closing on the sale, have revealed no trace of the electric current or the small circle and lines we saw emit the blue energy. But there is hope if we keep watch on the barn enough, or if Ollie can harness electricity in the correct area, we might see it again.

I park on the driveway, and Ashley pulls in next to me. She and Nanda jump out and tell me how nice the outside looks.

I unlock and open the front doors. 'Voilà. Go on in and see what you think.'

The house is newly renovated, with sandstone on the front and double doors leading into a tiled reception hallway.

'You guys go to the kitchen and put the kettle on. I'm going to talk to my sister real quick.'

I return to the car and pop the boot open. 'I'm glad you're here to help us set up this week.'

'I'm not running away,' Lara says. 'I just think it's better not to get settled. Don't overdo this friendship thing.'

'We're getting on great.'

'Huh? Things might peak too early. Make sure they don't get sick of you. It's hard to build something long-lasting.'

'You want to meet her, right?'

Lara smiles and I can tell she's hiding a laugh. 'Ashley Garvey, who doesn't have her shit together? Can't wait.'

I nudge her and pull the suitcase inside the hallway. 'Be nice,' I whisper before we enter the kitchen.

Ashley and Nanda introduce themselves to Lara. 'Nice shoes,' Ashley croons at Lara's high-heeled black sandals that lace up her naked calves.

'Lara's sense of fashion has taken priority over all tasks since we got here,' I tell them.

'Oh, don't act like there's no fashion in London, Erin.' Lara eyeballs me for my slip. 'Excuse Erin. She's not much for dressing up. I'm the one you want to call to borrow club gear.' Lara smiles next to me. 'I didn't take up all the room in the moving truck. You should meet our brother, Ollie. He almost filled an entire car with computer equipment.'

'Some of us made sacrifices to keep everyone else quiet.'

'Stalker Rian Butterly has infiltrated your life.' Nanda points to a bouquet of flowers and a fruit basket on the kitchen table.

I retrieve the card. 'He works at the bank that handled the sale,' I tell them. 'Turns out he was looking over this house when we got here.'

'Why the hell would he want a five-bedroom family home?' Nanda asks.

I toss the *good luck in your new home* card on the counter and Ash notices he's left his number for me there, too. She picks up the card and makes a swit swoo noise.

'Since we keep

bumping into each other,

maybe we should bump

into each other

on purpose sometime.

Give me a call.

I'd love to get to know you.

Fate might just

Be bringing us together!'

'Stop it.' I snatch the card and place it under the fruit basket, out of sight.

'He started all that "fate brought us together" crap with me too,' Nanda says. 'Not that he's possibly not genuine when he says it to you. You should totally go out with him and see where it leads. Just because I freaked out doesn't mean anything.' She's rambling, and honestly, I don't care what she thinks about a man I've bumped into a few times.

'He is seriously hot, and you obviously like guys with accents,' Ashley says. 'Scottish and Irish are practically the same,' Nanda says.

The idea is ridiculous.

Lara asks about local places they hang out and what Nanda's going to study at Newcastle University. Lara keeps the

69

conversation going about their shared impending departure and how to settle into a new town when they get there. Lara's strong point is putting people at ease and finding common ground. I go upstairs to dump my bag outside my new bedroom, do a quick sweep of the upper two floors, and rejoin them in the kitchen.

'Well, ladies, it was lovely to meet you, but I have to go.' Lara pours the rest of her tea into the white Belfast sink and rinses her cup. 'Dad's ordering the rest of the furniture today, and I want to be there to make sure he doesn't fuck it up.'

'The house is beautiful. I've always wanted to live out here, and you got one of the few places high enough for a view. I can't believe you bought it. You're not even farmers. What are you going to do with all this land?' Nanda asks.

'We've an installation business that requires a lot of storage space.' Lara's voice has a no-nonsense tone to it. Like she's switched to her business voice. 'You girls should stay a night after we have it all sorted. Meet the family. We want to get to know the people our sister has been spending so much time with.'

'I don't think Dad is going to want the house filled with women, especially when he's trying to start a company. He'll be working a lot,' I say.

Lara purses her lips and croaks, 'Ruin all the fun, why don't you.'

My phone rings, and I pull it out of my back pocket. 'Speak of the devil.' I say to Mark, 'Lazy much? I'm about two hundred feet away from you.'

'Ollie's trying to get more details as we speak,' Mark says, 'but he can confirm Garvey's unit was taken out overseas at least twelve days ago.'

I knew it was coming. I was preparing for it since I walked into that bar and met them two weeks ago, but it's still a punch in the gut.

'There are no names yet, but almost half the unit, and most of the US backup, were killed. Just like last time. Ollie is monitoring chatter about bad intel. Do you know anything else?' Mark asks.

I indicate to the girls I'm taking the call in the other room and wait until I close the door before letting out a breath. A tear falls, and I swat it away.

'I never knew the details.' I don't want to repeat what happens to Garvey, about the spiral of depression and PTSD, therapy and rehab. The dismissal of his career and the new direction of helping the families of lost servicemen.

'Why haven't we seen this on the news yet? A UK Special Forces unit would've made the news.'

'It means someone is hiding things. Did Garvey ever mention anything to you about being double-crossed or any cover-ups that happened?'

'I was a kid. My dad wasn't going to tell me things like that. Hell, you used to be his best friend. You know as much as I do about what happened.'

I cringe at his silence. 'Is he okay?' I rub my thigh. 'He must be okay, but is he in rehab already?'

'Ollie can't find any info on where the survivors were sent, but we assume they were brought back to the UK after debriefing. He's going to keep digging, but we will proceed as expected. Garvey will be along in two years.'

'Dylan,' I tell him. I don't know where the stab of jealousy comes from, but I suddenly realize I don't want the younger, cockier Dylan Garvey to take our leader's name. When survivors talk about Garvey, it's with awe and respect, and they are thankful for him taking them in, saving their lives, and for fighting for them. 'Tell the others we call the one in this timeline Dylan. He's not our Garvey yet.'

He will be, just after he goes through his own personal hell.

I stand up like movement and action will make the entire process less painful to deal with. Lara was right. People here deserve a fighting chance too, and we just let them die. 'Have Ollie send flowers to the families. Those soldiers deserve our respect and remembrance.'

'Will do, and, Erin? You couldn't save them, so don't feel bad because you met them once.'

I nod even though he can't see me, and my face crumbles.

'I didn't expect it to hurt.'

It's silly to grieve for a man I never knew and was never supposed to be with, but the loss of what *could* have been is stronger than I realised.

# nine

Darlington, UK

Six months later        June 2019

### Erin

Insomnia means I volunteer for most night shifts. Long after the sun rises, I sign off at 8:30 a.m. and drive into town to bring Ashley her morning coffee.

I'm standing in line at the coffee shop when she texts me: *Hurry up. I have gossip.*

She always has gossip, so I don't reply. It'll only take a minute to walk around the corner to her salon.

I don't think Ashley appreciates having a job under where she lives. No commute, no travel expenses. She works eight to four and is late every day.

Leaving the coffee shop, I see Rian approaching on the other side of the street. I could put my head down and take the long way around, but he's already seen me and is smiling like we didn't break up. I've been avoiding him ever since.

'How ya,' Rian says.

'Nanda was right. You are a stalker,' I half joke as he joins me.

Dressed in a suit for work, Rian is handsome. He has height and piercing eyes. Add a good job and charisma, and he

73

never has a problem getting a date. His problem is keeping someone around. Nanda was smarter than me and knew there was something off during their first date. Disappointingly, it took me longer to realise he was a possessive jerk, looking for someone to show off.

He glances at the coffee shop behind me. 'Only good place in town for coffee, and the bank is right over there, so maybe you're the one who is stalking me?' He smirks, like he hasn't been texting me crap about us being fated to be together.

Honestly. It's a coincidence.

Rian showed up at our house the week after we moved in to 'officially' ask me out for dinner. Before I knew it, weeks turned into months of dating, and it was a nice distraction from what was going on in my life.

'We should get a drink this weekend,' he says.

'No. This is annoying.'

'What's wrong with being friends?'

'You're being weird, and I don't have time for this.'

'Your family is really *weird* about keeping their business under wraps. Do you know how many places I had to check to see what finances you're pumping into a business that isn't even turning overyet?'

My jaw drops. 'This is exactly why we can't be friends. You don't even realise how many lines you're crossing.' I step closer to him. 'You might think you're some kind of junior bank manager hotshot, but my family will remove their business accounts from your bank. And if you keep making life difficult for me, I'll let your boss know why we're leaving.' I move off. 'And if that doesn't work, I might have to ask my dad to kill you!' There's laughter in my voice, but he doesn't know that Mark would kill him if he knew how much Rian has been stalking me since we broke up. Add that to the interference with our work, Mark wouldn't hesitate.

Rian yells down the street after me, making a scene. 'Just a friendly warning, Erin. That's all. Whatever tax evasion or what not you're up to, you're not as careful as you think you are.'

Outside Ashley's salon, I climb the two steps to bring me to the beautician's door, and the bell chimes when I enter. Ashley has the treatment room open and is clearing up her station when I stop at the threshold.

She turns. 'You look exhausted.'

'I need sleep, not caffeine.' I salute her with the cup and take a large swig, despite knowing I shouldn't.

'I thought working for your father was supposed to be easy, not sixty hours a week.'

I chuckle. 'I'm under a lot of pressure to keep the family business open. Every one of us relies on it,' I lie. 'The business runs twenty-four-hour shifts. Sometimes it feels like having the weight of the world on your shoulders,' I joke.

'You guys need to hire more staff.'

'Can't. Our clients like the small team we have. It offers more security, which is our main sales pitch.'

'Burying survival bunkers for rich people is a weird-ass business venture.' She scrunches her nose. 'You should do what Nanda did and get your dad to sack you so you can go back to university. Or take a job with no responsibility. Nanda was always complaining about "fate of the world" stuff.' She sighs.

I raise an eyebrow. 'Fate of the world?'

'That's what she said. If you asked her or her father, defence technology and support win wars, hence the fate of the world or whatever. "*Don't screw it up. Don't miss a day of college*".' She screws up her face. 'Yada yada, lots of pressure. I think it's why she took every opportunity to screw the local soldiers. She was trying to piss Daddy off.'

'Nanda, who left you with no roommate?' I ask sarcastically.

75

'I'm managing just fine.' Ashley shrugs.

'What's so important you tore me away from Phil and Holly? Some of us work in the evening so we can watch daytime TV.'

'Remember when I said I was going to quit when Susan told us we were now taking bookings for male treatments?'

'Back, sac, and flash us your crack. I remember.' I swirl the remaining coffee to see what grounds made it through the filter.

Ashley jumps up on the treatment bed and swings her legs back and forth. 'Obviously, I didn't think it through. I figured all the weirdos would come in and flash us their cocks.'

I hold up a hand. 'But you got a hottie in here. I get it. And now you want to see his cock when you're not ripping hot wax off it.' First-hand gossip about my mother's sex life is not something I thought I would have to deal with in the past.

'I never said I was going to ditch the hot wax.' She winks. 'Guess whose balls I just waxed?'

'Is this the gossip you texted me about?' I try not to gag. 'Because I have no idea.'

'Take a guess, because we have dates tonight. Both of us.'

I groan. 'I told you, I don't want to date. I just broke up with Rian. I want a break from men. From people, actually.'

Ashley snorts. 'You never spent that much time with Rian, so you don't need much of a break. Besides, the best way to get over your ex-fiancé is to get under—'

'Rian wasn't my fiancé. He asked me to marry him, so I broke up with him. He's my ex-boyfriend. That's all.'

'That's not what he's telling everyone. He's saying you left him in the middle of planning the wedding.'

'Christ, he's so dramatic. This is why I should never date. I don't have time for this. I have to go home and watch TV for another hour, sleep for six, then haul ass back to work before my sister kills me.'

'Is Lara back from Scotland?'

'No, but she'll be calling with her daily report, and I have to be there to answer.'

'Text her and reschedule. I need you back here at seven, dressed to impress.'

I head to the door. 'I'm not going out with some random whose balls you waxed.'

'No, you're not. You're getting back in the saddle with Finley tonight.'

I freeze and turn around. 'Excuse me?'

She holds up a used wax strip. 'Dylan came to visit. Our little soldier duo is back in town, lass.' She tries to mock Finley's accent.

'Dylan was here? Already? And he said Finley was— *alive*—with him?'

'Dylan is on like a month's hiatus before he has to go back to wherever, and Finley's being discharged for an injury, so he's renting a flat at the new build down at the train station. They want to go out with us.'

My heart beats faster, and I feel tears in the back of my eyes. I need to lock this down. I run my hand over my hip. *Don't give up*.

Ashley drops the wax strip in the pedal bin, crosses to the door, where I'm still frozen in shock, and takes my hand. 'Erin, are you okay?'

I nod, and that damn tear rolls down my face.

'God, girl, you never cried when you and Rian broke up, and you get upset over someone you met once?' She tries to make light of the situation, but there is concern and wonder on her face. She nudges me. 'Is this why you were always holding back when we tried to set you up?' She gasps. 'Are you in love with Finley?'

'No.' I've calmed myself enough to pass it off as something else. 'It's just... he reminds me of when we lost

77

Blake. Everything was around that time, and he was a breath of fresh air at a tough time. Don't make a big deal, okay?'

'Okay then.' She gently drops my hand. 'We're going out, so come to mine to get ready.'

Outside, I pull my phone out as I cross the road and beep my car lock. I pour the rest of the coffee out and open the driver's door. Ollie answers my call before I've buckled up and set the phone in the cradle. 'Can I talk?'

'It's just Mark and me. You're on speaker.'

I pull out of the parallel parking space and work my way around the one-way system to get back on the main road. 'Things are fucked up.'

'What happened?'

'Dylan's back early, and some people are alive that shouldn't be.'

I notice the recently filled flower boxes at every window of our house, pick up one of the heavy rectangular trays overflowing with climber flowers, and heave it inside with me. I go into the dining room, our makeshift meeting place. The wide oval table allows us to spread out paperwork and lets Ollie plug in more than one device at a time.

I drop the flowers on the edge of the table and sit. It only takes me a minute to tell them about Dylan and his team's mission.

'How the hell did we miss this?' Mark asks Ollie.

Ollie closes the laptop. 'We missed nothing. We interpreted what we got with the knowledge that Erin has from the future.'

'Meaning?' I ask.

'We assumed they were dead. We never found names. Everything was hidden. Hell, we were working on the assumption Dylan was a survivor.'

'Because he was,' I snap.

'But the dead? The details you had were basic. What if Finley and Cameron always survived?'

'They didn't. Everything is different already.' I click my fingernail back and forth between my teeth, trying to focus. I get a flash memory of a fingernail being yanked off during interrogation, and I manage not to gag as I move my hands to my lap. 'Dylan is supposed to still be in rehab. His best friend is alive. I'm going to assume he's dealing with whatever happened better than he did the last time, because it's not had as much psychological impact on him.'

'We need to get the timeline back on track,' Ollie says. 'Wait and see if he leaves Ashley again and comes back in eighteen months, like he's supposed to. Maybe sabotage your date tonight. Make sure you and Ashley don't go, and they might leave town.'

I argue, 'If he leaves her again, she's going to be so pissed she might not give him another chance.'

'I agree,' Mark says. 'Ashley and Dylan might have been made for each other, or whatever.' Mark rolls his eyes but tries to hide it by leaning forward. 'But this early in a new relationship, Ash is the kind of woman to throw you to the kerb if you screw around.

'Those men came back for both of you,' Mark says. 'If they're renting a place, they signed up for at least six months. That's some serious confidence to think you two are going to hook up with them again.'

I cringe. I can't go on a double date with my parents and their friend. It's too weird.

'Or they're in town for another reason,' Ollie says calmly. 'Think you can figure out what other business they might have in town?'

'Go tonight,' Mark tells me. 'Find out as much as you can about what happened. We'll dig up everything we can on Finley and Dylan.'

I drop my head on the table.

Mark crouches to speak to me at eye level. 'Dylan Garvey's in active service. He's at risk of being killed on missions he was never supposed to be on or his service history being stretched so far into the future that he's flagged as a threat in the first wave of takeovers. His relationship with Ashley is also a year and a half early, which means their timelines may have changed.'

'What the hell does that mean? What if we've already changed too much?' I ask.

Mark places a hand on my shoulder. 'First things first. Get those men out of the army. If the attack on Dylan's unit was as serious as the last time, an option to discharge from active service might be a possibility if he fails his next psych test. Find out when his contract is up. If he hands in his year's notice now, with a bad psych report, we might get lucky and keep him in the country. They both need to be off the government's radar when the time comes, then we'll deal with the teeny-bop romance dilemma.' He winks at me.

## ten

**Erin**

I parallel park into a space outside Ashley's flat at six. I'm giving her minimal time to poke and prod at me, and possibly inquire about my waxing before we leave for our double date. Yey, go me, dating two different guys in the wrong timeline and possibly fucking up the whole universe in the process.

I let myself in, dump my bag on the floor, and shout for Ashley. There's music on in her room, and I can hear her singing. I pause to listen. She has no problems, and you can hear that in her voice.

She opens the door, mid-verse, and screams when she sees me leaning on the bathroom doorframe. 'Shit!' she yells and claps her chest. 'Didn't hear you come in.' She nudges me out of the way as she enters the toilet and rummages through her makeup bag.

'The front door's unlocked.'

Ashley rolls her eyes.

'You're like a kid who can't see the danger they're constantly putting themselves in.'

Perfume invades my nose when she sprays it in my direction, pretending I'm an annoying wasp that needs to be shooed away.

81

'Stop it.' I pout like a two-year-old and check the beep on my phone. Great. Rian texted again. I don't read this one and slam my phone face down on the bathroom counter.

Ashley leans over the sink to get closer to the mirror and applies powdered shit to her eyebrows.

'Why didn't Dylan call you instead of coming to get his balls waxed?' I try not to gag at the visual that brings.

'I didn't give him my number.'

'You never ever told me that. I thought it was love at first sight.'

Ashley looks at me in the mirror. 'I told him where I worked, and he knew where I lived. If he wanted to see me again, he'd find me. He asked for my number a million times, and I told him he could find me when he was done with enlisted life. I didn't want to be the girlfriend left behind while he was off screwing around or, you know, dying and stuff.'

'You said that to a soldier right before deployment? That's kind of crass, Ash,' I say louder than I mean to. 'He went off to fight for our freedom, and you didn't give a shit. He almost died.' Frustration boils through me. 'Did Dylan say anything about Cameron or the others in their unit? How bad their injuries were or who made it home?'

Ashley stops curling her eyelashes or whatever the fuck she's doing and stares at me. 'What's going on?'

'Nothing.' I take a breath. 'Living this close to barracks, seeing soldiers come and go, you should be so blasé about what they're doing.'

She shrugs. 'I'm not. That's exactly why I didn't give him my number. I see groups of friends getting smaller and smaller as they pass through this town because some of them don't come home.' She tries to smile to let me know we're okay and continues abusing her eyelashes. 'Why do you think Nanda left her dad's company? It's a lot of responsibility to know if your technology screws up, a bunch of soldiers might die. It was all she spoke about for the months leading up to her quitting. A full one-eighty in moral code turnaround, if you ask me.' She takes a deep breath. 'No one ever died of a bikini wax.'

A bar across town that favours cocktails over football is where Ashley takes me. Finley is sitting in a booth along the back wall, and I've never seen anyone so radiant. He's alive, and I can't take my eyes off him.

Dylan says something to him, and he turns to the door, then stands. His smile is relaxed. My heart kicks up a beat. I don't even notice I've crossed the room until he's right in front of me, looking dapper in designer jeans and T-shirt. Nothing like his well-worn denims and army issue boots the first time we met. The smell of him makes my head spin when he leans in for a hug. I inhale him. I breathe him. And it feels like we haven't been apart all this time.

Part of me was hoping Ashley got it wrong, that history hadn't changed, and I hadn't screwed up everything by being here. Because one glimpse of him, and I'm pretty sure I'm falling for someone I shouldn't be.

The grin that spreads across his face eases my heart for the first time since I've been in this shitty timeline, and I'm totally screwed. I pay no attention to what's going on around me and hate myself for allowing someone to consume all my focus. It's all him and that gorgeous panty-dropping smile.

God, I forgot how good-looking he is. And nervous, apparently. His smile is a distraction from the red scar on the side of his neck, and he notices as I find it. It's puckered and raw, and looks like it will take years to heal and fade. Halfway from the top of his neck and follows the entire way down to the base. I bet it follows his tattoos under his shirt. He shifts and tries to hold his smile in place.

'Well, well, well, they return.' I make myself look at Dylan, relieved he's in one piece.

Dylan practically pulls Ashley onto his lap, and I hear that giggle of hers.

Finley takes my hand and leans in to kiss me on my cheek. 'You look good, Erin.' He holds out his hand. I take it, and we slide into the booth.

Finley's strong accent feels more like home than being in England, where my parents were raised. I think that's why I didn't go to Scotland with Lara. I didn't need a constant audio reminder of what I lost.

My jaw tightens. Fuck. Rule number two: don't concentrate on one thing so much that you forget to focus on everything. I took my attention off the room, and I need to re-evaluate.

Forty-six people in the place. My original headcount on entry has increased, with people spilling from the toilets and trickling in the front door. That has me on edge. It's more people than I'm used to seeing spread across a city the size of Manchester. I'm still getting used to so many gathering casually in one place.

I glance in the mirror behind the bar, dismissing the rows of bottles in the way and the dark ambience, the low lighting and dark-stained tables and chairs and support beams. The walls are freshly painted and there's heat coming from the fireplace, a popular location with the customers. Everything here screams nonchalance and freedom. The main entrance is behind me. The second egress is along the bathroom hallway, where a faint green light near the top of the door indicates the emergency exit sign hiding around the corner.

The intoxication going on around me is startling. No one is paying attention to their surroundings. I'll admit freedom is a potent substance. You can get drunk on it. Being able to walk on a crowded street, go out in the evening and see people laugh—hell, even picking up a newspaper that's not censored by

NewGov—is an eye-opener. Journalists are bold in 2019, because they can't be hanged for their words.

Not being chased or shot at is a relief.

But this false sense of freedom could be what gets us killed if we start to act like the people of this time. Their utter obliviousness of what's going on is why the first wave of takedowns was so successful. Three full days before people noticed and then it was too late.

The sheer number of people in this space, acting as a mob barrier, is a concern, but no one moves like they're trained. Most men have a slightly stooped posture, a typical lifestyle hazard of this era. Guess it's more favourable to *our* lifestyle hazard of dying. A fighter wouldn't stand so sloppy. Most people here are inebriated.

A round of drinks is ordered, and I sit in silence, waiting for someone to speak. Nothing's going to make you feel more awkward on a date than doubling with people who have the responsibility of keeping me alive in the future. And a tingling desire to screw their not-dead friend.

'You guys are going to be on TV? That's kind of cool.' Ashley picks up her third cocktail and twirls her straw. 'Actually, I take that back. Not when all the girls throw themselves at you. Remember, we saw you first.'

Dylan pinches her side and tugs her closer. 'I remember.'

Finley puts his beer down. 'A local investor is in partnership with a production company and approached the garrison for ideas of who might be suitable. Our names came up, and since Cameron and I have been discharged, it seemed like a good opportunity.'

It took me a minute and a half to find out Cameron came home alive with Dylan and Finley but is currently in France visiting friends and not expected back for a while. Two others we met at the bar that day are also okay, but three of the team were killed, like they were supposed to be. They never said it, but I deduced as best as I could from the headcount and whereabouts of the rest of the guys this time.

Finley raises his glass to Dylan. 'We're trying to convince this one to quit and come over to the reality TV star world with us.' He chuckles.

It'd be a good way to convince Dylan to retire from service, but the public eye is not the place for him either.

Dylan says, 'Nah, I'm staying until my time is up, no matter what's offered by some pissing little bank manager or the army.'

'What's the army's offer?' I ask.

'Early retirement, full pension—like Cameron and me,' Finley says.

'Why? What happened on your last mission? The government fuck something up? They don't normally let servicemen go that easily.' I glance between them.

Finley narrows his eyes and doesn't answer the first part of my question. 'Cameron and I were discharged because of our injuries and recovery time. Dylan was a greyer area.'

Dylan leans forward. 'Doc says I was only borderline crazy, so the government gave me an opportunity to stick around.' He winks.

I turn to Ashley. 'Didn't you say something about not coming back until he was back for good?' I'm stirring the pot, but Ashley was the only one who could ever get Dylan to consider serious life changes.

'I've got another month of leave, crashing on Finley's new couch, before I make my final decision. Thought I might come back here and see if there's another kind of life on offer.'

He says to Finley, 'No offence, but being stuck in a one-bed apartment with you wasn't on my life goals.'

Ashley eyes him. She must be mad he's alluding to a decision on the rest of their lives on the second date, but neither of them knows how pivotal this moment might be to them—and to me and the rest of us.

I slurp the last of my iced-down black cocktail and drop the straw in the glass. Finley's hand brushes the length of my arm as he leans back.

I can't help but grin at him, and for fuck's sake, I have to bite my lip to stop myself from laughing in relief that he's really here.

'When did you start drinking so much?' Finley asks.

I wave. 'It's only my second, and I've needed it the last couple of months.'

He smirks. 'Being friends with Ashley is that bad, huh?'

She snorts. 'Hell no, but dating Mr. Boring drove her to drink.' She chuckles, and I widen my eyes at her to shut the hell up.

I quickly change the subject. 'If you retire from service, Dylan, you'll go on TV and document everything you can and cannot do? Seems a little stupid, if you ask me.' My heart bangs, a combination of alcohol, espresso, and adrenaline. The most significant advantage we had was that no one knew who Garvey was. He hid, and eventually found and recruited others for the rebellion. If those who take over our so-called government come across documents and TV footage of Dylan and his level of skill set, they'll have more information than they had before.

'Whatever happened to *blend in*? *Don't give the enemy too much information*? Can't you do something else, like charity work?'

'I don't see me sorting through second-hand clothes in a high street shop, thank you,' he says.

'You could help those who come back from overseas service or fundraise for the families who've lost someone in the war.' The table quiets down. 'Not all of them get full pension, you know.'

'Don't mind her,' Ashley says. 'Her granddad was in the army or something. Guess paranoia runs in the family.' She smiles at me, but I can tell she's trying to figure out what I'm freaking out over.

'I come from a whole family of servicemen *and women*,' I say. 'And in the job we're doing, we hear a lot of stuff. That's all I'm saying. Might want to reconsider the TV thing.'

'And what, get an office job?' Dylan asks. 'What jobs are out there for ex-Special Forces guys who were discharged 'cause their heads are fucked?'

'Is that how you view yourself? With a fucked head? All I see is a soldier who was strong enough to ask for help.' I grew up around mental health. Paranoia, PTS, psychological warfare. I probably know more about it than Dylan and Finley do. 'You can't do this. You have no idea what the future is going to hold. You're still young, both of you. If you put yourselves on TV, you'll become targets.' I correct myself. 'Maybe not targets, but job opportunities will decrease. Sure, it sounds glamorous, but was that why you signed up? For fame and glory? Some people won't want to hire a famous SAS soldier. It might damage your career.'

'Our careers are over, Sunshine.' He's speaking to me, but smiles at Ashley. 'Plenty of us didn't come home. No need to tempt fate anymore. I should probably hang up my boots first chance I get and go after one of those office jobs.'

'Don't call me Sunshine,' I say flatly.

I know the pain in Finley's eyes, the guilt of surviving. Knowing your friends are dead and you're alive is something you can't be relieved about. The guilt of knowing that others will have to continue to risk their lives while you're safe.

'What if I could get you a job?' I ask. 'Speak to my dad. We could use someone with the contacts you might have.' My offer is two-fold selfish. We could use additional highly trained men, and by helping Dylan and Finley, I can alleviate some of my own survivor's guilt, knowing I'm helping a kindred spirit. Having Finley working with us would be a great reason to hang around him a lot too. I guess that's three selfish reasons, none of which have been through tactical analysis or safety consideration—for my unit here, as well as those stranded in the future.

Dylan says, 'We don't need any pity jobs.' He storms out, and Finley nods at me as he follows his friend out. It strikes me there's a possibility to bring Dylan Garvey and his friends into the fight sooner. I leap out of my seat, and Ashley calls after me but stays in her seat.

I catch the rebound of the door and tear out after them. 'I need gun runners.'

Finley and Dylan turn in slow motion.

Well, that stopped them.

## FINLEY

Missing brother, stuck in town, doesn't feel safe—
looking to employ gun runners. Everything says I should stay
away from Erin, but something about her makes me believe
she's not the bad guy in this.

The taxi drops the girls off at Ashley's flat. I let Erin out
while Dylan kisses Ashley at her front door. I want to kiss Erin
like that. It's all I've wanted to do since I saw her again. Hell,
she's all I thought about since I left her all those months ago.
Thoughts of her were the only thing that kept me going through
rehab. The person I wanted to be with to ground myself in
reality. The person I could see the possibility of a future with
and worth fighting through those awful days. I've wanted to
come back for her before I even left.

'Thanks,' she says.

'Sure I can't drop you at home?'

'I usually stay here after a night in town.'

'And I'm sure the fam don't want guys and taxis driving
up to the house at night. Especially if they are into something
questionable.'

Her smiles fades.

'I'm sticking around for a while. Maybe you'll explain
everything to me. Since you offered me a job, right?' I lean on
the taxi door and call to Dylan. 'Let's go, man.' Leaving's the
only distraction I have. I want to kiss Erin. I want to body slam
her against the car and lick down her neck. I want to tug that
dress higher to see her legs better.

She senses the awkward moment.

'The job offer was too soon, huh?' She tries to laugh, but she's still digging for information.

'Little bit,' I deadpan. 'But I also want to see you again.' Preferably alone next time, but I also need time to figure out who the hell she is. It's entirely possible I've spent the last six months building Erin Cooper up in my head into a fantasy that doesn't remotely represent the real woman.

Erin tilts her head. 'I'd have preferred it if Dylan was a little more cautious too.'

I glance at Ashley and wonder if I should pull him off her.

'Don't worry. Ashley knows nothing about my family's business. He's in safe hands.'

'Am I?' I ask.

She whispers in my ear, 'With or without the job, Finley.'

My dick hardens when her breath hits my face, and I grip the doorframe more tightly. Keeping my hands off her is tougher than it should be. As she moves back, I turn away. She catches her breath as my lips brush her cheek.

'Till tomorrow, emissary girl. Date two. I have something fun planned.' I get back in the car and tell the driver to honk the horn to get Dylan's arse moving.

We wait until the girls are inside before giving the driver our address across town. Dylan is texting as the taxi pulls out.

'Don't hit send.' I glance at my watch and groan. 'It's 0230 hours, 0330 in France. Cameron needs to sleep when he can. No point in his brain working overtime through the night. We'll call him in the morning.'

'Back here again, with a dodgy offer from someone we met the day before we got betrayed, can't be a coincidence.' Dylan leans back. 'Cameron needs to look into this from his end.'

91

*The bottom drops out of my stomach. Please, Erin, don't be involved in this shit.*

Dylan and I wait until after our morning workout and run before calling Cameron. A late night means a slow start, and it's after lunchtime before we've showered and discussed the best way to break this to him. He answers straight away, breathing hard like he's running, even though he's months away from being able to do physical activity to that extent.

'How's the sun? Meet any hot French girls?' Dylan asks over the speakerphone.

'If only I had enough time to chase a girl, rather than dealing with this,' Cameron replies.

Dylan's eyebrows shoot up. He never believed our conspiracy theory, but he let us use it as a distraction while we dealt with our careers being over and the death of our teammates.

I suspect the latter was why Dylan wanted some of our crazy talk to be true. Revenge against someone tangible is motivation, but Cameron and I were the only witnesses to things that could never be true.

'You visit the prison yet?' I ask.

'My contact at the embassy will let me see the prisoner soon. I'm wearing her down, but she's talking a lot about our people being involved in some psych test score for active servicemen.'

'What the hell does that mean?' Dylan, the only one of us still under contract, leans forward.

'I'm trying to get info from the prisoner over the phone, but she won't give me everything until she trusts me.'

'She's in jail for treason. Of course she's going to jump on a conspiracy investigation.'

'Arson,' Cameron corrects. 'Insists it was a setup to discredit her and keep her out of the way when the time comes.'

'Yeah, well, she burned down Notre Dame Cathedral. The whole world discredits her,' Dylan says.

'Let's not argue about why she's in jail. She knew our orders would be changed at the last minute. She had details about both sets of orders we got and that we were deployed out of Catterick Garrison, which we never are. That's enough for me to find out what else she knows. Why do you both want an update? Normally it's me calling Finley.'

We fill Cameron in on our dates with the girls and the job Erin offered us.

'You guys were supposed to be there investigating the lead the senior officer gave us on Wilson Tech, not dating.' He sounds annoyed but not mad.

'I know, but it was Dylan who set it up.'

Dylan punches me in the arm for ratting him out, and I chuckle.

'We're looking into the list you gave us,' Dylan tells him. 'And the TOP is helping. He doesn't know much, but he's getting us involved with some stuff happening at Command Training with Wilson. He's also trying to get us a TV job with a local investor and producer from London. It's a good cover to explain why we're in town, and it gets us access we need.'

'You're staying in Darlington then?' Cameron asks Dylan, knowing *I* was always going to stick around as long as he wanted me to.

Dylan says, 'It's a possibility, and with Finley getting involved with girls and illegal jobs, it might be good for him to have me around.'

'The date went that well, huh?' Cameron chuckles, and I laugh when Dylan's neck reddens.

'He's going to uproot his life for a woman. Someone call the papers,' I say. 'I'm thinking of taking Erin up on her offer or at least finding out more.'

'That's a good idea. It can't be a coincidence. It's a small-town gun-running job next to the largest garrison in the UK. Her family must have dealings with someone there. It's worth looking into, even if they're not directly involved.'

'She's not bad, Cameron. She was talking about helping soldiers. She mentioned creating a charity for those that return home and need help.'

'Those fucked up like us, you mean?'

'Hey, talk about yourself,' I joke. 'But seriously, a lot of them don't want help but need it. Even for the physiotherapy. She recognises that. It has to be a good thing, right?'

'Monitor her before you get involved personally. Scope her out, follow her around for a couple of days. Watch yourself.'

'Will do.' I disconnect the call.

We spend hours that afternoon looking up everything on the Notre Dame fire. The forty-five-year-old British woman, known only as Suspect A, was given full anonymity even after sentencing. The media tried and failed to get pictures, a real name—any details at all—but the whereabouts of the convicted woman were kept secure.

The UK and France happily denied her request to transfer to a prison in England and kept her in France to serve out her sentence. There's nothing to connect this incident with an intel bust in Afghanistan.

'Where are you going?' Dylan asks when I put my laptop on the table and lace up my boots.

'To scope out my girl,' I tell him.

# twelve

## Erin

Two mercenaries are alive in this timeline, and I invited them to work in the family business. I'm mad at myself the whole way down the high street.

Propositioning allies outside a pub last night was reckless. Mark's going to flip, and I've hidden out at Ashley's all day to avoid the inevitable. It will be dark soon, and I shouldn't keep information from my team.

That Finley and Dylan brought nothing else up later that night makes me nervous. It means they were planning to research me. It's the only smart thing *to* do when someone offers you an illegal job. God, I hope they do it and aren't completely incompetent.

I shoot Mark and Ollie a text after I'm inside the car: *Meeting. 10 min out.*

Eight minutes later, I'm rounding the street corner that follows the sandstone wall that encompasses our land and pull up at the bottom gates.

I enter my code and the iron gates open. My tires crunch up the gravel driveway, and I park alongside the fleet of family cars. Inside, I stride to the back of the house to the dining room we use for debriefing.

There are two mahogany doors on runners that I slide open. I sit at the head of the table. Mark and Ollie are opposite each other, at my left and right hand.

'Alarms?' I ask Ollie.

He taps his tablet screen. 'All set.'

We always double-check that the house and surrounding property are locked and alarmed before we meet. The walls and gates to the front of the house offer privacy from the road. The proximity of the neighbour's seasonal workers is becoming an issue. They're working so close to the barn.

I fill them in on my impromptu job offer, and Mark rolls his eyes. 'Was the job offer to solve the problem with Dylan being in the army, or was it for your boyfriend?'

I laugh, because it's not often Mark relaxes enough to tell a joke. 'He's not my boyfriend. If you think about it, he's older than you, and that's gross.' I pat him on the arm, and he sighs.

Ollie snorts. 'And apparently your dad's bestie. Don't think Garvey would be okay with his mate fucking—'

Mark cuts Ollie off. 'Stop. I don't need to hear it.'

I can't have a future relationship with a friend of my father. Throw in being not-dead, and a time travel loop, and it's far too complicated to work out.

Mark says to Ollie, 'I'm more concerned about the things we don't know. There are people we've influenced or interacted with over the last few months. How do we begin to document what we might have changed?'

'You mean every time you bumped into Ashley?' Ollie snickers. 'Everything we do might change someone's life. We have to live with it.' He leans forward, lowering his tone. 'I have a theory on why we might not have harnessed the time travel energy yet or even found it in the barn.'

Mark gestures for him to continue.

'It might only exist in 2042, and at this end, where we landed, is the drop-off point.' He leans back and stretches his arms out. That's always a sign he's been bent over a computer longer than he's realised. 'We're in a town with an active wormhole. It's next to an army base and a well-funded defence technologies company. I've been snooping around, and there are some things I've been able to decode, but most of it is blacked out. There's chatter about coils and crossed times. Events speeding up when there's an anomaly introduced in the original path.'

'Clarify.' I cross the room and flick the switch on the coffee pot after adding water and throwing two large scoops of coffee grounds into the filter.

'If Dylan is back early, it might be because events in this timeline are now progressing more quickly. He returned a year and a half early.' Ollie twists in his seat to talk to me while I perch on the windowsill, waiting for the caffeine to brew.

'We sped up the timeline by a year and a half?' Mark asks.

'Not just that. The timeline will speed up proportionally in relation to the event that interfered. The closer to the trigger, the faster it happens.'

'If my interference was meeting Dylan, and somehow saving Finley and Cameron, the farther away we get from that will slow the timeline, which will eventually return to normal?'

'If that's the trigger, then yes.' Ollie points at me. 'But the moment we dropped through time from 2042 could also be the trigger. This end of things is only the beginning. A drop of water has been separated from the ocean, and it's going to try to make its way back to where it belongs as quickly as it can.'

Ollie shuffles papers and goes over the equation he worked out. 'If my calculations are correct, the first takeover wouldn't happen in 2026, as it did for us. It'd be much sooner. Extrapolating from the time difference already noted, it will happen in 2021.'

'So basically we're running out of time?' Mark asks.

'No. I just screwed with Dylan and Ashley's whole future.' I swallow.

We're not ready for any of this to happen in two years.

Ollie says, 'Imagine reality and time are endless options and decisions, and the probable outcomes are coiled tightly next to each other.'

Ollie draws a picture of a spring on a pad. 'Endless possible realities, each one taking place in an untouchable space next to us. Some people like to think of it as a never-ending staircase.' His finger traces the circle of the spring to emphasise his point. 'Each step is a different reality, with the edges touching but never overlapping. Like a Slinky.

'An action in someone's life could, in theory, widen the coils, pull them farther apart. What if something in the universe, man-made or otherwise—pulls the stops and comes to rest? Before we know it, there's enough space'—Ollie points to an open space drawn between two coils—'enough of a pause in the pull, that something or someone could tip over the edge into the next reality, thrown along a path to a different time.'

He takes a Slinky from his laptop bag and puts it on the table in front of me. 'If something, like a drop of water, was to start at the top and the coils in the Slinky were loosened, the water droplet would follow a natural line to the end, like a timeline.

'If someone were to manufacture a way to keep the Slinky wound tight, that water droplet would roll down the side, crossing numerous realities at the same time.'

'That's what happened?' I ask.

'Fuck no. Someone figured out how to wind the spring tight but only in specific locations and for a certain number of split seconds. The second phase was to join those seconds long enough together to get someone to fall down the side of the Slinky. The fucked-up part was when they flipped the Slinky upside down, and we all landed in the past.'

'We're the droplets of water running down the wrong timeline.' I sit down, not understanding the analogy I'm making. 'Can't we, like, jump off the edge? Go back to where the droplet of water started?'

'Sure. How do you suppose we work out how to do that? I've tried to energise the spot where we came through. Clean it, dirty it, add static, tension, electricity. Lara even sent me crystals to charge it. I don't even know if it's controllable in any time zone or a pure act of nature.

'What I do know is with us here in the past, it's adding more pressure to an already unstable timeline. We added another drop to the water and made it heavy, and heavy water drops faster. We're moving down the pre-determined path faster than we did last time, with the possibility of changing it a little each day we're here. Nudging it out of its true position. Everything we do is adding more interference, and we can't stop being here. It's like we broke it. We snapped the top of the Slinky, and now we're trying to stop the jagged edges from ripping new holes in things.' Ollie pulls the Slinky apart and tugs at a piece in the centre, distorting the natural curve of the toy and distorting the plastic so it doesn't fall back into position. 'The part that really freaks me out is us staying here and the effect it will have on the world.'

The drip of the coffee into the jug next to me has slowed almost to a stop, but I suddenly don't have enough energy to pull the cups from the sideboard to fill.

'Time and reality are precious. I think the world still has its plan, and it's heading in that direction, but it's going there faster and with more speed and determination behind it, because we accidentally added more fuel to the fire. And with this broken piece in the middle, we can't go back to where we started.'

'So what are you going to do to fix it?' Mark asks.

'We can't fix a broken Slinky or even know we'll ever get home, but we can sand down the jagged edges. Work out how to keep our interference here in the past to a minimum, and put a plaster on what we broke. Help that drop of water stay on its path, because that'll lead us back to our people—and this time we're going to be ready to help them help themselves. All we can do is stay here and wait.' Ollie gets up and nudges me aside. Opening the cupboard door, he takes down three cups and picks up the coffeepot. We sit at the table while he pours three black coffees and slides a cup to Mark across the dining room table.

'At least here we're not dying like flies,' Ollie says.

'Easy for you to say. My entire family is hunted in a future we can't get back to.' I avoid his eyes and give him a blank sheet of paper to take notes on. 'You signed up to be in the resistance. You went through the screening. You ran with us, and you survived.' I look at him. 'You don't get to quit the cause just because your life is a little more comfortable now, understood?'

Ollie leans forward and takes my hand. 'I'm not quitting, Erin. My husband is stuck in a dying future too. Dylan Garvey said he was going to save us, and some of us are saved.'

'For now, but the future is coming,' I say sternly.

'I'll work on it. See if my theories match up before I come back with a possible answer, okay?'

I sigh. 'Thank you.'

'What were Finley's injuries?' Mark asks. 'Can we use him?'

I shrug. 'He's going to want to fight when the war comes.'

Mark asks, 'What're you going to do, tell them you're from the future and hang tight until we can use him?'

'Better than being dead, like they were supposed to be,' Ollie says.

'I'm going to bring him in as an arms dealer.' I make use of my original plan. 'Cameron is on holiday, visiting friends in France. That might be useful so Finley can tap the European connection. They'll have contacts and weapon knowledge. It's the only thing we've not been able to source safely.'

'They're soldiers,' Ollie says. 'How are you planning on flipping them?'

'I'm not. I'm going to show them the business side of what we're doing. Set up a briefing. I want a backlog for the website to make the business seem more established. If we show them the emergency bunkers and supplies, we need to stock them—'

'They might overlook the whole illegally buying and selling weaponry thing?' Ollie asks.

'They'll understand better than the average person.'

'Will they understand we're hiding shit in secret rooms of our customer's bunkers that we're selling to rich people?'

'If they're any good, they'll teach us how to hide it better,' I say. 'We just have to make sure Dylan quits the army, and soon. Ollie, we need more funds.'

Ollie taps his keyboard.

'We're going to have to pay them and get together an attractive package. Contract and pension. Those men just had a near-death experience. They're going to be thinking long-term, and we want to give them a career opportunity that they can support a future family on.'

'Got it. I can put together half a million and set up a payment schedule all the way to their retirement. If we all live that long. I'll call the payroll company in the morning and get them to start the paperwork. Oh, shit!'

'What?' I jump from my seat.

'Cameron Swan registered for NHS acute PTSD therapy six months ago. He attended six out of twelve appointments.

The last one he attended was when he was discharged for physiotherapy.'

'He never finished his therapy?' I ask.

'Nope. Neither did Finley or Dylan.'

'I ran the basic history psych programme I created when we got here. Warfare and humanitarian scenarios put both Finley and Cameron on a par with Dylan.' He looks up at me. 'They even scored ahead of you.'

'Bastards. Just 'cause they had better training, I'll bet.'

A few more taps of the keys and Ollie is zoned back into whatever he's looking for. 'He's hot.' Ollie hands me the file he compiled on Finley this morning. 'Since he's supposed to be dead, you two might as well hook up. It will limit the interference we're having here. Who knows what kind of interference you created while dating Rian?' Ollie grunts.

I shudder. 'Rian and I weren't that close. I doubt I'd have any lasting impact on his life.'

Mark snorts. 'You were close enough that he popped—'

I hold my hand up. 'Jesus, will you just stop? I don't want to talk about him or anything he may or may not have popped. Understood?'

'Yes, ma'am.'

Ollie sighs. 'There's a problem, though. I can't find Finley or Cameron in the UK for the last six months. They disappeared and didn't come back until last week. No port records, air departures, or arrivals. Either they left the country covertly, or they went underground.'

Mark pulls a cigarette from his pack on the table. 'Ask Lara to dig deeper and tell her I want an update about what she's doing. It's been too long since she made progress.' Mark exhales smoke. 'A silent signal, hidden in plain sight, but only decipherable to our people? It's a tall ask, Erin, and a risky one. Anything she can think of a whole load of people might decipher it as well.'

I smile at him. 'That's good. It means you're cautious. There's no point in trying to leave behind a landmark or a newspaper article to tell our families where we are or that we're okay if everyone is going to be able to understand it.'

'You two should come to terms with the fact we might never get a message back home,' Ollie says.

'While we're on the subject of bad news, lay your moral compass down for a moment and think about how to set things back on track,' Mark says.

My heart is hammering, my mouth is dry, and I try to act nonchalant. 'Go on.'

'If your dad was in a position that threatened your future, your very existence... I know the thought would cross his mind.'

'Oh, you know my dad so well, do you? Well enough to fuck his wife and try to parent his kids?' I twitch my head at him, baiting him to argue with me.

'While we're discussing theories, it's a possibility that if Finley and Cameron die, it might push things closer to the original path. Sooner rather than later, I'm guessing.'

I get up and push my chair in. 'Turn the alarms off. I'm heading out.'

Ollie says, 'Fuck.'

'What?'

'They're already deactivated. Someone's inside.'

## FINLEY

The sound of weapons being drawn has me cursing myself for jumping the front gate and snooping around. Goddamn Cameron's ideas.

'There's no activity in the shed,' a male shouts.

I swiftly move away from the double doors being opened and try to act like I wasn't listening to the last five minutes of their meeting.

*I try to act nonchalant, like hey I always break into a girl's house before asking her on a date.*

'Hold your fire,' Erin commands, and I freeze.

My throat tightens.

'Finley.' Erin's voice is calm.

She's sexy when she's holding a gun. That shouldn't be the thought passing through my mind right now, and she's not the first woman to point one at me, but she is the first woman I've full-body snogged who has argued for *not* killing me and seems to have some rank. Her dad and brother are doing what they're told, and haven't shot me—yet.

She flips on the safety and tucks her handgun in the back of her jeans. The fabric of her shirt shifts around her belt as she adjusts the weapon. My attention's back to her legs. I remember the feel of her body pressed against mine. Six months ago, she was ripped, and now I know why. She's a fighter, and god I hope she's one of the good guys. Her blond hair falls across her bare arms as she slowly brings her hands into view and opens them to show they're empty.

'Ollie?' Erin's dad asks the man next to him.

'The guy's a white hat.' Ollie—Erin's other brother, I assume—is a young black guy about my age. He stands at the back with a tablet in his hand.

'Everyone get back to work.' She comes towards me, and when she looks me in the eye, it's like everyone else disappears. 'Did you drive here?'

I tilt my head sheepishly, knowing I have to confess to stashing my car. 'Jeep's down the street. I rang the gate bell,' I lie, 'but there was no answer.'

'No, you didn't.' Ollie looks at his tablet and swipes a few times.

Erin takes me by the arm. 'You can give me a ride into town.'

'I need to know how he got in here,' Ollie calls after us.

We leave via the front door, and Erin says, 'Don't worry. No one's going to run up behind you and put a bullet in your head. You go snooping around after you got offered a slightly illegal job. It's good. It means you're cautious. You just have to work on not getting caught next time.'

'Only slightly illegal?' he asks. 'I've never known a family meeting to take place where everyone's armed.'

'We take our clients' privacy and security seriously. People pay us a lot of money for what we do, and we make sure things are kept secure.'

'So you pack weaponry for a family meeting about your dates?'

She opens her mouth to speak, then smiles, obviously giving up on her protest. 'How much did you hear?'

'Only your brother, talking about how hot I am.' I smirk and hope the bravado covers the truth.

'Liar. You heard a lot more. Why did you break into my house?'

At the end of the driveway, she covers the keypad as she types the code into the pedestrian gate next to the main one, and a latch opens and allows the heavy grating to swing inwards. We go through, and she closes it behind us.

I dig my hands into my pockets. 'Wanted to know what you were really offering us.'

'You're relaxed now that it's just us?' She grins. 'I'm still armed, you know.'

'I know, but if you wanted to kill me, you would have. You offered us a job, and by the sound of it, you need us. "Pension and everything", you said.'

She chuckles. 'I did, and you shouldn't underestimate me 'cause I'm a girl. My dad taught me not to draw my weapon unless I'm prepared to shoot the fucker in the face.'

'And have you?'

Cameron's right. We have to figure out who the Coopers are. Not their names or their agenda, but deep-down what kind of people they are. Have they taken lives in their work? Was it justified? Has Erin killed someone, like I have? More than one? The first time you take a life, it's out of necessity. You can justify it. The reasons are solid. People support you. It's the second kill that fucks with your head. You realise this is who you are now—someone who ends lives.

She stares at me. 'More than you need to know. If you want to make up for breaking in, you could speak to my brother, Ollie—tell me how you got so far inside without setting off his alarms. He's probably having kittens in there, and I need him to focus on other things.'

'Does all the security have anything to do with your other brother, Blake, going missing?' We stroll down the road.

'You remembered his name,' she says. 'Most people don't ask about Blake. I think they're afraid of upsetting me, but it's nice to talk about him sometimes.'

I nod at her.

'It's just the job that keeps us on edge,' she says.

'Ah, yes. Selling and installing emergency bunkers, from a one-person survival pod to a fifty-man bunker. Fully stocked and ready to outlast anything.'

'You looked us up?' Erin elbows my side. She must hit a nerve as pain shoots through me.

I try to hide the wince and shift my weight to the other side. Stretching and strengthening exercises normally help with random nerve pains.

'I was keeping track of you while I was gone. It was impressive how quickly the business grew. Almost overnight.' I give her my best suspicious look and point to my car, parked on the side of the road. 'I brought you something.' I beep it open and go to the boot. I hand her a paper shopping bag, and she peers inside.

'You bought me clothes?' She pulls out combat trousers and boots, followed by 1000 Mile socks and a technical T-shirt. 'What the hell?'

'I have a bet to win.' I open the passenger door. 'You can change when we get there.'

'What are you talking about?' She gets in.

Leaning over the door, I'm feeling pretty good with myself. 'I'm going to take you on a date. No high heels and tight dresses, no matter how good you look in them. Get your training gear on.' I gesture to the back seat. 'Promise I won't peek.'

I give her my best no-bullshit grin and pull out my phone to text for confirmation.

The mud is heavy and wet, and our feet squelch with every step as we cross the training field.

'How the hell did you get us in here?' She looks around the outside training course of Catterick Garrison.

'Oh please, I know a guy.' The sun is low and is about to set, but the floodlights will keep the course visible. Mostly.

'Of course you do.'

'This is it. Two acres of obstacle courses. You think you can beat me in the dark?' I grin and lean against a railing.

She leans in after me and rests her hands on my belt. Stretching up into my face. 'I might not beat you, but I'm fast. The important thing is I beat the person chasing me.'

'I can chase you if you want.'

'How many times have you run this course?'

'Scared I'm going to put you at a disadvantage?'

'No. It'll be better, actually. Sometimes you're running from guys on their own turf.'

She leans back and bounces up and down. 'It's been a while since someone's challenged me like this. You can chase me, old man. Give me a five-second head start.'

'You got it.'

She faces the course. 'And try not to injure yourself.'

I laugh. 'Oh, baby, that's not what's running through my mind right now.'

'You ready?'

I turn my watch around. 'Whenever you're ready, you can—'

She sprints off towards the high tower, and I curse, watching five seconds tick over. Then I take off after her.

My first mistake was taking my eyes off her. She's farther up the wooden ladder structure than I expected. Halfway up the thirty-foot tower, and she's not slowing down. The sprint at the start will keep her ahead of me. I sprint up the ladder, gaining on her, but she is over the top before me.

She runs over the top of the structure and pauses at the other end, bends down, and looks over the side. A lot of recruits are afraid of heights. You can be fast going up, but when you have to come back down, people are slower.

I catch up and run beside her. My adrenaline's pumping and I was getting a kick out of chasing behind her ass.

She looks at me, smiles, and jumps.

'No!' I scream, run to the edge, and lean over. She's swinging down a black safety rope and drops to the ground. She doesn't glance up; just keeps belting over to the tire run and makes quick work of it.

I look around the top of the tower. A rope is missing from the right edge of the structure. I never saw her snag it on the way past. Does she have a knife with her? She still has her gun tucked in her trousers, so who knows? I laugh.

I grasp the rope but don't know if it'll take my weight. That's one advantage she has over me, like she said, and she had the momentum to keep her free-falling. I'd have to abseil down. I decide to take the old-fashioned ladder down, but slide most of the way. The chase is still on, and she's winning.

After darting across the tires, she's scaled the wall, and I can't see how far ahead of me she is. I run, jump, and catch the top of the eight-foot wall, roll across it, and drop to the other side. How the hell did she get up there? That was harder for her than it was for me.

She's at the end of the two hundred metre mud crawl. The advantage of the wall has allowed me to catch up to her, but I throw myself under the barbed wire and slither, my weight and bulk slowing me down. She scrambles over the net tower and is halfway across the monkey bars when I finish the crawl.

Erin's covered in mud, and I've never been turned on in a training sprint before. A dash across twenty hurdles slows down her distance, but I've to cover all of those too.

She's in the rope pit, using one leg as an anchor and the other to push her across, saving the strength in her arms. Smart girl. A two-kilometre sprint lies ahead, through mud and water

109

and tunnels, and over hurdles. This is where I gain on her. That, and the final wall. She's not getting over it alone; no one does.

The whole point of the exercise is to build teamwork. Everyone needs pushed over, and the team has to pull the last man up. It was shitty of me, 'cause she can't beat me. But I never expected her to get there first.

The race to the end is impressive. Her body is agile. Her muscles flex in her back, and her arms and legs, as her strength helps her manoeuvre where she needs to be. As I close in during the final sprint, she's pushing out harsh breaths, giving it her all, running for her life, and part of me dies when I realise she probably knows what that feels like.

'You better not be holding back on me, soldier,' she pants.

I push harder.

She falters when she sees the height of the last wall and checks her surroundings. She's looking for something to give her height or a boost over. There's nothing.

I catch up, grab her around the waist, and lift her off the ground, still running. She throws an elbow in my face and uses her feet to push off my knees.

'Fuck,' I shout and try not to drop her. I let her go as we both tumble, and I roll, but she's still pushing away from me.

She gets up. 'Oh, crap, I'm sorry. I reacted without thinking.' She leans over, rests her hands on her knees, and breathes hard.

'Uh-huh. Teaches me never to jump out at you in the dark.'

She checks the side of my nose for damage, and I unexpectedly feel tears well. Damn, she got me good. 'I'm kind of proud of that one,' I tell her.

She looks at the wall. 'I was never going to get over this.'

'No, but first one to reach it is the winner. If I'd told you this was the end, you wouldn't have hesitated, so you did kind of beat me.'

'Nah. If this had been real, one of us would be dead. I'm just pissed I let you grab me. I changed my strategy when I figured I wasn't getting over the thing.' She kicks the base of the structure like she's angry at herself, but she tries to hide it by bending over to catch her breath.

'Come on, let's get some water.'

She shakes her head. 'We're not over the wall yet.' She stares at the thing, making it a personal challenge.

'There's no way in hell you're going to pull me up to the top.'

'That's why you're going to have to stand on my shoulders and get there first, then pull me up.'

I look at her and laugh. 'I'm six-foot-two and about three stone heavier than you. I can hardly stand on your shoulders and lunge up there.'

She looks at me, then at the wall. 'I'm five-foot-six. You're six-foot-two. That's tall enough to get you up there.' She braces her feet a comfortable distance apart, leans against the wall for support, and taps her thighs. 'Come on, big guy. Don't tell me you don't want to get on top of me.'

'Why is this so important to you?'

'Because if you're going to work for us, I have to know you'll get us both over a wall if we need to. Think of this as an interview.'

'I'll get you out of any situation if we're ever in trouble.'

'I said *both* of us.' She winks. 'I don't take my men into a fight unless I know they're capable of getting themselves out, too. Sometimes that means you go first.'

Christ. I put one foot on her thigh. 'I'm going to break you,' I say half-heartedly, knowing that she could take my

111

weight better than some of the skinny-ass teenagers who come through the army.

'Do it quickly and smoothly, and I won't even notice.'

'Ready?'

'Go.' Her order is measured and precise, like a team leader.

I use her body as a step ladder and quickly move from her thigh to her shoulder, and lunge for the top of the structure. She gets out of the way in case I fall back. I catch the ledge and pull myself up.

'Let your belt down,' she tells me.

I unbuckle it, lie flat on top of the wall, and lean as far over the side as I can.

She grabs the end and tugs, testing my hold. 'You good?'

'Yes.'

She takes a few steps back, runs, and jumps, latches onto the belt, and climbs the wall with her feet as I haul her up.

We lie on top, catching our breaths.

'Fuck me, that was tough,' I say.

She leans her hand on my chest. I take hold of her thumb and twiddle it around mine.

'It was fun getting all sweaty with you, Fin.'

'Best date ever.'

'How the hell do you get down from this thing?'

'We're abseiling, but right now, I want to look at the stars with you.'

She gazes at the sky. 'One thing that'll never change in this fucked up existence is the sky. It's huge and vast and goes on forever. The possibilities for life and dreams in the sky can't be contained.'

'Can I kiss you?' I whisper and push strands of hair off her face that loosened during the run. She flushes. I lean on my elbow and look at her. She's chewing on her lip, trying to hold back a smile, and I can't control mine. Her happiness is infectious, and I want to make her happy all the time just to feed off it, to keep my shit at bay. 'Is that a yes?'

She stops breathing. I can't help it when my tongue darts out and wets my lips, and she practically chokes when she breathes again. The pulsing in my shorts pushes against the fabric, and I can hardly wait for the answer. She raises her arms and laces them around my neck. My lips crash with hers. I slide my tongue in her mouth, and one of us moans. Maybe it's both of us.

I roll on top of her. When her legs open, I settle between her thighs, the friction and heat through our clothes making me crazy. I taste her mouth, her lips and struggle for breath when I try to stop. Kissing Erin is going to be my new oxygen. I don't mean to when I roll my hips and grind against her, but god I want to feel more of her. She locks onto my ass and pulls me tight against her, and I can't help but chuckle.

'Something funny?' she asks, breathless against my mouth.

I nibble along her jaw, to her ear, then down her throat. I bite down on her skin and not only does she gasp, but I swear her pussy clenches under my cock. Fuck. I roll us over so she's on top, changing position so I don't come in my pants, and give us a breather.

Doesn't help much when she sits up and straddles my hips, sitting on my dick and resting her hands on my chest.

'Well, that was an intense first kiss.'

Shit, that was like taking burning shrapnel. 'You wound me, Erin. That wasn't our first kiss.'

'I never thought I'd see you again,' she confesses. 'I'm counting that as our first kiss.'

'What time do you finish work tomorrow?'

'Why? You want to talk about that job offer?'

'I want to take you to lunch.'

'Two dates in two days? Don't you have any pride?' She chortles, and I grab her around the waist and sit up to lick her lower lip.

Erin lies back down and looks at the sky.

'You're trying to figure out how to fit swim training into your schedule, aren't you?'

I lean over her. 'Three dates. The bar earlier and now are two different dates.'

She raises her eyebrows. 'And just what do you think's going to happen on the third date?'

I bite the side of her mouth. 'Lady's choice.'

## fourteen

### FINLEY

I take measured steps back to the Jeep, my hand entwined with Erin's. I bet she can feel the slight tug as I pull to the left.

Erin says, 'How bad are the injuries, exactly?'

'It's not a problem, if that's what you're asking. Just been a while since I ran a full course flat out.'

'Is it a weakness? If we employ you in some questionable stuff, we need to know you can get out of the way quickly. None of that hobbling to the car crap.'

'I wasn't expecting it, is all. You moved quicker than I thought.'

Erin stops and turns me around. 'Don't underestimate us.'

'Noted.'

'The injury?'

'It's not serious.'

'It was serious enough to get you discharged, or was that not a physical thing?'

'My head's not fucked up.'

'Well, that's disappointing. Half your crew killed on a mission, and you're okay with that?'

I tug her into an embrace. 'What the hell do you know about friends dying?'

'More than you.'

I drop her arm. 'I'm dealing, and I'm okay. Cameron suffered the most, and I'm helping him.'

'It was his fault.'

'It was the enemies' fault,' I tell her as we approach her car.

'I know, but when people are dead, and you survive for no other reason than because you were standing in a different spot or there was a two-second time difference, it *feels* like your fault. That's what he's dealing with. Dylan too. He's relieved you guys are alive.'

'You're all pretty interested in Dylan.' We stop at the passenger door.

Erin's phone rings in her pocket. 'That's Ollie's emergency line.' She doesn't pull the phone out. 'Keys!'

I place them in her hand and she runs to the driver's door while I jump in the passenger seat. She tosses me her phone as she peels out. 'Tell them to open the gates in ten minutes.'

She drives full speed back to the outskirts of Darlington, and a twenty-minute car ride is completed smoothly in less than fifteen. The gates to her driveway are open. She circles around to the back of the house and slams on the brakes at the barn. After we jump out, Mark hands me a gun.

I check the weapon while Erin opens the shed doors. 'What the fuck is going on?'

'You're going to find out who the hell we are.'

In the centre of the barn, surrounded by security cameras, Mark, Ollie, and Erin take up flanking positions around a space that flickers with electricity. A miniature lightning storm takes place in mid-air, suspended in darkness, and the storm grows. The area grows, and negative space in the middle of the charge appears.

Flashbacks are a bitch.

PTSD is debilitating when it hits you like this. When my mind takes me somewhere else, I can't control it and it's not a safe time for me to be incapacitated, but the visions in my head want me to relive our last mission.

I concentrate on the overhanging lights of the barn. Watch them flicker, trying to keep the power surging through me in the present.

'It's okay,' Erin tells me. 'Whoever is coming will be disoriented for a moment.'

'*Pfft*.' Mark scoffs behind me. 'Let's hope so.'

'This is how we got here,' Erin says.

I falter in my step as I join them. 'What do you mean?' I hiss over the noise, weapon drawn to mirror the rest of the unit.

'Me, Mark, Ollie, and Lara. We dropped here seven months ago,' she says. The blue sparks spread wider. We adjust our perimeter to match its size.

'Something big is coming through. A group of people maybe,' Mark says.

'You're telling me you know that a person is going to pop out of this?'

'Sometimes it gets fired up and nothing happens,' Erin says. 'But there're so many bad guys where we're from, we can never assume. This place is always attended.'

'Bullshit. You're playing with me.' I holster my weapon and look around the barn at the ceiling, the stalls, the power cables.

'Don't touch them,' Ollie cautions, anticipating my next move. 'That's our security. We monitor the power flowing through here. If someone comes through and we miss it, security doors are set up to contain them until we get here.'

I'm going to call their bluff. People talking about crazy shit. I need to take out their source of pretence.

'Don't!' Erin shouts when I reach for the main cable.

I catch the main cable and rip the system apart. There's a dullness in power, but the light and buzz from the source are still alive and kicking.

117

There's a flicker of movement as someone materialises in the electric storm. He comes into focus as the electricity falls off to nothing, and we're left in silence.

The room fills with tension. Ollie, Mark, and Erin have the man surrounded. I'm next to her.

The soldier in the black uniform is less concerned about the people pointing guns at him than he is with where he ended up.

He flinches. 'Garvey!' he snarls, moving for his gun.

fifteen

*Erin*

I wanted to wait. I hate taking the first shot. There's always a chance that an Apostle soldier might want to flip. Not all of them are as dedicated to the cause as NewGov pretends. Some of them only need a way out, like the rest of us did. Like Ollie. He was a gem I found because I waited.

When the soldier reaches for his weapon, he's already too late. He shouldn't have hesitated.

Mark, Ollie, and I fire and the Apostle soldier drops to the ground, dead before the first thermal pin had been clipped. We move in, and when we're confident he's no longer a threat, Mark bends to strip him of his weapons. 'Do you know what this means?' he asks.

'We have a thermal pin weapon to stash for the others?' I ask.

'We just got a leg up.' Marks takes a knife from Ollie.

I turn to Finley. His gun is drawn, and judging by the angle, he must have been shooting over my shoulder. He had my back.

Mark hands me a holster. I attach it to the side of my jeans.

Finley has a vacant stare, like he's not focusing on anything.

'Fin?' I ask. 'Are you okay?'

I move closer to him, snap my fingers in front of his face, and yell his name.

Awareness returns, and he pulls me to one side. 'What the hell is happening here?'

'We're from the year 2042. There's a war going on, and from the looks of this soldier, it's safe to assume it isn't over.'

'What war? That guy was English.'

'There are no borders in the wars of the future. There are only good guys and bad guys. Trust me when I tell you we're on the good side.'

'Why did he shout *Garvey*? He's not even here.'

I sit on a bench next to the wall and lean back, then motion for Finley to sit in the chair opposite. He picks it up and places it parallel to mine, keeping his back to the wall so he can watch the others.

'Dylan Garvey is our leader in the future. We're part of a group of survivors on the run, a makeshift revolt sort of thing. The *Garvey* and *rebel* are synonymous. When the war started, he'd been out of the army for a long time. He wasn't considered a threat and had kept his head down over the years. He wasn't tagged in the first wave of take-downs.'

'Tagged?'

'All military personnel with a sense of morality were flagged on an internal test score, to be taken care of during the takeover. Anyone who might stand up and fight for the people were eliminated. It was only during the second wave of assaults that retired personnel like Garvey were targeted. He'd already packed up his family by then and was on the run.

'Ashley once told me it was like he knew something was wrong, even before a significant number of people were dead.'

'Ashley told you that?'

'She's his wife in the future, and she's goddamn fierce. He taught her basic fighting and keep-fit routines when they were dating. Even more after they were married. He pushed her

to perform better. Gave her the same training he—you guys—
had. He was good at that.'

'What?'

'Finding regular people and training them how to
survive.'

'He found you?'

A smile tugs at my lips. 'He taught me everything.'

*'Don't forget how to interrogate people and figure out
who you can trust to join the gang,' Ollie calls over.*

'In the future, there's only a small population of people
living outside London. Garvey and the others move around a lot.
We use the resources that were left behind, and we steal the
rest from storage areas. Flipping a farmer to our side is the best
means of survival, but then we have to protect them.'

'Protect them from who?'

'The government. They culled the human population.
They're still controlling lives but for their own gain now. Garvey
is trying to get our freedoms back. The world could be a better
place again, but those in charge run the country like dictators.
Death penalty for minor crimes, scaremonger tactics.
Kidnappings and forced marriages and executions. Slavery for
most and the pick of the population for those in power. They've
taken away the right to live outside London so they can control
everything and everyone. We're fighting for the right to live.'

'And this?' He waves at the dead body. 'Did he come
through some kind of portal?'

'You could call it that. Ollie is the tech guy, and he can't
figure it out. There's no way to control it or move it or know it's
there until it's active.'

He touches the injury on the side of his neck. 'Is that
why you're building panic shelters around the country?'

I shake my head. 'Those are for the future. Our main
struggle there is food and water, then weaponry and a safe

121

place to sleep. If they all stay intact for twenty-five years, and our people can find them in 2042, it'll save people's lives.'

'As long as NewGov doesn't find them first,' Mark says. 'If you guys are all rested up, we need a hand moving the body.'

Finley stands with me.

I put a hand on his arm. 'You don't have to do this. We can make it like you were never here. Delete the security feed from your car, erase your traffic camera locations. That tech is standard stuff for Ollie, but if you pick up a shovel and dig graves, that shit stays with you.'

'That shit's been with me a long time.' He returns to where the soldier lies, staying a couple feet back, and examines the scene. I follow him.

'No personal effects in his pockets,' Mark tells me.

He must be about my age, barely in his twenties. 'Once upon a time, Apostle soldiers were people.'

'Who do they fight for?' Fin asks.

'That's complicated,' Ollie answers.

'No it's not,' I but in. 'The quick answer is that NewGov, the dictators who took over the UK, decided it would be apt to name their now killer soldiers as Apostles. Give people the impression that they were saviours, starting over in a new world. But really, they are just cold-blooded killers who do the bidding of those in charge.'

'Not all of them,' Ollie says. 'A lot of people in London, Apostle recruits included, are forced into their jobs. They either work for NewGov or they're killed. Sometimes even those that look like the bad guys are searching for a way out too.'

'They're people who chose the wrong side,' Mark snaps. 'There's always a choice. He could've died instead of signing up.'

'And he would have. And NewGov would have taken out his family too. Don't try to make it sound like it's an easy choice, Mark.'

Mark crosses the shed towards Ollie. 'They're not all innocent,' he snides.

'Are you winning the war?' Finley asks.

'We're still alive. We're keeping them busy and distracted from their primary goal, which is killing us. They know more about everyone in the rebellion than I think my mother does.'

Mark takes a step back to Finley. 'You'll have to keep your mouth shut. You can't go spilling to Dylan yet. Not until we know the consequences that might have.'

Finley frowns. 'Do you think I'm going to talk about this? I just saw a guy appear out of thin air.' He throws his arms wide. 'A moment before I watched my girl and her family kill him, and hey, don't forget the whole PTSD thing from seeing most of my unit killed on the job. No one is going to believe me. Everyone already thinks I'm crazy. Even if you don't trust my integrity, trust my self-preservation.'

'Alright, cool off,' I say. 'This is a conversation for later. Right now we need to sort this out.' I point to the body.

'What are you going to do with him?' Finley asks.

Ollie fills him in as he rolls the guy over and strips off the NewGov-issued element survival kit. Handgun and bullets, outdoor uniform to withstand the elements and energy meal bars, as well as explosive tech that can work both as a hand grenade, and a transmitter back to their base; water purifying tablets that can last a month in the wilderness outside London; antibiotic tablets for infections, and cyanide tablets for capture—don't mix those up, like some of the poor young ones do.

'Strip the useful things. Leave the underwear, but everything else can be reused. Collect weapons to a pile over there and dump the clothes into the empty water barrel. They'll be washed and preserved in vacuum bags. We can store them, and hopefully they'll be useful for whoever finds them in twenty-five years.'

Ollie unzips the black jacket and rolls the body to one side, pausing at the *London Apostle Soldier* logo and ID number on the shoulder.

Mark takes a hunter's knife out of his boot and pushes the blade one inch under the guy's heart.

'What the hell are you doing?' Fin asks.

'Removing his tracker. It might come in useful,' Mark tells him. 'And since the past is getting all sorts of fucked up, we need all the help we can get.'

I face Finley, demanding his full attention. 'You and Cameron were supposed to die on the last mission. Where I'm from, it threw Dylan over the edge. You're his best friends, and it destroyed him that you guys didn't survive. But it ultimately was a good thing for the future. That didn't happen this time around.'

'Erin,' Ollie shouts. 'We have a problem. This one's still blinking.'

He's talking about the tracking device and not the dead body.

'What do you mean? There's no light on those things.' Mark looks at the chip in Ollie's hand.

'It's pulsing. I can feel it.'

'What the hell does that mean?' I ask.

'It means the tracker's still working in this timeline. Someone here has the technology to pick this up.'

Ollie leans into me. 'Our security system was fucked. The alarms weren't working. We only realised there was activity in the barn because Mark was checking the perimeter.'

'This was always risky,' I say. 'Darlington is Ashley and Garvey's hometown, for god's sake. This whole place has been pulled apart a million times.'

'If an Apostle soldier fell through our portal, you can guarantee that the future has eyes on this place. We're not safe anymore,' Mark says.

'If Apostles compromised our system, there's no way to start over from that, just by moving somewhere else, and we can't risk leaving this portal unmanned,' Ollie says. 'Let me work on reverse engineering this thermal pin. When have we ever had access to some of their shit and the freedom to research it? Let's see if there's anything we can use from this.'

'Find out why our security failed and fix what you can.' My tone is curt. Finley tore apart some of his wires, and I let him. Now Ollie has to add it to his pile of things to do.

'Holding on to their tech is risky, Erin.' Mark looks at Finley before he lowers his voice to speak to me. 'Our security system being disabled a couple hours before these guys came through is probably not a coincidence.'

'Finley crashing our meeting might have saved us,' I say.

Mark huffs like he doesn't quite agree. 'That would mean there's already someone here, working for the Apostles— someone who knows where we are.' Mark grabs hold of my arm, and Finley tenses. 'Don't get cocky because Dylan's back. He won't protect you the same way here. Not yet.'

'If Garvey were here, he wouldn't change the timeline by murdering his friends. He'd bring them in, protect them, and try to save everyone.'

'Casualties are inevitable, Erin. You don't have to slaughter people to get the job done, but we're never going to save them all. That's why Garvey kept making the decisions, even after you were old enough. He didn't want you to have to live with the mental anguish of getting it wrong.'

125

## sixteen

*Erin*

Finley follows me through the back patio doors and into the kitchen. 'You can crash here tonight.'

He groans as he eases out of his hoodie.

I help him lift it over his head. 'You okay?'

'It's been one hell of a night.'

I can tell by his voice he is physically and mentally exhausted. I pull out a chair from the table. 'Sit. I'm making everyone food before we sleep.'

It took us well into the night to help Ollie search the internet for any chatter on the thermal pins we extracted from the body. When life-altering tech is in production, there's always someone trying to black-market the design to a rival company or country.

'The adrenaline crashes me quicker than it used to.'

'Because you're on meds?' I ask. 'We pulled all records on you and Cameron. We needed to know who and what was coming back to town with Dylan.'

'I tried going without prescriptions, but it turns out I can keep my thoughts straight when I take what the doctor ordered.'

'It's nothing to be ashamed of. You're strong to survive the things you have.'

'So are you.'

'This is my normal life. For soldiers, it's different. It all comes along in a condensed period. It's harder to process.'

'And people popping out of the air, trying to kill you, apparently that's all real.'

'It is indeed.' I push him to sit on the chair and move to the fridge. Cooked chicken and ham are a staple in our house. Protein is always needed. I place the packets on the counter and pull out a pan and packet of pasta. 'A quick meal of carbs and protein will have us all healed up.'

'A lot of your life makes sense now,' he says.

'This makes sense to you?' I smile.

'Blake's still in the future, isn't he?'

'Yes, and some days I'm okay, knowing that we're doing everything we can to help him and my parents and everyone else back home.'

'Your mum and dad?'

'Mark is my stepdad. My parents divorced last year, but they're stuck in the future.'

'Your whole family is gone.'

'They're not gone. I am.' I turn the hob on and put on water to boil. 'It's my fault everyone is here,' I whisper. 'We all have loved ones we miss. Mark's heart-broken and trying to get back to my mum but also look after me while we're here.' My voice breaks. 'It was my fault he followed me into the damn shed.'

I sit at the table next to Finley, folding one leg under the other. 'This is the longest we've ever stayed in one place.'

'Jesus, so you don't even have somewhere to call home. Somewhere to settle down and take a breather?'

'Some places we have long-term allies who we trust. Those are the places we can stay the longest. There are lots of abandoned towns and villages. Everything of use has been stripped and sent to a different storage location for London to use when it's needed. National parks are good for us, though. They're already thick with trees, so the drones can't spot us as easily. Those were my favourites as a kid. There was often a

127

swing set left behind. The terrain is rough and overgrown. We set up a lot of blockades around us with fallen trees and make it seem like weather disruption.

'But we survive by stealing food, and that gets noticed, especially since everything is run so tightly by NewGov.'

I kick off my trainers and stretch my toes. Exhaustion hits me immediately. 'Mark had been part of our group for a long time. When he and Mum hooked up, I took it badly. Mark and my dad fought side by side for years. They were friends. Blake and I felt like Mark just swooped in the moment Mum and Dad separated.' I roll my eyes at my childish reactions. 'Now I understand he was simply a man who fell in love.' I look at Finley. 'Sometimes you can't control the people you fall for.'

Finley gets up and takes over the cooking, giving me the precious seconds I need. He adds salt from the salt pig that Lara insisted on leaving on the counter to make us look like we're used to fitting in to 2019. I help him find a jar of sauce, and we dice the cooked chicken and ham pieces in silence.

After I drain the pasta, and the meats are lightly fried, we add everything to one pot.

'It's scary being here and watching everyone change their behaviour.' I fill two plates and leave the rest in the pot for Mark and Ollie.

'That's social media for you,' he says. 'People are addicted to their phones.'

'It's the content and behaviour around it. Step out of line, and they will publicly bully and shame you online. Report you to your boss, do anything they can to prove that *they* would never make such a mistake, that they're the ones who do as *they* are told. Do you remember being taught about the Second World War in school? They use the same "reporting on your neighbour" tactics.'

'Sure.' He looks at me cautiously.

'Imagine knowing the government is behind the way we think and act towards each other, with social media shaming us at every opportunity. We're conditioned not to step out of line. With fear of crimes being committed in our homes, they convince us to buy high-tech security systems and cameras, which can be accessed via the internet, for you and any good hacker to view.'

'The government's not behind that. It makes people feel safe.'

'And cheap too, if you store all the recordings in the cloud. You are willingly inviting big brother into your homes, and you're the one forking the bill. Ever in a road traffic accident? Install a dash cam—the government can use the footage to find who hit you, but what they really want is access to more surveillance.

'Human to human interactions are dwindling. You can go days or weeks without speaking to anyone if you want. You can go to the shops and use those self-service machines or the internet click and collect systems. It'll isolate people even more in the next decade, and it makes it harder to have someone to turn to when things fall apart.'

'That's a little out there, Erin. I mean, it even sounds crazy for someone who just saw someone jump through time. You're telling me *1984* is going to happen for real?'

'I don't know what that is, but if it means the government is going to reduce the human population to ten percent and keep them on a lockdown in London by providing scraps of food under the guise of safety when the world is actually getting better—then yes, that's what happens. People are being killed. Forced into slavery type jobs or marriages with those in power—all because they can. When world leaders are bullies, it doesn't take long for that mentality to fester, and a lot of people show their true colours.

'We could survive in the rest of the country again, but the people on top won't allow it. They'll lose their power and the perks that come with the division of the classes. NewGov continues to kill to maintain a certain population quota that doesn't matter anymore. They bomb and kill and blame it on the rebels to make London citizens afraid of us. But we're the ones fighting for freedom.'

'Then that's a cause I want to get behind,' he tells me. 'Twenty nineteen is a good time to live in, and if we can keep the world like this a little longer, I want to help. I wish you could take the time to see it. I've always known something was stopping you from totally embracing life. I came back for you.'

'We can run until the first wave of culling is over, and then we need to stick to the original plan and keep fighting. Keep our friends alive and take down the monsters who are exploiting everyone.'

'Wait.' Finley asks, 'You're not trying to stop the first takeover? Why are you waiting until world leaders kill ninety percent of the population? That's billions of people,' he shouts.

'Just over 6.5 billion people.'

Finley pales. 'That's okay for you. You survived the first wave of culling, but everyone outside of London is going to die, according to you.' He throws his hands up. 'So guess what? That's everyone I know. All my family and friends are in Scotland. How many of them are going to survive?'

I whisper, 'A handful, if they're lucky.'

'But you can stop it. You can have Ollie start something about the government on the dark web, until it festers and grows into the main domains. Hell, you could help us move our families to places they're likely to make it.'

'And what about the other billions, Finley? Like it or not, the ninety percent population cut was necessary. And it worked.'

'What do you mean, it worked?' He screws up his face at me.

I push the pasta bowl away and recite what I know of what will happen. 'In the late 1990s, information became available that the world could not sustain the current population growth and pollution. Governments around the world were talking to one another about how best to combat this. China recommended against the one-child rule it previously tried. Over the years, ideas of inducing terrorist events, "natural disasters", and even infertility drugs in pockets of society were trialed. But it wasn't quick enough.' I pour us two glasses of water and place one in front of Finley. 'Drink.' I wait until he has taken a few gulps of water, then do the same.

'In 2010, the Doomsday Clock towards the world's ecosystem collapsing sped up. It was agreed that in ten years, each government would induce population culling. How each country tackled this was up to them. Some saved people in a lottery style. A lot of European countries opted for the UK way, which was isolating the capital's water system and poisoning the majority of citizens via a quick one or two-day death. Some countries were a little more—volatile.'

'Volatile? Murdering your own people en-mass wasn't enough that some places got upgraded to the definition of volatile?'

'They screened for the most suitable gene type for survival. Some governments, like ours, didn't hit the ninety percent mark on the first try. London had a high population. They also underestimated how many people used an independent water source. They let people fight to the death in the first few months and later encouraged it before bringing back the death penalty, hoping to reduce numbers to the ten percent quota. Disease and resistance, people turning on each other, and as a death sentence for committing crimes is bringing the UK down to six million people.'

I push the plate in front of Finley. 'Eat.' Ever the good soldier, he ignores his emotions and eats to fuel his body. Like Garvey, he knows when he needs to eat, stop, and sleep. And like Garvey, I copy Finley. After a few bites of food, I think it's

131

safe to continue and tell him when the world really got fucked up.

'After the first five years, there was no longer a need to reduce population. The planet was habitable. Global warming was no longer at threatening levels. $CO_2$ had dropped to levels that hadn't been seen in a hundred years. The resources we had could now sustain the remaining population for a very long time. Food, for the most part, was not scarce.'

'What do you mean, for the most part?'

'There's enough to go around, but NewGov is controlling the food to control the people. Capital punishment is used and argued that the "resource" could not be spared on people who break the law.'

'But there's enough to go around?' he asks.

'There are smaller farming teams issued all over the country—lands needed for agriculture, bees, bird, fruit and veg, animals, trees for firewood, turf. Entire cities like Manchester filled with mechanical parts so that there's no need ever to build new ones. When London needs something, it's looked up in a database, the location is found, and then those nearest fill the order and send it to London with the next Apostle pickup. Birmingham's filled with clothes and shoes that were collected from every home and store in the country. Luton is the frozen food storage centre. Newcastle had toilet paper and cleaning products. There's even a section in Brighton filled with stationery. The problem is NewGov has too much power and they don't want to give it up.

'Trade between countries opened back up about eight years ago. We're only allowed to use tall ships for shipping. Once a month, a train through the Eurotunnel is commissioned. But NewGov officials still use air travel when they want a game of golf in Ireland or a summer with their Italian counterparts.'

'Most countries are self-sufficient?'

'We use our collection of resources and grow the rest. People's needs are back to basics again. We don't get a new wardrobe every year or fruit flown in from New Zealand. Survival takes precedence over wants and desires. Unless...'

'Unless what?'

'You're at the top of NewGov.' I swallow the last bite of my dinner and push the plate aside. 'Then there's nothing you desire you can't have, including people. Sex and labour trafficking of our own people is big business between those at the top, and they don't bother to hide it.

'London is still crowded, which means if we need to make a hit or scavenge for something in particular, we can blend in. It's pretty easy to hop on a bus while keeping your face hidden from cameras. The reduced size of defence forces means they can control people in London, and most Londoners are well-behaved. Smaller units of Apostle soldiers staff the farmers' communities and fight rebels.

'There's less security outside London—CCTV and drones—as they don't have the working hours to review all the footage. People are scared to leave London because of the possibility of being arrested by a soldier whose testimony outweighs your own. They're also scared of the rebels, who might capture and torture them for access to London.

'There's no need to continue population reduction, but NewGov promised the world leaders, and they want to deliver so they can look like the tyrants they are. And that needs to stop.'

'Right after you let them murder billions of people,' Finley says.

'Right after they save the world.'

## seventeen

### FINLEY

Erin shows me where I can sleep for a few hours until the sun rises.

'This is the bedroom Lara will use when she comes back, but you can sleep here for now. It's the only one that's made up.' She points to a door. 'We're sharing a bathroom, so if you need anything, shout for me, and I'll hear you.'

I sit on the edge of the bed, more than ready to sleep but unwilling for Erin to leave. I want her to keep talking. I've learned more about her in these past hours than I ever thought possible. I know more about her than people I've known for years and I want to know more. She's lived through hell, and she's still fighting and sometimes smiling. And I want to know more about the good stuff in her life.

'Tell me, what's the future like? I've heard the bad stuff, but give me some good things.'

She sits on a small couch near the window. 'I love the forests most. The trees hide us, but I like them because they're pretty. Imagine being the only people at the Lake District for three months. The trees are overgrown with ivy, and the dead leaves lie on the forest floor. It doesn't need maintenance, like the streets here do. It's quiet without humans and machines, and you can hear for miles. If we're lucky, and the wind carries it, we can hear animals and know there's food nearby.'

'You should take me some time. I've never been.'

She widens her eyes. 'Seriously? It's only an hour away. How have you never been?'

I shrug. 'I joined the army when I was sixteen, and during furloughs, Cameron and I took Dylan back to Scotland. We never got the bug for going on holiday.'

'Well, I've got a whole host of places I can show you. Places you probably never knew existed. There are small islands off the west coast of Scotland with populations as small as five. The fishing there is amazing. You're hardly ever going to go hungry there.'

She's quiet for a while, and I hear a truck go by on the road. I'm getting tired, but I'm still not ready to sleep. I stretch out on my side on the edge of the bed. 'There are good things about living here, too. You must have seen that?'

She thinks about it. 'Being able to buy things.' Her eyes soften. 'I've focused so much on what we've left behind and trying to avoid the pitfalls of the surveillance that I forget to appreciate the freedoms here. It's what we've been fighting for my whole life. To order too much food and eating so much, my stomach hurts from being stuffed, not hungry.'

The fury runs through my blood and I don't have one tangible target to take my revenge out on. There are so many people responsible for the downfall of the world, and for Erin spending days of her life without having her basic needs met.

She gets up, settles on the bed next to me, and takes my hand. 'We could buy anything here. I mean like an exercise class or daily usage of the internet, or pay someone to paint my nails.' She laughs softly. 'Imagine making a career out of painting someone's nails. It's crazy but kind of wonderful.'

'Who knew emissary girl would fall in love with makeup and beauty services?'

She sobers. 'I never expected you to survive. That's why I could open up.'

I've not had much time to process my death in another dimension. I can't help having limited feelings about it, 'cause, well, it didn't happen, right?

'I'm sorry. This must be weird to talk about.'

'Dylan's the only one of us who's alive in the future?'

'Garvey. We call him that in the future. The one here with you is Dylan. That's how we keep some sort of semblance about who's who.'

'Future Dylan is Garvey. Got it. You should tell him. Bring him and Cameron in on this. We can all help.'

'They won't believe it unless they see something, like you did. There are other reasons too.'

'Dylan's going to be a problem. He'll never quit the army.'

Erin crosses her legs and rests her elbows on her knees, the tension easing out of her. 'I've never seen that man quit anything in his life. That's not always a good thing. But that's a problem for another day. Right now, we need to sleep.'

Erin shuffles from the bed and pulls down the blackout blinds on the window. 'The fighting is far from done, but if anything happens, we'll know about it.' She faces me. 'Unlock the bathroom door on my side when you're done. Otherwise I'll be storming through here to take a piss.'

I don't want her to leave. I tug her down to eye level. 'Stay,' I whisper.

Erin holds her breath, and I brush my lips across hers.

'I've been thinking about you for six months. When Dylan came back from the salon last week, he told me Ashley said you were engaged to someone. My stomach flipped, and I thought I'd missed my chance.'

She gulps. 'I never said yes to him.'

'I know.' I pull her down on top of me. Holding her around the waist, I kiss her neck and slowly make my way to her mouth. She lets my tongue in, and it's the best damn kiss I've ever had. My hands are all over her body, and she grinds against me.

When I feel her tug on my shirt, I panic and still her hands. 'It's not pretty.'

'What's not?'

'You were right. My injuries were bad.'

'It's okay.' Erin runs her hand over the side of my face, her fingers teasing the scar at the base of my neck. 'I've shown you a side of me I never thought I could share with anyone, and you didn't run off screaming. I can handle war wounds.' She looks sad. 'I'm used to scars. If you trust me, I promise I can handle it.'

I don't think there's another woman I'd be more comfortable with seeing me like this. My tattooed torso has an angry red puckered scar, disrupting the multiple designs that once bled into one another. Erin bites her lip, taking it all in.

'You should be dead, and this scar is proof you're alive.'

'Cameron got the brunt of it. I was behind him and got mostly shrapnel. If I hadn't grabbed him and moved, we wouldn't be here today. One piece of metal was stuck deep in my neck, but the burns on my side are the pain I remember. It was horrible.' I wince at the memory.

'You're alive.' Erin runs a hand over the thin skin. 'It's damn pretty when you think about it.' She smiles. 'That's what my dad always says.'

I chuckle. 'That's someone we don't want to talk about right now.' I grin and tug on the end of her shirt.

'I mean, I have scars too.'

Erin pulls her shirt up and shows me a small scar beside her stomach. 'This one's old. Maybe ten years ago.'

'It's a bullet wound.' I gulp. 'You got shot when you were a kid?'

'That's when we knew they had upped their game. We ran harder and faster after that. In a way, it saved our lives.' She pulls the shirt higher and adjusts her bra so I can see the knife wound circling the side of her left breast. 'Got caught about a year before we came here. The guy was using me for cover to escape. Something snapped in him. I think he knew he was

137

screwed. My dad and brother had guns on him, and he wasn't going to get far, even if he let me go. He realised it too, and I think he was taunting them more than anything. He sliced me, and my dad shot him in between the eyes before he could even laugh about it.'

'Jesus.'

Erin drops her shirt back in place and undoes her belt. She's not done showing off her war wounds. She opens her jeans and shrugs them down, then shifts her underwear aside, revealing a burn that runs from hip to pelvic bone. 'This is the one that pisses me off.'

'What was it?'

'Candle wax. I'm not sure what happened. I was a kid, thirteen. I don't remember much. I was asleep, and all I know was it was one of ours that was responsible.'

'One of yours?'

'It's when I realised that sometimes the good guys, the ones who are on the run with you, can be bad guys too.'

'What did he do?'

'We were staying in an old boarding school. Had been there a few weeks, and we each had a small single dorm room to ourselves. We were all on the same floor, right next to each other, doors open so my parents could hear us patrol. We should have been safe. I was sleeping when someone covered my mouth and tugged at my clothes. There was a shadow behind me—it must have been from the candle. Then there was no more tugging. My dad must have yanked him off me, 'cause there was a big commotion in the hall. Everyone was awake and wondering why the best data analyst we'd ever had had a gun to his head.'

'Your dad shot him in front of everyone?'

'No. He was beating him. Mum was the one with the gun.' Despite the tone, she smiles at the memory. 'She walked up and pointed it at his head and told everyone who had come out, *"It doesn't matter what you're good at. You fuck with anyone here, and you're done."* She pulled the trigger.

'Everyone was silent for about two seconds and then my brother shouted for help. He was the only one who noticed my trousers were on fire. The candle had accelerant in it, and it landed on my crotch during the fight. I think I was in shock about what had almost happened to me.' She narrows her eyes. 'I'd been training for years, and I was letting some asshole leave me in a state of shock that I didn't even realise I was on fire.'

'Suddenly my one near-death experience feels like a walk in the park,' I say lightly.

'Just 'cause some people have experienced worse, doesn't take away from what you're going through. Consider yourself lucky but don't belittle your own experiences.'

'I consider myself lucky right now. We're both alive, aren't we?' I stop smiling. 'I could give you a life here, in this weird, fucked up version of the world.'

'I think I'd like that.' She rolls on top of me, her awkwardly angled trousers preventing her from straddling me. She laughs, and I move her aside me and pull her trousers the whole way off. Halfway down her body, I blow a breath over the centre of her underwear.

Her breath catches and then she slowly breathes out and sinks into the mattress.

I hitch her hips and pull her underwear off. Before she gets her ass back on the bed, I grab hold of it and pull her closer to my face to bury my mouth inside her and kiss and suck at her core. When I look up, something on her hip catches my attention. On her hip bone is my handwriting.

*Don't give up.*

I meet her eyes. 'You've my handwriting tattooed on you.' My breath catches and a guttural growl rolls at the back of my throat. 'I'm alive because of you, Erin.'

139

She lets out a moan that turns into a gasp when I push a finger inside her and flick her clit with my tongue.

'Fuck.' She wriggles against me. 'Do that again.'

Adrenaline and fear, sorrow and lust are pumping through me, and I feel as warm as fuck. I lean up and drop my trousers to the floor. Erin sits up and unclips her bra, tossing it while I fetch a condom from my wallet. Erin pulls me by the waist down on top of her, my naked chest pressing against hers. I move up, kissing her stomach, while I tear the foil and pull the condom over my dick. I kiss her bullet scar and stop at the angry red mark left by the knife, where I kiss it and knead the flesh before sucking her nipple into my mouth. I'm pulling and tugging while Erin squirms, grinding herself around me.

I push her into the mattress and adjust myself between her hips. I lift her legs around my waist, tucking her ankles around my ass and kiss her deeply before leaning back and pushing all the way into her.

Erin screams and buries her head into the crook of my neck, hiding her face so I can't see the pain.

## eightteen

**Erin**

He stills inside me. 'Why the fuck didn't you tell me?' Finley slowly pulls out of me and rips the condom off, then curses when he sees small spots of blood on his hand.

'The last time it stopped you, didn't it?' I pull the blankets over me, mortified.

He pads naked into the joined bathroom and rummages in the cabinet. The tap turns on and off, and he appears at the foot of the bed, holding a damp flannel.

I grab the wet towel. There's no way I'm going to let him clean me up.

'How can you be engaged to someone and not have sex with them?'

I stare at him, open-mouthed. 'Unlike you, I'm picky about who I have sex with.' I spit the words at him like I used to do when Blake and I fought as kids.

Finley slides his T-shirt over his scars and sits on the edge of the bed but doesn't get back under the covers.

'I can't do this.' I run a hand over my face and snatch at my clothes. How could I ever think this would be okay? Garvey would never be okay with it, and Mum would freak at me shacking up with someone thirty years older than me, even if that's not the case now. When I start for the bathroom, he catches my hand and runs his fingers over mine in a caress.

'I'm angry I hurt you.' He looks tormented and tries to pull me closer. 'Don't go. If you want to stay, we can still do this or take it more slowly. I promise I won't hurt you again.'

I speak clearly. 'If we're going to work together, we need to sort this over-sharing thing out. We clearly get carried away after a near-death experience. There's a lot at stake, and we don't get luxuries like fuck-buddies where I'm from.'

He nods, but I see his disappointment. 'Fair enough. You're right. Last thing we need is awkward sex getting in the way.'

A sly grin hides under Finley's eyes. He's trying to goad me into a reaction.

Leaning in, I whisper in his ear, 'Ditto.'

Finley turns his head so his face is in mine. 'Sex with us will never be as mundane as fuck-buddies, Erin.'

The smell of him will always be my undoing. I want to taste him as much as possible, and I lean into his body as my mouth comes down on top of him. I let the blanket fall to the bed as the house alarms go off.

Jumping off the bed, I pick up my clothes and hear Finley gather his things behind me. Out the bedroom door, I have my underwear on and am hopping into my trousers as I try to get down the stairs. Mark appears at the bottom of the stairs and doesn't flinch at the sight of us half-dressed.

'The energy in the barn is flickering again,' he says.

Out of the house and fully dressed, we sprint to the shed.

'What happened?'

'Ollie was doing a visual assessment. He wanted to do some tests, but it flickered. It's small, but it's growing fast.'

The barn door is ajar. I hear voices. Ollie is conversing with someone. Nothing sounds tense or like a fight is in progress. My throat constricts. It might be something good.

Mark takes a step forward. His posture straightens, but his shoulders deflate. The woman he loves, maybe even more than I do, isn't on the other side of that door. He smiles tightly and opens the door fully.

Ollie is hugging someone. I smile. Flanked by two others from our camp, looking as freaked out as we were, is JT, Ollie's husband.

JT finally releases Ollie but snags his hand and looks at the three of us. With him are his brother Nivek and his wife Eleda, who are always on watch together.

'Your dad is going apeshit trying to find you.' JT frowns but then swings me around in a circle. I hang on to him, a link to our past, and let out a sob.

Dad is still my dad. Despite our time here, we hadn't impacted on that seemingly insignificant detail, and that gives me hope. We can still save them all.

I turn and smile at Mark, who looks sombre. 'What's wrong?'

'If they're here, that means those left behind lost another three of our best fighters.'

# nineteen

### FINLEY

When I get back to my apartment, Dylan is sitting on the couch, talking on his phone. He holds up a hand for me to wait.

'He's home. I'm switching to speaker.'

I sit on the arm of the chair, kick his foot, and point to the clothes he has strewn over the other end of the couch. Renting a one-bed with Dylan crashing on the couch sounded like a good idea. He was only going to crash for a month, tops. But we should've sprung the extra hundred a month for a two-bed for the sheer tidiness factor.

'You look like shit, man,' Dylan says. 'After the first night at your girl's place, you were supposed to come back refreshed and happy.'

'What's up, man?' I say over the speaker and ignore Dylan.

'I was ringing for a favour,' Cameron says. 'My mum's not doing good lately. I was wondering if you were free one weekend to drive up and check on her for me. Maybe give my sister a hand?'

'Sure. Been a while since we've had some proper bacon sarnies,' I say light-heartedly.

'How the hell can someone make bacon sandwiches taste any better?' Dylan asks.

I groan. 'I've no idea, but I swear they melt in your mouth.' I talk to Cameron again. 'Call your sister and set up a time that works for her. I can head back every week if she wants. Do the shopping and stuff.'

Cameron hesitates. 'I don't think you need to go that much. It's a long way, but I'll tell her you offered. A couple times a month, if she needs it?'

'Of course.'

'That'd be great. Thanks.' He breathes out, relief in his voice when he speaks. 'What did you find out about your girl?'

I've practised this speech the whole way over, but it doesn't stop the roll in my throat as I prepare to lie to my two best friends about time travel and a war that's about to rip the country apart. 'She's legit. The business is flush with paranoid rich clients who want the A-class upgrades to panic shelters. The guns are mostly for show. Nothing more than what you can buy legally in other countries.'

'What's the job description exactly?' Dylan asks.

'They want me to start first.' Another lie. 'Set up a training programme and make sure clients know what they're buying and how to use them. Only later do they want to get into the movement and storing of weapons. That's when they want to bring Cameron in and maybe Dylan too. If you want in, I can tell them I need someone overseas to help with logistics. The rate they're charging their clients means we can all get salaries by being consultants in defence tactics or something.'

'I'm a little busy here, but I'm making progress.'

'Why the hell are things going so slowly, Cameron?' I ask.

'A British Embassy liaison officer is helping me get prison access. And she's busy—she covers all the British citizens incarcerated in the country, so she's not always in Paris. I think the prisoner knows exactly what happened to us. She's talking about plans going back ten years. Whatever's happening in the world isn't just confined to us. A deadline is looming that a lot of governments are taking seriously.'

'She has knowledge of a setup?' Dylan asks.

'Nah.' He hesitates. Dylan never saw what we did when we walked into that courtyard in Afghanistan. He was too far back and only made it across the threshold when the bullets were already flying. 'She knows what I'm talking about, with the whole light show thing. I swear she doesn't think we're crazy.'

'I know,' I tell him. *Because I've seen it again.* 'We need to exchange info in person. There are things I can't discuss here, not even on a secure line. But what I can tell you is that yesterday I had to disable Erin's security alarms to get inside the house and eavesdrop on one of their meetings.'

'Yeah?' Dylan says.

'I had to wait until I was parked outside their property before I could get a look at their programming system. There was already a Wilson Tech software installed.' I leave out the part about people appearing out of thin air because I need more information from Erin first. I can't accidentally give away her location to anyone who might be listening, here in the past or in her future. I need to keep her safe.

Dylan sinks back into the couch.

'What the hell does that mean?' Cameron asks harshly.

'That was the single most complicated insertion job we've ever had.'

Dylan sits forward.

'That shit takes time and money and access onsite. It's not something an amateur or someone out for business sabotage does.'

'It means someone else is already spying on them.'

Mark is right. Someone from the future is already here. 'Someone who works for Wilson Tech,' I realise. 'I didn't tell Erin or her family yet because I wanted to speak to you guys first. We're not even supposed to know that a WT bug exists, let alone that it was the job that nearly got us killed.'

'Why is someone with that kind of money and resources watching a family?' Cameron asks.

'Because they're a threat.' Dylan looks me in the eye.

After a shower and a three-hour nap, I ease myself onto the couch and jot down notes for my new business venture cover story. Dylan's getting ready to go out.

I want to tell him all about the leader he's going to become. My admiration for him has kicked up tenfold. Dylan's the right man for the job, even now; looking after his men's mental health after the mission, following us around, and letting us investigate our paranoia.

Dylan folds his scattered clothes and puts them on a shelf he's cleared out under the TV cabinet.

'You decided living out of a bag wasn't permanent enough for you?'

He shrugs. 'Things just upped a notch. You're going to be staying now that Erin may be in danger. I thought I'd prepare to keep an eye on you a bit longer.'

'And keep an eye on your own girl, right?'

Dylan smirks, and regardless of the future knowledge that Ashley will one day be his wife, I know he's smitten with her.

'Need to keep an eye on you, more like. If you guys believe half the stuff you've been looking into. I wouldn't trust anyone in this town. No matter how hot they are. Did Erin say anything about a business connection with Wilson Tech? Or anyone who's helping them hide their activities? This could be a coincidence.'

I shake my head. 'Her brother Ollie runs their online and IT stuff. He's pretty good, and they're too damn paranoid about industrial sabotage to outsource anything. Whoever is spying on them... this is bad, Dylan.'

147

He sits on the windowsill and looks over his shoulder, out across the manicured estate gardens towards the train tracks. 'Monitor her if you're worried.'

I sigh. 'Nothing's officially happening between Erin and me. We still have the job offers if you want to take them up on it? It'll give us a foot in the door to see what else is going on.'

He glances at the pad on the table. 'Is that what you're writing?'

'I'm thinking up a cover business that could help us bring in other ex-servicemen that might be interested.'

'You're going to take down more of our boys with you?' he snarks.

'Anyone who's trustworthy and wants in—I think we should give them the opportunity. At the very least, it isn't an office job and doesn't qualify as a—what you call it? A pity job?' I show him what I've written down so far. Pointing at the first entry, I say, 'Her family has the funds to start something big, like an adventure company. Skydiving particularly. It would give us access to planes and airfield drops around the country.'

'And who doesn't love jumping out of aeroplanes better than soldiers forced into early retirement?'

I grin at him. 'We'd have to run the company for real—have customers and the day-to-day grind—but it just might work. It would make moving guns around the country a little easier. The aircraft will be light, and we can hire people to help with flight lessons if needed.'

Dylan stands. 'Who the hell needs flight lessons? We're hiring pilots, right?'

'Let's just say it wouldn't hurt to learn new skills while we can.'

'Erin's hiding something big,' Dylan warns me.

'They're up to something illegal,' I answer. 'And she offered us a job helping her. The way I see it, there are some bad people in this world. And if a bunch of civilians want to spend hundreds of thousands of pounds to protect themselves, why would we want to get in the way? The guns are out on the street anyway, so let's gather them up and lock them in bunkers. We're lucky. We can secure our homes and defend ourselves. Other people understand the threat, but they need a different type of weaponry to protect their family. It's like an insurance policy. Christ, did you see that crazy guy on the news who's stabbing girls he meets in nightclubs? You can warn women, but how well can they protect themselves against a crazy like that? If we can help someone, I'm in.

'Someone tried to kill us, Dylan, and it looks like they were trying to take *us* out, not the team. Don't you think it's time you think about getting discharged?'

'I'm good.' He takes a deep breath. 'No one tried to kill us, Finley. Well, no more than usual.' He chuckles without mirth.

I do something that's usually Cameron's role; I argue with Dylan. 'You're wrong. Implanting a WT on that mission was only the start. I've recently found out things I can't tell you while you're still enlisted, but there's so much more going on here. Someone in the government tried to kill us. Kill *you*. They're going to try again, and being an active soldier, it won't take a lot to make your death look like a job-related accident. It wouldn't mean dishonour if you accepted an early retirement. Psych was on the fence with you. All you have to do is ask.'

The apartment bell rings, and Dylan stares at me for a second before crossing to the door and picking up the video phone. 'Hey, babe.' He buzzes her in.

I place my hand on his shoulder. 'What would you do if it was Ashley who was involved?' I ask. 'Would you get on board?'

'Ashley's not involved in anything.' Dylan's words are harsh and there may be a warning there, too.

'Not yet,' I goad. 'But if she joins Erin, are you going to be *her* backup?'

He narrows his eyes. 'If you're trying to get my girl involved in this stuff, I'll get you and your girl out of the way.'

# twenty

## FINLEY

I bang on Erin's front door. They must know I'm here, given their security, but it takes a few minutes for someone to respond.

Erin leads me through the house to the dining room where they hold their meetings. The way she moves screams exhaustion. I wonder if she got any sleep.

At the table are Ollie and JT. Mark's sitting at the open window, smoking.

'Where are the other new arrivals?' I ask.

'Sleeping,' Erin says. 'We've made arrangements for them to join Lara in Scotland while we're figuring everything out.'

'You shouldn't be telling him everything.' Mark stubs out a cigarette in the ashtray on the windowsill.

'Leave him alone.' Erin lets out an exhausted breath and sits in a chair at the head of the table. 'We've got a shitload of work to do, and we don't have time for teenage dramatics.'

Mark stands. 'You've no idea what you're getting into, boy.'

'I'm on board.'

'You're on *her* more like,' he snipes. 'You better be prepared for what that means in the future. When this war starts'—Mark points at Erin—'that girl's family is going to be the

151

prime targets. You keep this relationship up and you won't even be able to stick around and help.'

'Hang on,' JT says. 'Erin hooked up with Garvey's bestie? Can't wait for that firework to go off.'

I playing this cool. I'll show a bunch of insurgents from the future who recently introduced me to a whole new world that I'm not fazed by this kind of goading.

Mark looks at Erin. 'He's going to have to abandon you, one way or another. Garvey isn't going to let him hang around you in the future. Question is, are you going to leave with him?' He takes a step towards Erin.

Erin looks like she is chewing on her anger. Her posture is rigid, and she's staring Mark down without blinking. 'Sit down,' she says. Turning to me, her face softens. 'We've filled JT and the others in on where we are and our progress at finding a way home. JT was just getting us caught up on what happened after we left our time.'

'That was it.' JT entwines his fingers with Ollie's and leans back into his seat. 'Blake and Garvey searched the house and the land for you after they finished their recon and found nothing. No big fight or destruction. You simply disappeared.'

'The same amount of time has passed for them at home as it has for us here,' Ollie tells me. 'That fits into a theory I have about the timelines continuously moving. Why this one wants to speed up to get us back where we should be.'

JT says, 'Your dad went crazy trying to find you. He never gave up—he still hasn't. A lot of people are assuming you lot are dead.' He looks at Ollie. 'It was something we had to consider. That you all got in an accident of some sort. We had to search for bodies. Garvey couldn't find anything that said you were dead or captured and when no one ever came with a ransom, people were telling us we had to move on. We couldn't risk staying any longer. The camp's split in two, and most of the others retreated.'

'The Apostle soldiers. What would they have exchanged for ransom?' I ask.

'Garvey. They always want him,' Erin answers before JT gets a chance.

'Garvey captured ten government agents and tortured them for information before he finally believed they had nothing to do with your disappearance. We had to fall back until that shit storm calmed down, but your parents were hitting up every lead they had to discover who might have captured you.'

'They don't know we're safe,' Erin says, and JT shakes his head in confirmation.

'It's all so overwhelming.' She rubs her eyes and then places her hands flat on the table, stretching her arms and back.

The room remains silent and lets Erin have her moment.

'Mark says you're a good fighter,' JT says to me. 'You're exactly the kind of person we would snatch up.'

I chuckle. 'Yeah, *the Garvey bunch* would really eat me up.'

'It's not like that. We respect him for what he's done for us. We respect you too,' Erin says. 'You're his friend, and that means something to us. It's just a shame—'

'I was dead.' I hang my head, knowing no one will be happy with what I have to say. 'There's a mole in your unit.'

Mark grabs me, and despite the upper hand I thought I'd have because of my size, he wrenches me out of my seat and has me pinned to the wall, a hand around my throat, quicker than I expected. I refrain from punching him in the side.

'Never question our loyalties. You've no idea what we've been through together,' Mark screams in my face.

Erin touches his shoulder. 'Drop him now.'

When Mark doesn't ease up, the pain in Erin's voice is clear. 'Damn it, Mark, don't make me take you down.'

He releases me, and I feel the colour flood back into my face as the blood returns.

'It's the only explanation of how I got past your security systems yesterday. Someone's fucked with your system. I've seen it before. My bet's on a programmed delay to the alarm. Someone can get in and out in a specific time window, and the alarms don't activate. It needs to be inserted manually from the main service computer, so it's someone who's been here long enough to upload the bug.'

'How do you know this?' Erin asks.

'Because I've planted one before. I don't know future software and computers the way Ollie does, but I can work with what I'm shown. I know just how long it took to upload and get out. It's practically invisible unless you know what to look for. I can tell Ollie what I know, see if he can find it, but be prepared to look internally. It's government technology, developed by a private company here in town. Cameron is working the same trail in France, looking for whoever targeted our unit.'

Mark raises his eyebrows. 'Why didn't you tell us earlier?'

'Because when I suspected what I was dealing with, I still didn't know everything. And then I was distracted by people appearing through a time portal. Excuse me if it took a while for the entire day's events to unfold in my head.

'It's no secret what we saw on our last job fucked us up. We were betrayed by bad intel. Cameron's convinced someone set our unit up. We spent a lot of time tracking down leads and he kept talking about this woman in France who might have the answers, but I got tired of chasing something that made me think I was crazy. I let him go to France on his own, and I checked in with a company here that our senior officer hinted may have a connection to the intelligence leak.'

It's hard to take myself back to the day we were ambushed, when I lost most of my friends, but it's time we lay it all out. Cameron needs to push his contact in Paris, and I need Erin's people to know there's another portal that could be a threat to them.

'I only realised what it was when I saw what happened in the shed yesterday. It was the same thing we experienced when we were ambushed in Afghanistan.' It's the first time I've said that, knowing the people hearing it will believe me. It took Cameron and me days before we could speak about it to each other. Dylan never saw it, so he never fully believed us. We saw the pain and worry in his eyes as he tried to counsel us, but we both knew he thought we were crazy.

Erin straightens. 'Someone from the future tried to take out your team?'

'Looks that way. Cameron and I were in the courtyard first. Dylan and five others were behind us. The US team came in from the east. It was clear, and we gave the signal to move. Suddenly there were soldiers in front of us. They wore black uniforms, just like the soldier who came through here. Unlike him, though, they were ready for us. They were in position and firing the moment they appeared.'

Mark moves to a seat at the table and lights another cigarette. 'They didn't *try* to take the team out. They *did* take you out. On another timeline, they were successful. Someone's been coming after Garvey for a hell of a long time.'

'What changed?' Erin asks.

I made an impatient sound. 'How the hell do I know? You said I died in another life, but this time I didn't.'

'We're what changed,' Mark says. 'Erin's entered your life, and whatever happened between you two—or maybe it was something she said or did, made you react differently.'

'She saved my life.' I'm embarrassed that I fell in love with a stranger after one evening together. 'I had something to live for, and when I felt something wasn't right, all I could think of was coming back to her. I took cover. Cameron was closest to me, so I grabbed him and took him with me when I ducked.' I swallow thickly. 'Half the unit behind us got hit with bullets meant for us.' A shudder goes through me. 'About a week before we shipped out, Cameron said he received information from a prisoner in France. She said our orders would be changed last minute and even knew what they would be. She also sent an embroidered uniform logo. The same one that soldier had on his uniform last night.'

Mark and Erin exchange glances.

'What was the ID number?' JT asks. 'Each logo has one.'

I write the six-digit code and hand it to Erin. 'Cameron has the emblem with him in France, but this is the number.'

'I'll see if we can get any information on the Apostle, find out how it got in the past, and with this person in France.' She hands the paper to Mark, and he frowns.

'I'm going to need the actual logo to confirm this is real.'

'I'll arrange a meet with Cameron.'

I say, 'Even before we left for the job, the contact in France told us we needed to return to town and get inside Wilson Tech. *That the rebellion would start within*. Dylan, Cameron, and I were already involved in this. Someone tried to kill us. They killed members of our team, and we want justice. We want to stop whatever the hell their plan is.'

'Who's the prisoner?' Erin asks.

'After we returned to the UK, Cameron and I confronted our senior officer about the possibility of a setup. He sent us to investigate Wilson Tech. They manufactured some of the software we were using. We were to speak to a British woman who's in jail in Paris for reckless liability and arson that caused the Notre-Dame Cathedral fire. Turns out she was the one who tried to warn Cameron of a setup before our deployment. Cameron still hasn't managed an in-person meet and her identity is still under anonymity. When Cameron uncovers anything new, we can pass it on to you.'

'That would be helpful. Thank you,' Erin says. 'What Mark was trying to say was the mole isn't one of us. But we've made friends with people here that we need to look at. Ollie and Mark, take that chip we found on the soldier to Lara first thing tomorrow. I think it'd be useful for Finley to go. He can share what he knows with you on the road, and you can brainstorm with Lara when you meet her. Ollie and Lara are the best people to discuss the possible repercussions of another active portal.'

'The soldier's thermal pin is expensive and uses a lot of resources. This wasn't a run-of-the-mill operation. He was sent here,' Mark says.

'Through time?' I ask.

'I'm not sure, but he was specifically sent to this location. They were likely chasing someone important.'

'Like Garvey.' Erin's voice chokes.

'We should bring Dylan and Cameron in on this. They can help.' I say.

'There are many things in play with Dylan and Ashley. We can't risk changing the path they're on,' Ollie says.

'But you're not concerned about me knowing the truth?'

'You and Cameron.' Erin runs her hand down my face. 'You were both supposed to be dead. There's not much more we can screw it up for you, and we need people like you two fighting with us.'

'Plus, Ollie is concerned about you and wants to be able to watch you,' JT says. 'The impact of you being alive is wide and ambiguous. Ollie wants to monitor possible changes to the past. He's writing a computer programme to help him.'

'So we're homework?' I ask Erin.

'We're responsible for you. We brought you in, turned your life upside down, and threw time travel and government murder your way. If Dylan remains in the army, you can use this situation to your advantage. See who else you could flip.'

'If it was my choice, Finley, I might take your hand and run off into the distance. Take my shot at a normal life for a couple of years and be happy. But I know what's coming, and I know how to rally an army behind me. If we can fight this, maybe *everyone* can live a normal life.' She stands.

'We're finished here. You need to give us a minute.' While everyone is packing up their things, Erin goes to the door, and I follow her to the kitchen. She clicks the kettle on, opens the fridge for milk, and tosses it on the table.

She sinks into a chair at the table and looks at my shoes. 'Why are your boots unlaced?'

'I left in a hurry.'

'Movie night, huh? Kind of a big deal, all these official dates.'

'If you like that sort of thing.'

'I've never been.'

She sounds sad, and I kick myself for not thinking about taking her. 'The movies? Not since you got here?'

She narrows her eyes. 'Rian took me once, but I freaked out when they dimmed the lights. I've never sat in a dark room with so many strangers. I ran to the toilet and texted him I got called to work. He didn't care. He wanted a homer, and he didn't care who that was.'

'What's a homer?'

'It's what we call those who stay at a more permanent compound. They make comfortable for people to come back to. Cooking and cleaning and maintenance. Being in charge of those left behind. But for us it also means being in charge of emergency evacuations, and if the camp is ever infiltrated, they'll be the ones who step forward as leaders if the fighters are gone.'

'That's what Rian wanted from you, someone to step up?'

She laughs. 'God, no. He wanted a housewife who would thank him being the breadwinner. He tried to plant the seed about giving up work for family. Rian has new business investments that are paying off for him. He's doing well enough that he can afford to ask me to quit my job and stay home. Ashley told me he even tried to talk Nanda out of going back to college last year, and they only had one date together. He said, "It's best for women to let their husbands earn more money than them".'

I take her hand. 'You're a prize, Erin, but by god, he has no idea just what you're capable of.' I gaze at our hands and tell her what really happened. 'I freaked out when I hurt you this morning.' I look her in the eye. 'I was mad at myself, not you. I should've taken things slower. If I were a good boyfriend, or whatever the hell I am, your virginity would've been something I'd known.'

She blushes and averts her eyes, trying not to make a big deal out of it.

I stroke her cheek as the redness disperses. 'I want to know everything about you, Erin, and I missed one of the important things, at the most important time, and that made me angry, because maybe I'm not good enough for you. I wanted to be someone worthy of you.'

'It's complicated in places you don't even know.'

'Hey, I'm in this war now, right? So it's my decision.'

'You're always giving your life to war.'

'Right now, I'd like to give a bit of my life to you. You've been my priority from the moment you walked into that bar six months ago.'

She snorts. 'Why?'

'I was drawn to you. The moment I saw you, I felt a pull, like you were someone I knew. I've been thinking about it a lot these past months. I don't believe in auras or soulmates or any of that crap, but your presence was something I recognised—felt a connection to. Does that make sense?'

'Surprisingly, a little.'

'Plus, you're a fucking knockout.' I wink and earn a little more blush from her cheeks.

'If you spent months working out how people fall in love at first sight, why didn't you contact me?'

'I thought about it, but we were in hospital for weeks, followed by psych and the discharge process. It was something I wanted to be on the other end of when I came back. I didn't want to burden you at the start of a relationship with someone who needed so much support.'

'You wouldn't have been a burden, Fin.'

'You say that now, but we were only together one night. Besides, I needed to help Cameron too, and I didn't want to abandon him. He got the brunt of the injuries, and his recovery is still far from over. He's also not dealing with it well.' I take a deep breath, steadying myself. 'Do you think there's a version of your life where you might let me in?'

'Most definitely, but I'm not sure that's going to fly with Garvey in twenty years.'

'He doesn't like relationships getting in the way of the mission?'

'Sometimes they can do more harm to friendships and the survival of the unit. But what if Ollie comes up with a way to send us home? And we leave you here?'

My heart skips a beat, and I know that as crazy as all these possibilities are, she's right. The best choice for her might be to help her back to her family without me. Me and Erin, no matter the pull I might feel, were never meant to be together.

'Maybe that's why you didn't survive. If I'd known you in my future, we would never have progressed to this.'

'I'd wait for you,' I tell her. 'If you get home, you'll pop right into my future, and I'd wait twenty years for you on this side.'

She holds her hand out, and I slide my fingers through hers.

'There are so many reasons why we can't be together in the future, and the end of the world is just one of them. A hook-up six months ago was different. We didn't know as much then as we do now, and things have changed.' She traces my cheek. 'We've got these immense jobs ahead, and I need to get my head back in the zone.'

'I understand. You take all the time you need, emissary girl.'

'That makes me nervous, because I need your help with the war that's coming. You must convince Dylan to quit the army. I need you and Cameron. Your knowledge and skill and leadership are invaluable. And I don't want to go into a relationship with the slightest chance the job is the only reason either of us is dating.'

'You'll use me for work but not sex?' I tease.

'I'm trying to be upfront.'

I hold my breath. What's coming isn't good.

'I'm not asking for time to see how things go, Fin. I'm saying no.'

# twenty-one

## FINLEY

Erin had me meet with Ollie that night. He debriefed me on everything from our last mission: the change of plans for the WT, how I inserted it, and how I recognised it in his system when he couldn't see it. He spent extra time having me go over and over my account of the portal and how the soldiers were ready for appearing in the past. He suspects the shock of what I witnessed in the barn is causing my brain to fill in the blanks during an attack I haven't processed yet. I assured him that Cameron had a similar account. We just weren't confident anyone would believe us. The Apostle logo from the uniform is the only reason I think he's taking me seriously.

Ollie and JT are waiting for me in the driveway of the Cooper house when I park up at 06:55. I want to hear what they think of my idea for a skydiving adventure company to front for the gunrunning as well.

JT is wearing the same clothes he came through the time portal in. Though they've been cleaned, they still hold signs of wear and tear. Ollie has a bag slung over his shoulder, and his usual jeans and T-shirt have been swapped for a dirty pair of snickers trousers and a scuffed pair of steel-toed work boots.

'Thought you were the computer guy, not the workie?'

He hands me coffee in a paper cup. 'We all work crew when we have to. Erin changes things up now and then. I'm the whatever-Erin-tells-me-to-do guy.'

I hide a laugh; we're all a little like that. The Coopers work almost every waking hour.

'Erin wants me to show you one of the current installations. We have a crew on a site now, so when we're there, we might as well pitch in and help.'

He tosses his bag in the back of the Jeep, which carries construction tools and dirt. The thing Jeeps were built for.

'Mark's coming too. He'll be in the car behind us.'

'Right, I knew that.'

Ollie laughs at me. 'He's intense when it comes to his family. It's nothing personal.' He frowns. 'Actually, maybe it is. He's waiting for Nivek and Eleda. The three of them are traveling together, so that will give you breathing room.'

'Don't forget I want to grill this guy, too.' JT smiles, but I'm not sure how much of it is genuine.

Ashley exits the house and smiles as Mark comes around the corner.

'What are you doing here, Ash?' Mark asks.

'I spent the night. Erin wanted me to help with the interior design ideas for the attic conversion.' Her smile is tight, like she knows as well as I do that Mark's a moody fucker when he wants to be. 'Just as well I was here, because Mr. Computer Geek had a crisis with his social media accounts and *I* saved the day, right?' Mark doesn't respond to her teasing. 'I also scored these bad boys Lara left behind, so it was worth the trip.' Ashley holds up a pair of very high heels with about a metre of ropey string hanging from it. These are as sexy as hell laced up to the thighs. She glances around. 'Erin worked well into the night. Can I get a lift back to town? She fell into the bed, still fully dressed. I'm guessing she's exhausted.'

Ollie looks at Mark, who tosses his bag into the back of his car and answers without looking at her. 'We're on a schedule. I'll call you a taxi.'

'Why don't you give her a ride home?' Ollie says. 'We can meet you there. We might need a second vehicle anyway, so give Ashley a ride.'

Ashley looks apologetic. 'I would appreciate a ride. I don't get paid till Friday, and I don't have any money for a taxi.'

The tension is making me uncomfortable, but I have a simple solution. I pull my wallet out. 'I owe Dylan for a million taxi fares at this stage, so it's on him,' I say, a little too chipper.

Ashley looks at the ten-pound note a little sheepishly, but Mark slams his car door. 'Keep it. I can take her.'

'It's no trouble if Finley doesn't mind.' Ashley's caught between a pissed off Mark Cooper and pride at being offered cash.

'Get in the car, Ash,' Mark yells.

'Thanks for the offer, Finley.' Ashley mock whispers, 'Mark's never really liked me, but I get to talk his ear off the whole ride home until he does.' She winks and rolls the laces of the high heels around her hand on her way to the car.

'Wait,' I call. I remove the paper bag from my hold-all. 'Can you put this in Erin's room? I thought I'd see her this morning too.'

Ashley takes it and opens it before I can stop her.

'Space Raider crisps, Bikers, a whistle lollypop, and strawberry Hubba-Bubba?'

'She's never tried them before, okay? Just give them to her, and don't make a deal.'

'What kind of childhood did she have that she never spent 10p on *Space Raiders*?' Ashley says.

Ollie gets in the Jeep and yells at me, 'We need to get moving.'

I jog back and jump in the passenger seat as Mark and Ashley pull out ahead of us.

'Ashley was suspected of inserting the bug?' I ask. 'She's your leader in the future?'

'We're examining everyone who's been in the house since we moved here. We trust her—obviously—but someone may have gotten to her. She's a clueless kid in this time. Or she might have not understood what they asked of her.'

The car chugs when Ollie shifts a gear and I look at him, but he doesn't react.

'But it wasn't her, right?'

'I set up a problem with my social media accounts and watched how she fixed them. She didn't even do the elementary things. Basically, she has no idea how to work a computer. She had to switch to her phone and reinstall everything. It was an embarrassment to her future self, if truth be told.' He sighs. 'Along with Erin, she was the one who caught me in the future.'

'Catch you?'

'I run tech 'cause that's what I used to do for NewGov.'

'I thought NewGov was the bad guys?'

'Depends who you're asking. They can be the bad guys in every time, right?' He chuckles. 'Not everyone was born free. My mum was pregnant with me and didn't make it out of London in the beginning. Her and my dad were both software engineers and were forced into NewGov work. I showed some advanced computer skills when I was younger, and I was recruited into IT. Here, in the past, with your outdated machines and tech, and almost pre-historic approach to mass security, it's easy to manipulate and pre-empt what's in place. We were taught the mistakes made in your time and how to avoid them. I'm sitting at home, infiltrating the things I got taught in history lessons.'

Ollie's driving is a little ropey as he switches lanes, and I take a deep breath, wishing I had my own car.

'Mark never told you, but the ID number on the London soldier's emblem your friend Cameron has—it's mine. Whoever your contact is in France—they know I'm here.

'The real thing that makes me nervous is I might lose touch with current challenges. Or you know, future stuff. When the time comes that we end up going head-to-head with someone from our own time, I might be out of practice. Moving money and hiding people, though? Dead easy in your time.'

I raise my eyebrows. 'Yes, because making a person disappear from today's world is so easy.'

Ollie grins. 'It is. Top tip, you need to take precautions.' He points to the dash. 'Don't buy a car with a built-in GPS, for example. But it's social media and Gestapo-style policing tactics that's the real threat. I can hide documents and hack CCTV, but twenty-five people in a pub who post pictures on Instagram, with you in the background? That's harder to control.'

'But not impossible?'

'Nothing's impossible. Time travel, for instance.' He chuckles. 'We've got a list of people to check as the potential mole, but I'm going to have a different approach with them.'

'Are there many?'

'No. It's a short list. Then Mark is going to be killing someone.'

I snort in agreement.

He smiles at me. 'Erin'll come around, dude. Her head is full of what-ifs, but I've known her a long time. She likes you. And if there's one thing I know, is that conventional relationships can go fuck themselves.'

'You think we wouldn't be conventional?'

Ollie side glances me as he pulls onto the dual carriage-way.

'But we *are* conventional. Boy, girl, same age category, both of legal age.'

'*Now* you're both in the same age and peer category. But where we're from, you're not.'

'Where you're from, I'm dead.'

'But if you'd been alive…'

'I get it, age gap.'

'It's not just that. You would've been one of the grownups.'

'And what, you guys are a bunch of kids?'

'Ten years ago, we would've been. You would've been an adult, running in a tight circle of people, and she and I would've been kids. Hooking up, even when she turned twenty, would've been weird.'

I shiver at the thought. 'That is weird. But maybe I wouldn't have met you guys till she was an adult. Ever thought of that? How old was she when she met Dylan and Ashley, anyway?'

Ollie sighs. 'You're right. It's not worth stressing over since that's not how things happened. I told her that, too. Everyone can stress over a whole load of what-ifs. She has to concentrate on what's right in front of her.'

'Which is?'

Ollie shrugs. 'A good guy who wants to help. Someone she can trust to help, as well as be in a relationship with. A total-hot, good-guy, soldier type.' He grins.

I chuckle at him. 'I'm Special Forces, dude.'

'I know, but I didn't want to crash the car.'

JT clears his throat. 'Stop flirting. I'm sitting right here,' he calls from the back seat.

Ollie smiles at JT through the rear-view mirror.

'You're a good guy, Finley. Blake would've liked you,' JT tells me.

I tense. 'You say that like's he's dead.'

Ollie pulls up at the traffic lights leading to the exit of the motorway. 'Maybe he is. Maybe *we* are. By the time our timeline catches up, we could be.'

'What was Blake like?'

'He was a lot like Erin. A leader, a fighter. He looked after us, just like their dad taught them. A lot of the stuff we had to learn was second-nature to them.'

167

'Were they close? I get the impression they were like two peas in a pod.'

'That's a much nicer way to say *two babies sharing a womb*.' JT chuckles.

'They're twins.' Ollie swallows hard at the expression on my face. 'She didn't tell you?'

I shake my head.

'They never spent a day apart until we disappeared. He was protective of her. Always by her side, joking and laughing, and diving in front of her when the bullets flew.'

I tighten my grip on the door handle. 'Did that happen often?'

'More than it should have. You and JT should use this opportunity to get to know each other. He's staying in Scotland with Lara and will head up the construction team. JT and Blake were tight.'

'Why isn't JT staying in Darlington with you?'

'We have jobs all over the UK that have to get done. I need someone I trust on the construction team. I've a lot of paperwork to hide, and I have to make sure the person keeping me in the loop knows what they're doing.'

'That's not going to leave much time for you to be together.'

JT shrugs. 'Sometimes sacrifices have to be made. Sex and cuddle time is a luxury, and it needs to come second.'

'So I've heard.'

'That could be why Erin's reluctant. Thinks if no one else is getting laid, she shouldn't either.'

'How far north are we travelling?'

'Edinburgh.' Ollie sighs.

'Christ, no wonder you're on the road so early.' I push the seat back and stretch my legs. 'You could've told me you were building bunkers in Scotland. I should visit Cameron's family. Think I'll be able to swing by Glasgow on the way home?'

'We're not just digging a bunker. We're building a bridge. Want to know the first freaky time travel loop we might have uncovered?'

I straighten. 'Do I?'

'We spent a lot of time up north and in Scotland. A lot of farming land was used there, and the roads were easy to hide on. There was one spot east of Edinburgh that had a lot of abandoned construction supplies. It took about ten years for the entire country to be scavenged and organised by NewGov. They control who can have what items, transport, household goods. Everything needs to be used and recycled, no more throwing things away and buying replacements. Each city was assigned a storage category, and items were moved around the country. It took them a while to get the larger building materials listed for long-term repairs on existing buildings in London, like the materials on the Edinburgh site.

'When we were kids, like sixteen and seventeen, we hung out there—Erin, Blake, and me. There was an office onsite. The company was building a bridge and left a lot of machinery and materials behind. We raided the office paperwork for something to do—the company had a lot of engineering problems, delayed starts. If we needed a place where adults couldn't see us, we met there. It was next to the sea and only had one main road coming into the site, so we could hear anyone approaching for miles. We stole materials when we needed them. After it was finally cleared out by NewGov, we came back, and we found a door under the office.'

'What kind of door?'

'A bunker.' He looks over at me. 'We only found it because we were kids snooping around. We were looking for an adventure. The bunker was empty, but it became our new place to hide. When we realised how valuable it was, we told Garvey about it, and he used it a couple of time when we needed to hide.

'Anyway, when we got here last year, Lara went looking for that site. There was nothing there yet. The original plans for the bridge were submitted to council planning, but the company had gone bankrupt. Lara was devastated. She knew we needed that bunker. Ollie rolls his eyes. 'I chose the construction company name as our alias here. *The Coopers*.'

'No, it couldn't be.'

Ollie nods. 'Erin pointed it out, and it got me thinking. I dug around and found the name of the original company that went bankrupt was something else entirely. Erin wanted to make sure the building on this site would start and their resources get left behind for us to use in the future, with our first bunker hidden under the office.'

'She never knew you started The Coopers business when you stole their name?'

'We've no idea if we're living the same life we always did and making a difference or if we're in a transition place, where we can take the things we always knew and make them better. Either way, Erin wanted to intercept the build, make sure the bunker got sunk, and that all records of it are destroyed, and the materials left behind in the place they always were. Erin's given me a note to bury inside it, for Blake.'

'What did it say?'

'Didn't ask. Erin wants to let him know she's alive. That Lara is alive—so he'll keep fighting and winning.'

'Did you find a note when you opened the bunker in the future?'

'Blake was the first one in. He never said anything, and maybe that was the plan all along, or perhaps this is the first chance we have to stop from getting sucked through a time portal in the future. Either way, we became the Coopers—the building company that failed at building a bridge and left thousands of pounds' worth of materials and equipment lying around.' He chuckles. 'We always said the people who worked there were stupid to make so many mistakes, to screw up a job so badly.'

I swallow, knowing that Erin has to choose between staying with her family in a world that's trying to kill her or leave them behind forever and try to fix their world. As selfish as it is, I'd like her to stay here with me. 'One last question. Did Erin tell you to bring me back after the job, or is she shipping me off to the farthest location you have?'

'Don't worry, Edinburgh's not our most remote site.' He slaps me on the arm. 'The Isle of Skye is.'

# twenty-two

## DARLINGTON, UK

## 2019

## FINLEY

We arrive in Edinburgh, at the Coopers' building site, by late afternoon, and Ollie reverses into a spot and leaves the engine running and the driver's door open when he gets out. He slowly approaches the small crew of workers and casually greets them.

'Stay here,' JT says from the back seat and joins Ollie.

The two men are almost the same height, and although Ollie is stronger than you'd expect for a computer geek, JT dwarfs him in the muscle department. He's a fighter. I can spot a guy who can handle himself.

In a Portakabin, surrounded by mud and dredge, Ollie spends an hour showing me and JT blueprints of emergency bunkers customers can purchase.

I've already seen the ones they offer for sale online. They're finished to a high interior spec and start at studio size, with living and sleeping quarters, up to an eighteen-unit military-type underground survival command centre.

But these blueprints have details that aren't on their website: access tunnels and hidden floor spaces, panic rooms and supplies, weapons storage and hunting and fishing equipment.

'We've mostly sold units that sleep from four to ten people,' Ollie says.

JT produces a second set of blueprints and lays them over the ones on the table.

'These include hidden rooms or floors we keep off the customer's plans. When they inspect the work, or after the job's complete and they're jacking off in their new bunker, they aren't aware we've added sections only we will use.'

I shake my head. 'If they're that securely hidden, how will your people in the future know to look?'

'That's Lara's job, and she still hasn't figured that part out. It's not a problem yet. We haven't sold any big bunkers thus far,' Ollie tells me.

'But you think you will?'

'Doesn't matter. We're going to install them on the sites where we can dig deep enough,' JT answers. 'That's why we're going to expand our work to include the building of other infrastructure. We'll get a site that's big enough and in the right location to construct what we need.'

I sit down and rub my temple. Christ, I wonder if I can get one placed closer to my family, or heck, get them a berth in this one.

'Don't think about it too much. You'll have a headache for two years,' Ollie says. 'All of us have family or friends across the UK we wanted to warn or bring into the circle, but it isn't feasible and it might impact us getting home.' He squints at the computer screen. 'Black Jeep driving onsite.'

I glance at the small CCTV pop-up window.

'Looks like Mark,' he says. 'And Lara is with him.'

Ollie and JT rise, open the door, and move quickly down the steps, JT with his hand under the back of his shirt. I follow them out.

Ollie struts towards the Jeep, and Mark raises his hand in greeting.

Mark reverses into a spot and leaves the engine running and the door open when he gets out. Fuck, how did I miss that? They're checking that everything is alright before they settle in.

JT greets Mark. 'All good, brother.' He slaps him on the shoulder and gives him a quick hug.

'I dropped Nivek and Eleda off at Lara's apartment. There's enough room for the four of you to stay there.'

A petite woman gets out of the car behind Mark. Her long dark hair is tied back, and her tight jeans and cropped top bare half her stomach. Makes me think she won't be pitching in with the hard labour later.

Ollie pulls her in for a quick hug. 'Finley, meet our *sister* Lara.'

Lara smirks at me. 'You had to go and survive, didn't you?' She chuckles. 'Erin told me to work on the website for your cover business. We need names, tax records, and assets, then we can start marketing and running the day-to-day business. We'll keep it small, fully booked mostly, but it has to be functional. You'll ask me for everything you need, and I'll make it happen. Not gonna lie. I'm going to enjoy how this all plays out.'

'Lara,' JT chides.

She looks affronted. 'What? I'm being nice.' She turns to me. 'I think Erin is going to benefit from having you here.'

Mark grunts as he goes by.

'They're a little jumpy, burying guns and all,' Lara jokes.

'I see that.' I turn to Mark. 'Dude doesn't even turn his engine off. You know that's bad for the environment.'

Mark turns it off but doesn't lock up. 'Everyone in the office.'

When I'm up to speed, Ollie says, 'We know it's not ideal to go head-to-head in a gunfight with weapons thirty years more advanced than ours, but it's all we have right now.' He retreats to a corner with Lara to update her on everything I know about the WT bug in their system. Lara looks worried, and I catch occasional computer-related lingo I can understand. But these guys are on a different level. Ollie rolls the chip he cut out of the dead soldier's body between his thumb and finger as they talk.

JT and Mark prod me to focus on my new job, and I say, 'I don't see how the staff manufacturing these things don't notice the added areas.'

Mark says, 'They do, but it's none of their business what we put in them. Ollie upgrades the locking devices on the hidden areas. With some bunkers, we make the alterations onsite.'

JT slaps Ollie on the shoulder, then digs his fingers in and massages the muscle.

My gaze lingers on them, and the jealousy of not being able to do that with Erin irritates me.

'We need you to fill them with whatever Erin tells you to.'

Conversation with Lara over, Ollie rolls the office chair over to the table to join us, looking a little deflated.

Leaning forward, I speak, 'You're not just building bunkers on this site. Ollie told me about the bridge on the drive up here, but there're issues that're going to draw attention to this job, and soon.'

'Like what?' Mark asks.

I slide the blueprints across the table to him. 'Site's too big, and you're digging too deep and too wide. You've already reached the mile mark in length based on what we saw on the drive in. There's no product here yet, which means you're

175

nowhere near ready to start installation. You can't bury a large bunker this quickly before the public notices.'

Ollie shrugs. 'The Cooper Bridge is in planning stages, Objections and safety breaches meant that the project was never completed before the world fell apart, and means that the materials were left behind. The only thing we need to do is get the bunker in place, and leave behind all the bogus documents in this office

. It was enough crap to keep us entertained as kids for a while.
'

'But someone is paying attention to your family, here and now. There was a WT bug in your house, for Christ's sake.'

'Nah.' Mark lights up a cigarette. 'We don't have to build that damn bridge. Just need to make sure the supplies are here at the right time, and no one moves us off the land.'

'The business isn't relying solely on private contracts for places to leave supplies,' Ollie tells me. 'We're trying to branch out and get government contracts for public works and national parks. The best place we can hide things is in plain sight, in the heart of what will be closed public compounds in the future.'

'A Trojan horse?' I ask. 'You're looking for places in London to hide bunkers?'

'We're trying to leave messages and signals for our people in the future. It's harder than it sounds, but it looks like someone managed it with the WT bug you found in our system. Only the message wasn't from us. It was from someone else.'

'Whoever is the mole that made it into your house, for a lengthy period to upload a WT and left an encrypted message, is from the future?' I clarify. 'But you're confident the mole is not one of your guys.'

'It's not. It has to be someone else,' Marks says. 'They weren't able to send another message to say we'd found the bug. They haven't uploaded anything else, because we're watching the system now and know what to look for. If it were one of our own, they'd have found another way by now. They'd have sent more Apostles to kill us.'

'What he's saying is thank you,' Lara says. 'They had a way of communicating and knowledge of the portal and how to use it to kill us. You might have saved the future.'

JT has refilled my coffee and Mark has relaxed enough to take a seat at the table. With Lara permanently based in Scotland, she's been grilling Ollie and Mark on what they've been doing with the energy source in the barn to get everyone back to where they belong. JT's arrival with the others has only pumped up her resolve to make returning to the future a priority.

It's been a while since anyone has spoken. Ollie and JT keep making eyes at each other, like they've discussed it and argued about it many times in the last twenty-four hours and would much rather be fucking in the hotel we have an hour outside of town.

I don't blame them. If you think about it too much, you get one of those two-year headaches Ollie warned me about.

Erin will never get to go home and find her brother or her parents. I'm devastated for her and distressed that a little piece of my shit heart is relieved she'll stay here.

'I've been working on the mechanics of how people are travelling into the past. All I'm certain of is it's completely separate from how to travel into the future.'

'Surely they should work the same way,' Lara says.

'They're two different things, so no. Once you're in the past, you are in a new version of reality. The future hasn't happened yet. You can't jump somewhere that doesn't exist.'

'People can go to the past, but once there, they're altering things, so the universe is unsure which future to return them to,' Mark says.

Ollie looks at JT. '*This* life is going to be our future, and none of us knows for sure what it is.'

'But you can't stop yourselves from making the same mistakes that sent you here. That in itself alters things. If you never came here to build all the things you need to help survival in the future,' I say.

'Guy catches on quick,' JT says.

'But there's a chance others will come through.' I motion to JT. 'Each time someone arrives, they bring news, right?'

'Take a moment and look around, Finley,' Mark tells me. 'Our community in the future is getting smaller. Those left behind don't have as many protectors as they did.'

He's right. For every fighter that comes through here, those left behind are slowly getting fucked or killed. 'They might be dead already?' I ask with horror.

Mark's eyes glaze over. 'They're not dead.'

I've overstepped a line. I voiced the one fear they have—that this might all be for nothing. 'You left someone there.' I remember.

He slams his fist on the table. 'I never fucking left her.'

## twenty-three

*Erin*

Seeing Finley at my house after his trip to Scotland makes me smile more than it should.

'Sitting on someone's car can be considered stalking.' I walk around, lean on the bonnet of my car, and crack my neck.

'What do you know about stalking?'

'It's illegal in every time zone.'

Finley narrows his eyes. 'We need to bring Dylan in on this.'

I click the car fob. 'I told you it wasn't time yet.' I get in my car, and Finley follows. 'Sometimes we keep people in the dark in case there's a leak, and thank god for that.'

'Why, what happened?'

'We've received information about what's going to transpire in the future. Someone's going to screw us over.'

'Dylan won't. You can trust him.'

I drive to the road and turn towards town. 'What if the information leak is from more than one person? A compiled pile of scraps of information?'

'It's a possibility.' He lays his head back.

'And there's a possibility it's three or four.' I swallow. 'They could have us all captured at some point.'

'You can't take all this on and not have someone to talk it through with.' He reaches over and runs his fingers through

179

the hair at the side of my face. 'Keep too much bottled up, with the resulting stress and pressure, and people can go crazy. Trust me, I know.'

'My family help.'

'A fake family who you don't divulge everything to?'

I tense. 'It's not that I don't trust them. I do. Maybe some of it is fear. You know what it's like being on the front line. If you're captured, you'll break eventually. Everyone does. I want to make sure no one feels guilty when they do.'

'That's smart. Do what you can and take care of your soldiers, even if they get captured and you never see them again.'

'Mark's trying to keep the ones we love safe in the future. Sometimes, I think he misses my mum more than I do. He looks tough and scary, but he's not.'

'Just a man in love?'

I weave in and out of traffic in the high street. 'Mark should be with my mum in the future. She'd be happy.'

'I don't think so.'

'No? What the hell do you know?'

'I don't think she'd be happy knowing her daughter is missing.'

I smile sadly. 'But she'd have Mark. He would wrap her in his arms and tell her it was okay. Mark's good at taking care of her. He's always looking out for people. He doesn't sleep much. He... helps.'

'Then maybe it's a good thing he's here, and maybe your mum will sleep easier knowing he's with you.'

'Things are going to get bad.' I glance at him and look back at the road. 'And I don't want to be in love when that happens. I don't want to hurt as much as Mark is hurting right now.'

Finley lightly touches my cheek.

'Get out,' I tell him as I pull to the kerb.

He wraps his fingers around the door handle.

'You need to get out.' I unclip my seat belt, lean over him, and push the door open.

'Erin—'

Putting on my best happy face, I shout at Nanda and Ashley, who are walking towards Ashley's flat on the opposite side of the road. 'Fernanda!' I run across the street. 'It's so nice to see you again.' I hug her, despite only seeing her a few times before she moved. She was always kind to me. 'I didn't know you were coming back today. Let's do lunch, and you tell me all about uni.'

Nanda smiles. 'I quit my placement job and don't want to say a single word about that dreadful place.'

Shit. Ollie needs a foot in the door, and Nanda was going to be our way in.

'But I do want to talk about this delicious hunk of a man who's following you around.' She links arms with me and looks at Finley.

'That's my cue to take off.' He grins. 'See you later?' He touches my arm and walks off.

'Dylan is back. Finley is back. Is anyone going to find me a boy to snog tonight?' Nanda asks.

'I'm sure we can find Rian lurking in a club. You two can keep passing him back and forth each time you show up in town,' Ashley jokes.

'Shut up,' I drone, and Nanda and I shove Ashley down the street towards the pub.

## twenty-four

### Erin

I hate nightclubs. They're dark and disorientating even without the alcohol. The relentless thumping bass radiates through my chest and is giving me a headache.

'Cheers.' Ashley raises her glass, and Nanda and I clink ours against it.

'I love coming back to visit with you guys.' Nanda moves her arm, and her shirt lifts, revealing her perfect belly and tan. It appears to be accidental, but she has the back of the shirt tucked into the waistband of her short pleated skirt, knowing every move will show off her skin to all the hot-blooded men glancing in this direction.

One thing's for sure, Nanda and Ashley get male attention. They're beautiful, classy—most of the time. After lunch and drinks at the pub, we changed and reapplied makeup, and ended up here.

'Are you trying to make him jealous?' I ask Ashley and glance at Dylan, who's holed up in a corner with Finley.

'No.'

'Then why the outfit? I thought there was a one or the other rule?'

'My friend is home.' Ashley puts an arm around Nanda. 'I want to have fun, burn off some energy before she knuckles down, and I don't see her again for months.'

'I didn't realise the first few weeks of university were going to be so tough. Doesn't stress come at the end of the year, with exams and things?' I ask Nanda.

'Nanda's been approved to take on three extra modules, with the intention of getting her second degree in two years, instead of three.'

Nanda looks embarrassed. 'Suppose it helps if Daddy is funding the university.'

Ash says, 'It's you who's going to have to study and pass the damn course. Don't suppose you could swing another traineeship for Erin's brother at your dad's place?'

I keep quiet. No need to tell her we've no interest in expanding Ollie's career.

Nanda sips her drink. 'I'll ask, but to be honest, he might get stuck making the tea the first six months. My dad is careful about who he lets work on his projects.'

'But he let you work on his last project?' I ask.

Nanda smiles tightly at me, a non-committal response. 'It wouldn't be a bad idea to bring in an assistant, I suppose. If he weren't your brother, I'd tell you to call him up right now. He's got that intense bad boy radiating off him.'

I snort. 'Yeah, and his beau would smack you out.'

'His what?'

I swallow diet Coke the wrong way. 'Isn't that what the cool kids say? It's what the urban dictionary online says. Is that not right?'

'Wait, is Ollie gay? Damn.' Nanda finishes her drink. 'That's even hotter now.'

I make eye contact with Ashley, and she silently laughs with me. 'Let's go over there.' I gesture towards the men's table at the back of the club. 'You're going to go eventually.'

As Ashley approaches, Dylan gets up and waits for her, then bends her back for a full-on, movie-worthy snog. Eww. Nanda and I laugh as she pushes him off her and wipes her mouth and smeared lipstick. He regains his seat and pulls her down next to him. Finley hasn't taken his eyes off me.

'Don't look now,' Nanda whispers in my ear. 'But Mr. Boring is sneaking up behind you.'

Fuck. I keep my eyes on Finley as another man's hand touches my side. I knock it away and turn. 'Rian?' I ask, surprised. 'Nice you see you.'

'You too, babe.' He leans in for a kiss, but I move my head, and it lands on my cheek. I push him away, but he grabs my hand and places it on his chest.

From a distance, we must look like Ashley and Dylan did a few moments ago. 'What are you doing?' I'm shocked by his familiarity.

He moves his attention to Nanda. 'Heard you enrolled in university. Thought you were all about marriage and babies?'

'Fuck off, Rian.' Nanda gives him the finger as she walks away.

Finley's eyes are on me. I keep my eyes on him over Rian's shoulder and silently ask him for help, hoping by some miracle he can mind read. At the words, '... *give you another chance,*' I turn to Rian. 'Excuse me?'

It took a while to realise his serious face was anger in disguise. He hid a lot from me in the beginning, when I wasn't paying him all that much attention beyond his pretty face.

He's attractive. Not natural and raw and real, like Finley, but in a polished way. He's tall and muscular from working out in the gym, but not like Finley, who came by it because of how he lives. Rian likes to show off with button-down shirts on the clingy side, sleeves rolled up to showcase his buff arms to the girls who take second glances as they pass by, even now when he's trying to win me back. Because that's all I ever was to him: a prize to parade at charity dinners the bank organised.

He smirks. 'I'm going to take the stunned silence as a yes.'

I hate that smirk. He thinks he has me tied up with a bow and ready to swoon at whatever he offers. Like marriage and kids and moving to London for him to climb the banking ladder.

I pull his head down so I can whisper in his ear, and I swear I feel him smile. 'Leave me the hell alone.' I push off him for a dramatic exit and bounce off a solid hard wall of chest, and when Finley reaches out to steady me, I relax and sigh.

Finley feels it. He tightens his grip on me and pushes up against me. Christ. My head spins, and I follow Finley away from Rian.

'All okay?' Ashley, and I squeeze her hand and take a seat next to her.

Finley bends towards me. 'You want to tell me what that was all about?'

'Just a guy who can't let go. I bruised his ego.'

The insecurities Rian planted over the months we were together crawl their way to the edge of my skin and prickle inside.

'Talk to me,' Finley says. 'Ex-boyfriends are supposed to get you mad, not sad.'

'It's bad enough when the little voices keep you awake at night, telling you you're not good enough. You don't expect someone to be subtlety feeding the same things to you during the day, too.'

'That fucker.' Finley looks over my shoulder, trying to find Rian.

'It wasn't like we were a proper couple. Rian wanted a trophy wife on his arm at events. He was attentive to me when there was an audience, but on our own, he hardly spoke to me. Our dates were always in places that wouldn't serve him to be seen canvassing or bumping into the people he needed to mix with.'

'You were getting married before I came back.'

185

'No, I broke up with him.'

'You didn't want to run off with him?'

'Not even close.' I don't see Rian anywhere. 'He probably only wants me back for a few weeks so he can be the one to dump me and save his reputation.'

'And what do you want?'

Finley's face is beautiful and safe and honest, and everything I need when I look into someone's eyes and bare my soul.

The noise in the club is grating through my ears, my brain. Everything in this bloody time is so goddamn bright and noisy and intrusive. 'I want to go home.'

It must have been the croak in my voice and the tears I'm holding back that let him know I didn't just mean back to my house.

'This is going to make me sound like a selfish prick, but I did something.'

'What?' I practically yell at him.

He holds his hand up. 'Nothing bad.' He smiles. 'I was hoping it might help you feel settled here if I could show you some of the good things we have. Show you that maybe this could be home for you, too. But now I feel bad for trying to keep you here, so maybe we shouldn't go.'

'Go where?' Curiosity has always been my downfall.

'A weekend in the Lake District. I thought you could show me around, and I don't know—feel closer to home, with the trees and nature.'

'Can we camp out?' I ask before I've even thought about what his offer might mean. A weekend break away with someone. A chance to see what a life in 2019 might look like in the right setting, with Finley.

He smiles. 'Whatever you want.'

I shift towards him, to get some illusion of privacy at the small table.

Finley moves his legs and lets me get closer to him.

I put my hand over his. 'Sometimes I lie in bed at night and pretend I'm outside sleeping. We used to do that a lot. The dark sky and stars are comforting. Here in town, all the bloody light pollution dulls the stars. But when I close my eyes and pretend—I can hear them next to me.'

'Your family?'

'And everyone else. Bonds formed quickly under Garvey's leadership. He made everyone feel important. Each of us had jobs and responsibilities. Everyone was needed, valued. We looked out for each other.'

'He's good at psychology and human behaviours, the social sciences. It's all part of our training.'

'Sometimes I dream of them. I don't know what we're doing, but we're caught in this spell of happiness. That's why I know it's not real. If I ever went back, it wouldn't be all Sunshine's and laughter. The running and dying would still be there. Trying to get a step ahead, to rally more troops and flip some people high in the command. It gets so damn tiring, I wonder if it's worth it.'

'Freedom is worth everything.' He wraps an arm over my shoulders and interlocks our fingers.

I let myself lean into the crevice of his arm and relax. 'I know. And despite it all, we want to help. To save dystopia.' I smile at our hands. 'We want to save the shitty future we live in and keep our freedom, and I want to go home to my family and know they're all alive and safe. But recently'—I scrunch up my nose and sigh—'I want to stay with you too. That's scarier to me than dying.' I wriggle free. 'If I get comfortable here, I might decide this fight is something that can wait or someone else can fight it instead of me. And I can't do that.'

'I'll fight with you. Let me in, Erin. Dylan and Ashley made the deadliest couple, you said. And your mum and Mark. They have time to fight with the rest of the survivors and look out for each other. Would it really be that bad?'

187

'When we have to leave, yes, it'd be that bad.'

I get up and head towards the toilets where there's a fire escape door that leads to an empty porch no one knows about. The door is heavy, and as soon as I'm through, all the noise is blocked. I take deep, calming breaths. The door opens behind me, and I'm assaulted by the music again.

Nanda pulls me in for a hug, and I let her. 'You okay?'

I don't cry for the family I left behind or the possibility of a new love here. I let her hug me.

'Let's go dance. We can work out our frustrations on the dance floor. It's my second favourite way of relaxing.' She grins.

## twenty-five

### FINLEY

I pay the barman for the round of drinks and lean back against the bar with Dylan to watch the girls hovering near the dance floor. Nanda's trying to coax Erin into dancing, rather than her sway from side to side on the edge of the floor.

'This is bullshit,' I shout to Dylan next to me. 'She won't allow herself any time to enjoy what she's working towards.'

Dylan takes a swig of his beer. 'I thought you were giving her space.'

I bite the top of my bottle. 'Is it so bad that all I want to do is watch TV on the couch with her forever?'

He raises an eyebrow. 'That's not all you want to do.'

I dismiss his teasing. 'I like her.'

He smirks. 'The crazy shit she's talking about... maybe it's better if you let this one lie. I swear the girl thinks she has a higher calling.'

'And if she does? What if Ashley told you she'd something bigger than you and me? Something important that she had to do with her life. Would you let her?'

He looks at me like I'm crazy. 'Dude.' He turns back to stare at the dance floor. 'I'd be her fucking cheerleader.'

I know exactly what he means.

'But not over something that might adversely affect my mental health. We were offered the consultant role on the TV show. You said that's why you were back in town, but I know full well Cameron asked you to look into the info he got about people at the base.' He raises his bottle to his mouth but tips the end towards Erin at the dance floor. 'She shows up with a crazy story and a purpose for your life, right after a near-death experience. Don't you find that weird?'

'You think I'm being duped? Thanks a lot, man. What about you? You cruised back here for a fucking holiday during your leave, and now you're acting like a man in love?'

'Maybe I am.'

'Maybe it's fate.' His concern is touching. 'Erin saved my life, of that I'm sure. Our fate changed the day we met those two.'

'So why the hell will she not take you seriously?' he asks.

'Those girls need time to figure out they're going to spend the rest of their lives with us.'

'Dude, did you just ask my girlfriend to marry me?'

I laugh and slap him on the shoulder. 'Yeah.' I look at Erin. 'I did.'

Ashley passes by the girls and heads to the toilet. Dylan says, 'Did you book our flight to Paris?'

I swallow my sip of beer. 'Not yet. Was going to do it tonight.'

'Don't bother. Cameron is coming here instead. Says to stay put till he gets here. *"Don't leave town, Dylan".'* He imitates Cameron's Glaswegian accent. 'I hope this isn't a wild goose chase. He doesn't need anything else fucking with his head.'

'Whatever he comes back with, I'll hear with an open mind. But you two have to be receptive if I choose not to believe everything and suggest going back to therapy. Neither of you finished your course.'

'We're going to lose our table.' I deflect. 'Be a good barman. Take those back to the table. I have something to do.'

He salutes me and gathers the five drinks while I make my way to the edge of the dance floor. Erin sees me approaching, and Nanda subtly takes off, hips swaying.

'Dance with me.' I hold out my hand, expecting her to run. The fear in her eyes has me biting my lip to keep my smirk under control.

'I can't dance.' She drains her drink and shakily places the glass on the divider separating the dance floor from the tables.

Leaning in, I whisper, 'I'll only tell you to do things I know you'll love.' I lick her ear when I retreat and feel shivers run through her.

She presses against me, and I move with her to the railing two steps behind us.

'I say what I mean, and I literally can't dance. Never had a chance to learn. But if you're willing to take that sexy body out there and let every woman in this club know you're going to be dancing with me tonight, I'll let you teach me a few things.' She leads me onto the floor.

'What do you mean, you've never danced?' I yell over the music.

'We didn't have many parties back home. Not much music either.'

'No music? How is that possible?'

'Music's streamed over devices, but we keep our tech contact to a minimum. We try not to draw attention to our camps either, so no unnecessary noise, not that we could ever find many old CDs to listen to. But no gatherings or parties—not like here.'

'Well, that sucks, but I kind of like that you've never been on a dance floor with another man before.'

'How many girls have pressed up against you like this before?'

I laugh. 'Oh, baby. If I told you the truth, you'd run and hide.'

Her expression sours, and she shifts back.

I follow her. 'I don't dance with girls, Erin.'

191

'Then what the hell are you doing?'

'You looked like you wanted to be out here, so here we are.'

Erin slaps me lightly on the chest. 'Do you even know how to dance?'

'Not a clue, but it's pretty much like sex. You move your hips and go with the flow. If you're doing it with the right person, there's not anything you can do wrong.'

'You give that advice to all the virgins you meet or just the ones who are dance virgins too?'

My heart falls. I pull her off the dance floor towards the emergency exit, away from the speakers and the crowd. It's a lot quieter a few feet away. 'I like you, Erin. Why do you think I don't?'

She kicks the toes of Ashley's borrowed high heels at the ground and hesitates, stuttering to answer.

'Because I stopped?' I try to look her in the eye. 'You think I don't like you because I stopped fucking you when I realised you were a virgin?'

'No need to yell it, Fin.'

'You deserve more than a quick fuck after an intense night. If I didn't care about you, nothing would've been able to hold me back once I was inside you. If you don't know that already, Mark is right. We're messing things up trying to be together.'

As I'm walking away, Nanda runs over. She's pale and breathing erratically. 'Ashley's in trouble.' She leads us through the club, past the VIP curtains, and into a room where a bouncer is guarding a door. 'He's a friend. He can calm him down,' Nanda tells the bouncer.

The man moves aside and lets Nanda open the door. Dylan is being restrained on the floor by two club bouncers, and Erin and I lunge forward to help him.

'You have to calm down, pal,' the bouncer says calmly to Dylan.

Dylan needs to be kept under control, that much is clear, but no one gets to hold one of our team down but us. I push the bouncer off him. 'What the fuck happened?' I ask.

Ashley is sitting behind a desk in an office, a blanket over her shoulders and a female bouncer holding her hand.

Ashley looks up at us, a gash near her temple and blood oozing down the side of her head. A staff member holds something against Ashley's neck.

'Rian knifed me in the toilets,' her voice is grainy.

I understand now why Dylan went crazy.

'He had his hands around my neck and was cutting my throat.'

Nanda and Erin gather around her, and she sobs with her friends.

'Dylan was waiting outside the toilets for her, and she was taking ages, so he sent me in to get her,' Nanda tells us. 'When I started screaming, he came in and'—she stumbles over her words—'he n-nearly killed him. I've never s-seen a fight like that before.'

'Calm him down,' Erin says to me. 'When the police get here and see him like that, they'll arrest him to make sure he doesn't do anything stupid. Dylan can't have a record.'

They'll find him too easily in the future if he has a record.

'Give Dylan a job to do,' Erin says. 'He can take her to the hospital and then home after.'

Dylan has stopped struggling under me and is listening to the girls' conversation. I look down at him. 'If I let you up, will you be cool?'

He draws a shaky breath. 'I'm okay now. Let me up. I need to go to Ashley.'

I back off but remain alert.

Ashley steps out of the office, still clutching the blanket around her. 'Dylan.' Her voice is hoarse.

She moves down to Dylan. Her hands are shaking, and two of her nails are broken off as she reaches out and touches the side of Dylan's face.

Dylan holds her gently. 'I'm sorry.' Tears roll down his cheek. 'I'm sorry I didn't get there in time.'

Ashley clears her throat. 'Take me to see a doctor. I don't want to leave here alone. Help me, Dylan.'

Ashley sits on the floor, and the staff member is still holding a rag to the blood on the side of her head and neck. The bleeding seems under control for a neck wound, but Ashely is pale and her limbs are shaking, even sitting on the floor.

Dylan carries her out the door and through the club as sirens approach.

'Did you know about this?' I ask Erin. Nanda hovers, shaking almost as much as Ashley.

Her voice is low enough only I can hear what she says, 'Of course not. Ashley never told me about this in the future, or I'd have tried to stop it.'

'That's not what I meant.' I grit my teeth. 'Did Rian ever hurt you?'

'No.' She's suddenly in a panic. 'Dylan's going to kill him. He can't go to jail, Fin. And Ashley—Dylan wasn't here this early before, which means when this happened in the original timeline, it was much worse for her. She didn't have the emotional support Dylan is going to give her.'

'What does that mean?'

Chills run through her; I see the shivers run down her arms, followed by goosebumps. 'Your experiences define you. Maybe the Ashley Garvey of the future is such a badass survivor because she'd already lived through some nasty shit.'

'And now?'

'I need to ask Mark.'

twenty-six

*Erin*

At 3:30 a.m., Finley's name flashes on my phone.

I whisper 'Hello' when I answer, even though everyone else in the house is awake.

'I'm at the gate,' he tells me and hangs up.

I wrap my dressing gown around me and disable the alarm sensors at the bottom of the stairs. In the kitchen I pull up the front gate security camera and see Finley sitting in the driver's seat of his car, window rolled down, waiting for me to buzz him in.

I press the intercom speaker. 'What do you want, Finley? It's late.'

He startles hearing my voice and turns to face the camera and speaker. 'I wanted to check on you.'

'I'm fine.'

'Let me in, Erin.' He frowns.

I sigh and push the button. I monitor the rest of the cameras and watch him roll through and up the drive. I go to the front door and open it.

'Did you speak to your family?' he asks, coming in.

'Yes. We've spent the last three hours trying to figure out what this means for Ashley. After Mark smashed a bunch of shit in the kitchen, we cleaned up. We argued and shouted and wondered if there was any way we could've stopped or helped her, or how to help her now. There are various theories. Most

195

of them are crazy, but all of them are scary. The most hopeful one is that this always happened to her, and everything will be as it was.'

'That's the best? What about the worst?' He follows me along the hallway to the kitchen.

I blow in my mouth and my cheeks puff out. 'That it will break her. She was never supposed to be rescued, and that made her tougher. Or it never happened at all, and when you guys came back, it altered things for her. Or someone from the future is trying to fuck with Garvey through her. That one has double the fear because of the WT in our system and the active link we found to the thermal pin, the information on the bunkers, and the people who tried to take you out on your last tour.' The speed of my voice matches the anxiety running through my veins.

'What do you think?'

'I don't know, but I'm giving her a couple of days. Then I'm going to make sure she gets through this and turns into the person I've always known.' I unplug the battery pack that was charging on the kitchen counter and wrap the wires.

'I took Nanda back to her father's place. Rian's probably going to be released on bail Monday morning. I'm going, but call if you need anything.' He kisses me on the cheek and makes for the front door.

'Finley.'

He stops at the kitchen door. 'Yeah.'

'I wanted to let you know that you made me feel important,' I whisper. 'I previously dated someone who on paper was the best boyfriend I could ask for. Good family, great job and career path, and I didn't like him enough to let him get anywhere near me. Now look at what kind of person he turned out to be.' My smile is fake to hide the tears. 'I wanted you. I still do.'

'Then why do you keep pushing me away?'

'Embarrassment, mostly. The first guy I wanted to let in my pants turned me down twice.' I play with my thumb, hoping it'll turn into something very interesting soon.

'Stop punishing yourself. You deserve to be happy, you know. I promise it won't get in the way of your work. I'll help and support you, and I'll be your damn cheerleader.'

'You can't even dance, let alone cheer.'

'For you, I'll give it a go.' He crosses the distance between us and snakes an arm around my waist. I drop the battery pack on the counter. 'I'll get pom-poms and everything. Let's do this right. We date and have fun and go away for the weekend.'

'We're in the middle of a crisis.'

'Our lives will always be crisis-driven. I'd like to have time just for us, when we don't have to be quiet or get dressed in the morning.'

I smile. 'So sex with me is back on the table?'

He laughs. 'Christ, Erin, it was never off the table. It got postponed until we were in the right place.'

It's a new thing for me to relax when the world keeps tumbling around me.

Finley kisses me softly on the lips. I part my lips and wait for him to take the kiss deeper. 'Good night, Erin.' He breathes into me.

'Good—'

He chases my tongue with his and devours my mouth while pushing me up against the kitchen counter. Finally I understand the expression, *take someone's breath away,* because all I can do is gasp.

'It's been a rough night for everyone. I'll see you in the morning.'

'Will you stay with me?' I ask. 'Normally, I curl up and worry about everything until I fall asleep from exhaustion. It'd be nice to do that with someone I know is going to help me.'

He touches my temple, my cheek, and presses his thumb against my lips. 'Of course.'

I take the walkie-talkie pack and spare battery downstairs and leave them in the panic shelter off the utility room. Finley follows and lets out a whistle when he sees our mini-hospital supplies and food storage. 'Just in case,' I tell him.

'In case of what?'

'You know, the end of the world,' I joke.

I reset the alarms and we jog up the stairs. When I take off my dressing gown, I'm chilled by the night air in my camisole and thin trousers. Finley sits on the couch and takes off his boots and socks.

'That couch isn't comfy. There's no way you're going to sleep on a two-seater.'

'It's better than some places I've had to catch a power nap.'

I climb under the covers. 'Me too, but when there's no need, it's stupid. Being a martyr won't get you anywhere, you know. Sleep in my bed with me?'

He freezes.

'No funny business, I swear.'

'Okay, but I'm keeping my underwear on.' He takes off his shirt and jeans. I look at his hard chest, the muscles in his legs, and the bulge between them he's not trying to hide.

When he climbs in, I let him get settled before I move over against him and rest my head in the crook of his arm. I find the scar on his hip and the one on his neck. I take a deep breath and savour his smell.

'I get why Dylan and Ashley were so damn close,' I say. 'No matter what happened, they got to hold each other at night. It makes you stronger, knowing someone is there for you.'

Finley kisses the top of my head.

After a few moments of silence, I can feel my breathing becoming more profound and relaxed. I don't think I've ever relaxed in bed so quickly.

'Erin,' Finley whispers.

'Yeah,' I barely grunt at him, already sinking toward sleep.

'Do you think we were supposed to be together?'

That wakes me back up again. 'What do you mean?'

'You were born after I died, then got thrown back in time and landed in the one spot where you saved my life and turned it upside down. We're the only two people who aren't supposed to be here, and yet we met. If that's not the universe's way of saying we were meant to be together, I don't know what is.'

I gulp. 'Even if you'd survived, that relationship would never happen.'

He laughs. 'A fifty-year-old man on the run in a dystopian future with a hot twenty-year-old girl.'

'That's not why.'

'Oh. You don't think we would have been friends in the future?'

'You would've been friends with my dad. You would've been part of the resistance. I'm going to be born in a few years, and eventually we all become part of the same unit. We know there will be two versions of ourselves in the future, but we figured out a way to make it work, and when and how to split the group. But you dating me after seeing me as a child would be too weird.' She paused. 'My father wouldn't like it. He might just kill you,' I whisper.

Finley sighs. 'He can't be any worse than Mark, right?'

I shake my head. 'Mark's nothing compared to him.'

Finley's arms squeeze around me, and he sounds concerned. 'Is that why your parents divorced?'

199

I sit up, wide awake with from adrenaline. 'Oh, god, no. No.' I gulp. 'My father is the best man I've ever met. Even better that you. He's fierce and protective. He's never harmed us, and he would die to protect us.' That's not just a figure of speech. 'There're many times he's put himself in danger to help us. When it made more sense for me to climb down a cliff and find a tunnel, because I'm the lightest of the group, he stepped up and insisted he go instead. He caught a knife that was thrown at me once. Stepped right in front of me, and the blade went through his shoulder. He gave us his share of rations when things were bad. He'd lie and say he ate earlier or he was bigger so he didn't need any that day.' I look at Finley. 'Something like us could cause a knee-jerk reaction.'

'Sounds like a good guy.'

'He was.' I choke as I hear what I said. My eyes widen, and I cover my mouth with my hand, trying to claw the words back in.

Finley sits up and takes my hands away. 'He's not dead. There's no way a man like that is giving up when his daughter is missing. He's a survivor, and with Dylan and the rest of the people with him, he's okay. I know he is.'

Finley's phone vibrates in his shirt pocket. 'Shit, I have to get that.' He hops out of bed, and I turn on the light. 'A call at four a.m. is never good news. It's Dylan,' he says and swipes his phone. 'What do you mean, someone is out to get you?' Finley asks and puts it on speaker.

Dylan's voice is frantic. 'Ashley just fell asleep, but they're coming for her.'

I'm on my feet and pulling on my clothes when I press the alarm to wake everyone in the house.

'Who's coming?' Finley asks. 'What the hell is going on?'

Dylan says in hushed tones, 'Someone's killing my ex-girlfriends. It's on the news.'

Finley looks at me. Mark and Ollie appear in the doorway, pulling on their shoes.

'The serial killer that popped up a few weeks ago? What's that got to do with you?' Finley asks Dylan.

'They're all girls I've dated.'

'There's no connection between the girls. That's why they can't find the killer yet.'

'I'm the connection,' he growls over the phone. 'The first one was my girlfriend when I was fifteen. They're being killed in the order I've dated them. I can tell you who's next.'

I take the phone from Finley. 'Stop talking, Dylan. Get Ashley discharged. We're coming over.'

A safe extraction as smooth as a military operation is what we're used to.

Mark and I file down the stairs, closely followed by Finley and Ollie, while I fill them in on what to do.

I expected Mark to say something about Finley being in my bedroom or make a disapproving face at least, but Ashley being in danger trumps scolding me for screwing around with Dylan's friend.

At the car, Mark's tying his boots and Ollie is patting down his pockets for the keys. We're loaded with weapons and agree on an extraction backup. Mark doesn't hang around, and we've to jog to the car to make sure he doesn't leave without us.

'Why are you bringing everyone back here?' Finley asks from the back seat.

'It's the safest place we have. If we have to, we can run to a bunker close by.'

'Assuming they're still safe,' Mark says. 'This could be a distraction. Rattle us enough that we run and duck for cover.'

'People are dead, Mark. It's more than a distraction. Someone is targeting Garvey here in the past.'

201

Finley leans forward between the two seats. 'You can't possibly think random girls killed all over the country have anything to do with you guys?'

'Ashley and Dylan are in danger. It has everything to do with us.' Mark puts his foot on the accelerator.

On the first floor of the hospital, we keep our hands on our weapons but under the cover of our clothing. The hallways are empty, and we walk soundlessly up the stairs.

'Is that necessary?' Finley eyes the butt of my handgun, sticking out from under my shirt. 'Sometimes girls get assaulted in clubs and women get murdered by psychos. It rarely has anything to do with time travel complications.'

Dylan is waiting at the entrance to the ward room, and he looks at us and relaxes. 'At least some of you are taking this seriously.'

'Where's Ashley?'

'The nurse is speaking to her,' Dylan hisses and grabs Mark by the arm when he tries to pass him.

'What happened?' I step away from the ward and motion for Mark to do the same. He takes a step back but doesn't leave the doorway.

Dylan motions towards the TV screen attached to the wall outside the room Ashley shares with five other patients. 'It took me a while to get her to sleep and then I came out here and turned on the TV. I've not been paying attention to the news lately, but the serial killer has been going on for a month.' Dylan has a news feed pulled up on his phone, and the screen shows pictures of four different women, all seemingly in their twenties. 'They're dead, and I dated them all.' He hands his phone to Finley and paces. 'What the hell is happening to me? Ashley tonight... those other girls? Someone is coming for me through them.'

'It looks that way,' Mark says. 'We need to move you somewhere secure.'

'Who the hell are you guys?' Dylan looks angry. 'You show up here with your obscure backgrounds and go around with guns tucked in your back pockets. You've got my boy here all whipped and spinning lies for you too.'

The yelling has alerted Ashley, and she calls for Dylan. He abandons his fury and makes for the door, reassuring her on the way.

I follow him and pause at the closed curtain. 'It's Erin,' I call and stick my head around to get a peek at her sitting on the edge of the hospital bed, fully dressed, and a nurse packing painkillers and instructions on how to care for her wounds. 'Something's happened. We are moving you to my family's place, where you'll be safer.'

'Why wouldn't I be safe? Did they let Rian go already?'

The nurse says Ashley is all set to leave and excuses herself. I wait until she is out of earshot and keep my voice low, conscious of the other patients. 'We think the attack on you was to get to Dylan. Other people Dylan's dated have also been targeted.' I walk over and take one of her shaking hands in mine. 'There's nothing we can't survive when we're all in this together. Everyone here is going to take care of each other, but you need to trust us. We're leaving now.' I rise and turn to see Mark staring at me. It's the same bullshit words Mum used to tell me when I was younger and scared. *We're all in it together.*

Sometimes I think I can see Mark's heart break at not being able to be with her.

# Twenty-seven

## Erin

At the farmhouse, Dylan and Ashley sit on the couch in the living room that we hardly ever use.

She looks exhausted but has colour in her cheeks. The dressing on the side of her throat and top of her head are clear, which gives the impression there's not much damage.

I had Ollie go to her apartment and pack two bags of her things. She never questioned it when I handed her a change of clothes. Dylan helped her into fresh pyjamas and her dressing gown. Curled up against Dylan's chest, she almost looks peaceful, but her mind must be spinning after someone tried to kill her.

Mark hands her a glass of water and a pill the doctor prescribed her for the pain. I sit opposite her on the leather ottoman and lean on my knees. Ollie is on the couch at the opposite end of the room.

Mark and Finley hover around, too twitchy to plant themselves somewhere.

Dylan is nervous, but he's trying to keep everything bottled up. He does this when he wants to wait until later to talk about something important. He'll lean back extra casually, trying to give the impression of calm aloofness, but the constant shifting of his feet and touching of his face are all I need to know that he's cracking inside.

'You can't keep her in the dark,' I tell him. 'She has a right to know what's going on.'

Dylan gives me his pissed off look. He's thinking about how to chew me a new one.

Ashley sits up. 'Something freaked you out at the hospital. If I'm in danger, I want to know.' She swallows hard.

'You're not in danger anymore,' Mark says over my shoulder.

'Now that we know we have to protect you, we will, so don't worry, okay?' I tell her.

'How the hell are you going to protect me from a psycho and why would you? That's what the police are for,' Ashley hisses.

'Finley and I can look after you,' Dylan says.

I say, 'We all can. This is what my family does. We help people.' I take her hand. 'It's something I couldn't explain to you before, but trust us. Ollie? Sit next to Ash and show her our security system.'

He moves so smoothly, the couch doesn't make a sound when he slides over to one end and boots up his tablet. He turns his screen to Ashley and opens up our security system.

'Tell us what you know about the girls,' I say to Dylan.

'The first girl was the one I lost my virginity to. The rest were killed in order of when I slept with them—hook-ups when I was on leave. One of them was in Scotland. Finley and Cameron took me there once. The next one I remember is Lucy or Lucille or something. I didn't recognize her until I heard her name. Things after that got a bit'—Dylan shrugs awkwardly—'busy? What I want to know is how someone would know the order of the women I slept with more than ten years ago.'

Ashley listens, like we all do, but her attention sometimes turns to the computer, where Ollie is patiently waiting for her before moving on to the next feed.

'Busy?' My indignation is clear.

'I fucked around, Erin. A lot. I'm not going to remember every woman.' Dylan turns to Ashley, who is looking at him, too. She tries to smile, but it's a lot to deal with.

Finley goes to the dining room and returns with a pad and pen. He hands them to Dylan. 'Write down as much as you remember, including names, about as many as you remember.'

'We need dates, too, roughly speaking,' Mark tells him.

I don't know whether to be disgusted or relieved we're getting a long list of ex-girlfriends, one-night stands, and holiday romances from Dylan. We're all hoping this attack on Ashley has nothing to do with the murder victims, but we can't take the possibility lightly.

While Dylan does that, Ollie takes his tablet back and types.

'What are you looking for?' I ask.

'Checking police records.'

'How are you getting into those?' Ashley asks.

Dylan stops writing and looks in their direction.

I nod at Ollie, and he answers. 'I can hack a lot of things. It's one of the ways we keep people safe and find what we need.' He makes a face.

'What?' I ask.

He looks at me over the top of the laptop. 'Ran across victim photos.'

Ashley asks, 'Can I see?'

Ollie's forehead crinkles. 'You sure?'

'Yes. Show me.' He turns the laptop around again, and she recoils slightly.

Ollies moves the screen towards himself again. 'Sorry.'

'It's not that. I mean, yeah, it's disgusting, but it's the marks. It's what Rian did to me.' She turns to Dylan. 'He really did try to kill me.'

Mark and I are on our feet and over next to Ollie before Dylan has his arm around Ashley.

'We have a problem.' Ollie looks up at us.

I bend closer to the monitor. A deep cross is carved into the upper chest of one of the victims. *End the lies, not lives* is carved into the crosspiece.

'What does that mean?' Finley asks.

'It's the rebel propaganda slogan,' I tell him.

It's taken a long time for Dylan to complete a comprehensive list. The sun has risen, and Ashley is asleep on the couch next to him. She wanted to call the police with the new information we had on the victims, but Mark pointed out that if Dylan has dated all the victims, including her, he'll be hauled into custody and probably never get out of jail.

'We need to put a watch on the next girl,' Finley says. 'Ash is right. If we're not going to involve the police, then we need to protect her.'

Dylan nods. 'Fuck, yes. And if Rian shows up, we can take him out ourselves.'

'No,' I say. 'We already have people in Scotland we trust who can handle this. We'll put them on it. They have no connection to you. Best you stay out of the fucking country when your ex-girlfriends are being murdered.'

'Tell JT to get Lara, Eleda, and Nivek to make this a priority,' Mark tells Ollie, who closes his computer and leaves the room.

'It's a crazy thing to do to someone. I mean, who would know every girlfriend he ever had?' Finley asks.

'It's a thing.' I look at Finley.

'What thing?' Dylan asks. He gets up.

'It's a thing where I'm from.'

Dylan looks exasperated. 'What are you talking about, Erin?'

207

The intense exchange has stirred Ashley, and she sits up.

'It's research at a university where I used to live,' I lie. 'They were developing it into an app for dating histories. It's going to market for a joke, sort of like a "rate my date" sort of thing. But it also enables someone to check a potential partner's sexual health and history. In reality, the primary goal is a method of extracting information and checking DNA theories.'

'Who the hell did you piss off so badly, Dylan?' Ashley asks. 'And how did you ever get so close to someone without knowing they were a psychopath?'

'The same way I got so close to Rian without knowing who he was.'

Ashley's eyes widen. 'Oh, Erin, that's not what I meant.'

'Well, you should have known. That guy was in your flat many times, in my house. I brought him in. I trusted him.'

'And now he's a part of this murder spree?' Ashley asks.

'We need every detail you know about Rian Butterly,' Mark says. 'We've had someone researching him through the night, but memories can sometimes tell us more than internet searches and documents. Tell us about your conversations with him, stories he told.' Mark sits on the ottoman I spent most of the night on and talks to Ashley. 'Your ex-flat mate, Nanda, dated him before we arrived in town, correct? We should speak to her.'

She nods. 'She was planning to leave for Newcastle first thing this morning. She's busy, so you might have to talk to her over the phone. I don't think she knew much. She doesn't do deep conversations with guys. She was getting out of the placement at her dad's tech company, so she practically lived on base for a while. I can't imagine she'd remember any boring conversation she had with someone she dated once.'

'What do you mean, she lived on base?' Dylan asks.

'Lived in the lab. They had camp beds at the back of the office. You guys understand how crazy the army types can be when they're working on something,' she says.

I raise my eyebrows. 'Nanda was a soldier?'

'No.' Ashley chuckles. 'But her dad has defence technology contracts. I thought you knew? He's a big deal. Anyway, Nanda worked for him three or four years ago and hated it. The morality of building defence technology that can be weaponised was something that freaked her out. But there was a problem with one of the programmes, and because she was on the original team, she was "obligated"'—Ashley uses air-quotes—'to go back in and fix it before she went back to university full time. She plans to use enrolling at Newcastle University as an excuse not to keep working there.'

Finley is the one who asks, 'Who does her dad work for? Which company? There aren't many private contractors through Catterick.'

Ashley says, 'He doesn't work for anyone. He runs his own business, but he's contracted exclusively through the government. Has been the last fifteen years or something.'

'What's his name?' Finley almost demands, but she hesitates, and he adds, 'I've probably met him if he works at the base.'

She smiles tightly. 'Carl Wilson. He trades under Wilson Tech.'

'Nanda's last name is Wilson?' Finley says.

'Yeah. Oh, god, don't tell me Cameron knows her dad.'

'It's a large barracks.' Finley smiles thinly. 'We've probably crossed paths and not known it.'

I pick up the empty mugs of tea from the coffee table and take them to the kitchen. Passing Finley, I murmur, 'We already know who Nanda is, and we're working on getting someone inside.

# twenty-eight

DARLINGTON, UK

2019

### FINLEY

At nine a.m., all of Erin's family is in the dining room. JT is on a video call from Scotland, and Dylan is here, but Ashley's upstairs resting.

JT is reporting on his findings. 'Rian wasn't taken to the local police station last night. After a trip to Accident and Emergency, he evaded police custody. Ollie and I found CCTV footage of him returning to his apartment and taking his neighbour's car. Motorway cameras recorded him exiting the A1, heading towards Durham a few minutes ago.'

'Why would he be going to Durham?' Erin pulls the list of Dylan's ex-girlfriends out, which shows the next girl in Dylan's dating history to be a resident there. 'He's on his way to his next job.'

'We have to see if we can cut him off. Warn her, call the cops if we have to, but I can't just sit here and let someone else die because they knew me a decade ago,' Dylan says, agitated.

'There's something else,' I say. 'The contract offers and development idea for the TV show, which came through the barracks, arrived in the post yesterday.'

'And?' Erin asks.

'I read it before we went out. The appendix at the back has the main funding coming from GBE Banking, signed off on by Manager Rian Butterly.'

Erin looks at Mark. 'He was embedded in Ashley's life before we got here.' She closes her eyes.

'I have a question,' Ollie asks. 'Why attack Ashley? If they wanted to set Dylan up for murder, why warn us and leave us all these clues?'

'Perhaps he never meant to leave her alive.' Mark bends over the table to stub his cigarette out. 'Let's suit up and hit the road. We can call Nivek to meet us there. He might reach the location before us.'

'And if this is a distraction? Get us all out of the way while the real shit goes down here, with the two of them on their own?' I say.

'They're not going to be on their own. Erin's staying behind,' Mark tells me.

'Bullshit. If I'm staying, so are you.'

Ollie stands. 'I have a new plan. JT is closest, and he can take Nivek with him. Lara can check CCTV and traffic lights and organise an escape route. I'm going to stay here and monitor the house and the sheds. Some things can't be neglected. Mark, you're staying too. We need you, in case this is a distraction. Erin and Finley can stay with Dylan and Ashley on level three. We'll be in touch via intercom and keep you up-to-date.'

'Don't do this,' Erin tells Ollie.

'Do what?' I ask.

Mark lets out a frustrated laugh. 'He's evoking our backup chain of command. If anything happens here that can be categorised as too personal or has too much emotional involvement, the next in line takes over on an ad hoc basis.'

Ollie steps forward. 'The satellite crew and I voted this morning.' He looks at me and places a hand on Mark. 'You'd do

211

the same thing if the tables were reversed. If either of you goes in there without a clear head, you'll get killed or worse.'

'And me?' Dylan asks. 'I don't care who you guys think you are, where you're from, or what psychotic cult bullshit you've got going on here, you can't keep us here.'

'Actually, I can,' Ollie says. 'If you don't stay, we'll call the police and tip them off to your connection with the girls. You'll be picked up quickly. We can keep tabs on you and give them your real-time location.'

Dylan lunges toward Ollie, but Erin's team is slick. Mark has Dylan on the ground after Ollie spins out of the way and elbows him in the nose.

Ashley screams at Dylan from the bottom of the stairs.

'Calm down and look after your girl. She's still hysterical,' Mark hisses at Dylan. 'She needs you.'

'They're right,' Erin explains to Dylan. 'We have to maintain a low profile. It won't do anyone any good if we are spotted at a crime scene you might already be connected with. Let them handle it for now.'

Ashley tugs at Dylan's arm, moving him into the kitchen. I hear the tap running and cupboards being pulled open. She must be looking for a towel for his nose.

'Wasn't Ollie one of them?' I narrow my eyes at Erin. 'Hell of a lot of patience to join the crew, then wait until there's a family drama to step in and take command.' I turn to Ollie. 'But control over time and space seems to be one thing these Apostle soldiers thrive on.'

I don't see the head-butt coming. One hit from Ollie's head, and I'm knocked on the ground.

'Nice one, Ollie,' Erin spits out sarcastically. She helps me up and steadies me.

'I downloaded Rian's interview statements from the police server. There's something of interest you need to see.' Ollie says.

She waits for him to give her the tablet, but he shakes his head. 'A lot of it is nasty. I suspect he said it on purpose, knowing you'd get a hold of the interview.'

'How nasty?' I ask.

'Some sick shit for a guy to be taunting his victims with, and by victims, I mean us. The attack on Ashley was also on you. Us, too. But one thing stood out. He told the officers that "Erin can blame her brother for this one".'

My stomach rolls, and I feel vomit moving up my throat. I breathe through my nose.

Erin says, 'I never mentioned Blake to Rian. He shouldn't even know I have a brother.'

'Could he be referring to me?' Ollie says. 'We've been posing as brother and sister.'

Erin sits on the bottom step, and the rest of us linger nearby. 'What have you got to do with any of this?' she asks him.

He lets out low mumble. 'I'm not sure, but there are a lot of people in 2019 that we don't know. Bring in Finley, and he wants to extend that invitation to Cameron and whoever is involved in their conspiracy research. Now Dylan and Ashley, earlier than they should be. The timeline is splintering. One thing's for sure, Rian knew you'd hear that statement, and it would be enough to throw you off balance. He's either trying to fuck with things for us here or with Blake in the future. Either way—Erin, this guy's a loose cannon we can't afford to have running around.'

'There's another possibility,' Mark says.

'What?' Erin says quickly.

'It's a message. Rian might have found a way to communicate with the future, using officially recorded interviews that will survive the next twenty-plus years and always be at NewGov's disposal.'

213

Mark explains something the crew has been trying to figure out since they got here. 'A lot of people in the future think we're dead.' He exhales unsteadily. 'We've been trying to find a safe way to let our family in the future know we're not.'

'I can't let my parents know I'm still alive, in case the wrong people also find it. I get to live the rest of my life here and die, the way things are going—maybe even before I'm born. And that fucker gets to kill people and gloat about it for his comrades in the future,' Erin says.

'Get a transcript of the interview to Lara. We have to figure out what else he's saying between the lines,' Mark tells Ollie.

The house is a flurry of activity. JT leaves to break into Rian's home and see what he can find there, while Ollie concentrates on hacking Rian's office computer, which he says will be no problem to do remotely.

Erin is hunkered over a tablet, reading through what must be Rian's police interview while on the phone to Lara, discussing it.

Which leaves Dylan, Ashley, and me at loose ends.

When Erin sees us leaving the room, she hangs up and follows us upstairs.

The third floor of the Coopers' farmhouse is brightly lit. The top of the stairs has a floor-to-ceiling window and balcony door that overlooks the back of the property, all the way to the barn that edges up to the neighbour's field.

Erin turns right at the top of the stairs and opens a door. 'This one is yours,' she says to Dylan and Ashley. She points at the doors to the right. 'Shower stalls are through the last door, two lots of bathrooms before that.'

'What is this?' Dylan nods to the row of doors. 'Ten bedrooms? For what? Planning on opening a hostel?' Dylan, always suspicious.

Erin shrugs. 'Hostel, safe house. Whatever you want to call it.'

'Is that necessary?' Ashley asks as Dylan opens the door to a sparsely furnished bedroom with a double bed and two sets of bunk beds.

Erin takes her hand. 'You should sleep when you can.' She affectionately strokes Ashley's hair. 'Remember that, okay? Finley and I will be outside your door, so you know you're completely safe.'

Ashley hugs Erin and follows Dylan into the room.

'Wait here,' Erin tells me. I touch my temple, where Ollie smacked me down, and feel a short, sharp pain. Lesson learned: don't mess with Ollie.

Erin returns from a room at the front of the house, pushing two soft computer chairs on wheels. One chair faces the set of stairs we climbed. The other faces the large window and balcony door.

'What're the chances of you giving me the chair with the view?' I ask.

She points to the bathroom and shower room at the other end of the hall. 'You'll find towels there. Better get a cold cloth on that.'

I pass four doors on my left and nothing but unconverted space on my right. Another three doors on the left mirror the three rooms on the right. I open the first and find a row of five toilet stalls, with sinks and mirrors just like a shopping centre.

'I said the last door was the showers. You either weren't paying attention or you're nosey,' Erin calls.

'Yes, ma'am.' I close the door and continue to the shower room. Rows of towels and toiletries line the right-hand wall, and showers closed off by bright orange doors are on the left. I soak a hand towel in cold water, only realising how tender my head is when I press it against my temple. I open one of the mirrored cabinets and find medical supplies. Anti-inflammatory

215

tablets and Arnicare are just what I need, and I walk back to the front of the attic.

'You guys planning for an entire village to end up here?' I sit in the vacant chair.

'Maybe. Part of me wishes we could bring everyone here, but if it were that easy, enemies would show up too.'

'I'm sorry about what I said about Ollie.'

'Ollie is the most objective person in this situation now. It's right that he takes charge of this for now. But I'm not an idiot.' She looks out the window. The morning sun is high, in the harshest light shielded from our tired eyes. 'I'm sorry for the way things are going, Fin.'

She leans over the arm of the chair, and her face is next to mine. I hold my breath, praying she might kiss me, but she touches the bruise on my head. She places her lips on mine tentatively, testing how I'll react, and when I do nothing, she pulls back. Fatigue slows my reaction, but when she pulls back, I snap into focus. My hands go to her hips, and I haul her out of her chair and into my lap.

My mouth is on hers before she's settled, and she lets out a soft moan. 'Don't do that,' I murmur between kisses and move to the side of her throat. 'Never think I don't want to kiss you, because I always do.'

After a few minutes of tasting her and touching her, I hear someone walking into the bedroom next to us. I release her, and she scrambles to her chair as Dylan opens the door.

'You two need a room?' he asks.

Erin stands. 'I'm going to get Finley some ice.'

'Don't leave on my account, Sunshine. This is your place.'

She rolls her eyes. 'Stop calling people terms of endearment you don't mean. You don't even like me.'

'Don't trust you. It's not the same thing. You got my boy here all tied up in knots. Leading him around by the hard-on to get what you want out of him.'

Erin shudders.

'Watch your mouth, Dylan,' I say, and he holds up his hands, backing off.

'Just an observation. I can worry about my friends, right?'

Mark quietly lands at the top of the stairs. 'You don't really think I'm not going after the guy? Do you?'

Dylan rolls on the balls of his feet, ready to jump out the fucking window if it means he can catch Rian fucking Butterly.

'What about Ashley?' I ask.

'I'll be fine here,' she calls from inside. She comes to the door. 'I'd rather you leave it to the police, though. This is dangerous.'

'We've dealt with worse than him. We'll be fine,' Dylan says.

'She's right,' Mark says. 'It will be dangerous, and you've never gone into a mission with so little information on your target before and so little backup.'

'I'm backup,' I tell him.

'Me too,' Mark says. 'But we're on our own. No tech support or CCTV feed. Erin will stay with Ashley.'

'When are we leaving?' Dylan asks.

'Now,' Mark says. 'There are fire escape ladders in each window. We're sneaking out.'

# twenty-nine

## FINLEY

There's so much blood. It's all I can see from Lucy's front door, trailing through the hallway.

We crept silently through the house and found her body on the kitchen floor, face up, her shirt open and the word *collaborator* carved into her chest.

'This isn't the killer's MO,' Dylan says. 'Maybe it's someone else?'

Mark gazes at the dead woman. 'Either way, we need to get out of here unseen. Wipe down anything you might have touched.'

'We haven't touched anything,' I say. We can move through a building without leaving a fingerprint. Shoe prints and possible fallen hairs are the only things we might accidentally leave behind.

'Me neither,' Mark says. 'Ollie should be finished with Rian's apartment and workplace by the time we get back. Let's go see what he has.'

We leave the kitchen as quietly as we entered and nudge open the front door. There's a small creak, and Dylan and I stop.

Mark turns around and his eyebrows are a question: *why are we stalling*?

I point upstairs, and Dylan and I move while Mark keeps watch at the door.

The sound is so tiny it could be dismissed as a typical household creak, but given the circumstances, we have to check it out.

The obvious places to hide are in the wardrobes and bedrooms. In the bathroom behind the shower curtain is a stupid place a lot of people think they can hide.

Dylan takes the first bedroom, while I check the bathroom next door. Both of us keep an eye on the doorways in case someone runs from the second bedroom, but with Mark downstairs we should have all bases covered.

I'm only two steps into the bathroom with my gun drawn, ready to yank the damn shower curtain back, when someone rushes me from the other side, using a sheet as cover and knocking into me before I have a chance to brace myself.

Dylan arrives and punches the man in the face. When he falls back, I see it's good old Rian.

Dylan is about to knock him out when Rian catches Dylan's fist, pushes his legs against the wall, and flips, pulling Dylan farther into the bathroom. Dylan stumbles into me, and we both quickly get off the floor, but it's a second too late. Rian jumps over the banister and lands at Mark's feet, kicking out before Mark can prepare.

One thing's for sure. The gun sure as hell isn't scaring him. He's not going to surrender. He's going to have to be shot.

Running down the stairs, with Dylan at my back, I can't get a clean shot with Rian so close to Mark. Rian breaks Mark's nose with whatever weapon he had in his hand.

Mark doesn't falter and goes after him, but Rian must have stabbed Mark. Mark bends, protecting his stomach and covering the wounds pouring blood all over Lucy's already blood-spattered hallway.

Rian's out the door, pulling the front door closed behind him, and then it locks. Those precious seconds of turning the lock and yanking the door open is enough for Rian to vanish.

Neighbours are out in the street. They must have heard the commotion, and I don't think I put my gun away before someone saw it.

Mark appears at the doorway, hand on his gut. 'Let's go.' He takes the stairs two at a time and vaults into the car.

Dylan and I follow and drive out of the neighbourhood as quickly as we can, scanning the streets for Rian.

Mark calls home and speaks to Ollie, telling him to attempt to trace Rian before or after he made it to Lucy's house. Ollie isn't happy we went against his orders.

'How many things do you think you touched now?' Mark asks sarcastically.

My stomach churns. That entire house is full of evidence we were there.

# thirty

## Erin

Finley, Mark, and Dylan arrive back at the farmhouse by early evening. Mark debriefed us during the drive. Ollie tried to trace Rian, but he's apparently exceptional at keeping a low profile. Lara had to switch gears and erase all electronic evidence of Mark's car from traffic cameras and local businesses that picked him up on their security systems. It's a last-minute shit show, but we pull it off.

Battered and bruised, the men walk in. Mark's injury is not life-threatening; he was lucky. Rian doesn't care who he kills. It's surprising he didn't plunge the knife deeper or give it a twist.

With Lara and JT in Scotland via video call, we set up a meeting in the basement triage room, minus Dylan and Ashley. The less they know about the future, the better.

'Rian Butterly is a legitimate 2019 resident.' Ollie opens packs of saline solution over Mark's stomach wound to clean it. 'His history is patchy, but that's not uncommon in real life. There were a few years in his early teens when he falls off the radar, but a trip to Dublin might confirm he was born and grew up in this timeline. His work computer shows nothing unexpected aside from him monitoring our property purchase and business activity somewhat more than the average Junior Manager.'

221

I fetch Steri-Strips from a storage unit and hand them to Ollie, then dig for bandages and tape.

Ollie continues, 'There is search history on Dylan Garvey's financial records. Looks like he gathered enough information to offer Dylan a TV gig, offering enough money to make the proposition attractive.'

'Why?' Finley asks.

Marks sits up. 'He's tried many ways to get him on the list of assets that have to be extinguished in the first wave of takeovers.'

'Or get him locked up for life. Bye-bye future wife and kids and rebel life.'

'And then you would all be dead? Without him, you might not have made it?' Finley says.

I purse my lips at the thought of my future life disappearing.

'I have news about the WT bug Finley found in our security system at the front gate,' JT says.

'Nanda is our suspect on that.' Mark sighs as he stands and paces the room. 'Her dad created it. There's every chance she was involved and could have helped plant it.'

'It's no surprise now why there's a huge IT overhaul project, and the area around Darlington is sealed off in the future. We always knew something big was happening there, like an outpost for London tech development, but we couldn't get any solid information.'

'We have to find out who planted the bug and flip them. See if and how they are communicating with the future,' JT says.

'Don't forget Nanda has a history with Rian too,' Mark says.

'There's something else,' Ollie interjects. 'That WT bug isn't from here. That technology doesn't exist yet. I've seen parts of the system in the future, but it hadn't even made it into military testing at this time. Whoever planted the bug brought it from the future. If Rian is a legit 2019 resident, as you said, then someone else sent it here or is here with him.'

Finley says, 'I saw it three years ago. It was used for a job in London and again in Afghanistan, six months ago. That's why we were there.' His mouth dries, and he takes a swig from a water bottle. 'I could be tried for treason for what I just told you.'

'Three years ago?' Ollie asks. 'Time travel rebels who saved your life should be given all the info they need to stop a war, correct?'

'This means someone from the future has been interfering as far back as what, 2016? And they've infiltrated the military already,' Mark answers. 'Tell Ollie everything about your orders for the London job. Who gave them to you and who was part of your team on both missions. We can look into this further.'

Ollie nods. 'We can start with the London job since geographically it might be quicker to gain a physical eye on it.' He keeps talking despite me shaking my head.

Finley purses his lips. 'I can't do that. I can't give you details on other soldiers. I'm sorry, but if this all turns out to be a coincidence, or heck, something that should stay out of the public domain, I won't be the one who gave up other soldiers.'

'We're fair,' Ollie tells him. 'If they're clean, we leave them alone. If it looks like they're on our side, we'll look after them. The bottom line is someone had you plant that software, then killed you.' He clears his throat. 'Well, you know what I mean.'

'After the WT link was activated, it left our system vulnerable. You saved our lives by snooping around our house, Finley. If we hadn't seen you in the main house, we wouldn't have been looking at the system, paying attention to the barn, or checking the perimeter. The soldier would've got through the barn undetected, and I bet he'd have come straight to the house. I've already apologised to the others, and I want to extend a heartfelt thanks to you.'

'Apologised for what?' Finley asks.

'I got cocky. I thought I was the smartest one in this time, and the programmes I wrote and the tech I recreated would be beyond anything anyone could use against us. I got lazy. We assumed we were the only ones with knowledge of the future, and it nearly killed us. If we die here, without making a real difference, everyone in our future unit dies too.'

'It's so much worse than we thought. If there's a time travel hole in Afghanistan, that indicates they're all over the world.' Mark's voice always remains even, no matter the seriousness of the information he's imparting. 'People are trying to infiltrate military operations and war zones here in the past, and it's been going on for a while. The WT was not just a bug in someone's system. It's a call sign. When you uploaded it on your mission, you gave someone the exact time and location where you could be killed. You were set up by someone in the future, Finley. They didn't only want Dylan Garvey dead. They were coming for others on the team, too. That means you.'

thirty-one

## FINLEY

When Cameron's name flashes on my phone, I excuse myself from the meeting and answer the call on the stairs to the kitchen above.

'I met her today.' Cameron's voice is tense. 'I finally got into prison to meet her.'

'Did she have any information you were looking for?'

There's a moment of silence. 'I know her, Finley.'

'Who is it?'

'She looked familiar,' he rushes on, 'but it took me half an hour into the conversation to realise I'd met her before. Something was wrong, though.' His tone changes from uncertain to confident, and I know he's leaving out information he doesn't want to say over the phone. 'It was like she was interviewing me, rather than the other way around. Remember hazing week?' He chuckles. 'And those mad power play interviews? She analysed me. I tell you, bro, whatever's going on, I need to stay here a while. This woman is in charge of something bigger.'

'Why the hell did she set fire to the Notre Dame Cathedral?'

'Someone lured her to France with information about her daughter and set her up. The fire at the Cathedral was the easiest, fastest, most public crime they could deliver.

225

'I'm close to something. Before I left the prison, she said something to me that didn't make sense. "*Find out why you're still alive and get back to me*".'

My heart skips a beat. 'Do you think you should come home? If your contact is getting edgy, it might be time to pull out. You don't have backup close by.'

'No, I'm staying.'

'We were supposed to die on our last job, Cameron.'

'No shit.'

'I know why we survived, but I have to look into something here first and check out this woman's identity before we play ball, okay?'

'I'm not giving you her name over the phone.'

'If we start information sharing, I have to know we can trust her. In the meantime, ask her about London in 2041.'

'What the hell does that mean?'

I purse my lips. 'Ask her, gauge her reaction. See if she knows what you're talking about.'

'Will do. How's Dylan and Ashley?'

'They're okay. I didn't realise Dylan filled you in already. Ashley seems to be healing up okay.'

'That's good.' Cameron seems distant. 'What are they like as a couple?'

'Good.' I hesitate. 'That's a weird question to ask.'

'Just wondering if you like her, is all. Dylan's never had a serious girlfriend before. He seems to be thinking long term.'

'I think they might have a future together.' I think of the overall ramifications of that thought. 'Hey, remember how your mum always wanted to move somewhere quieter, with no neighbours?'

Cameron chuckles. 'Yeah.'

'I was thinking about looking into that.'

'What the hell are you talking about?'

'I'm not sure. Just thinking it might be nice to find land somewhere for everyone, maybe become self-sufficient. Like one of the west coast islands.'

'I think my mum's too old and too sick to be working farmland in the wilderness.'

I nod. 'Just a thought for the future.'

I disconnect the call, stand, and see Dylan in the doorway. That sneaky fucker made it down a flight of stairs without me hearing him.

'What do you know?' he says. 'The girls we hook up with before our unit is hit seem to know stuff about what you and Cameron have been obsessing over the last six months. You know shit, and you're not sharing.'

'We can't bring you in yet.'

'Can't or won't?' He takes a step away and rubs his face. 'I don't need to be in this for you to confide in me. I've always backed you guys. I can be your sounding board. If you're getting involved in something, we should talk things through so you make the right decision.'

I lay a hand on Dylan's shoulder. 'You're going to have to discharge and get involved.'

'For some illegal operation?'

'It's something you have to see to understand, but being in the service is a conflict.'

'If I need to pick a side, why do I have to stop defending my country?'

'You'll be fighting for your country in a way you never thought possible. I'd never take you down a path you'd regret. It might seem like the wrong choice to someone on the outside, but when you know what's going on and how connected everything is, you'll be the first in line to lead us. But we can't risk you having too much knowledge and going back on tour. We can't even risk you taking another tour and getting killed. Trust me, when the timing is right, I'll show you everything.'

'I'll need more than that if you want me to discharge. I can't make a decision this big based on that.'

'You have two more weeks off before you report in. We'll see what we can do, and we'll get Ashley set up with some security while you're gone.'

'You never said you only had two weeks left,' Ashley says through her sore throat on the bottom step.

Damn.

thirty-two

*Erin*

When Finley leaves to take a call, Ollie keeps feeding us info. 'I found a strong signal the thermal pin was connecting to. The location is scattered. We just need time to find it.'

'How is that even possible?'

'It means the Apostle technology and chips are already in place *in this time*. From what I gather, it's still at trial stage, meaning it's not live yet. If the system detected the soldier who landed here, it didn't recognise what it was. It might have thought it was a glitch, maybe picking up a similar signal from a bunch of phones GPSs. If I can get access to the primary system, I might be able to make changes. Set up a back door, at least screw with the development, delay it, make it less effective. We all know what else uses these chips.'

'How the hell are we going to access the Apostle mainframe? We've tried before, and a lot of people died.'

'That's when it was fully operational, with a million people guarding it. In 2019 it's only development.' He looks at me sheepishly. 'It was a Wilson Tech product before the government confiscated and took over the plant.'

Mark asks, 'Can you get inside Wilson Tech? If thermal pins and WT bugs are circulating in the past before they've even been manufactured, someone at Wilson Tech must be involved.'

229

'Wilson tech has an intern programme. I can enrol and see how far I get.' Ollie shrugs. 'We always thought the Apostle soldiers searched this town high and low because it was where Garvey and Ashley started out, but maybe it's someone else they're here for.'

'Someone?' I ask.

Ollie taps on the tablet and pulls up a file. 'I ran Nanda Wilson through a testing system I created when I arrived. It suggests which side they're likely to choose when the takeover comes.'

'How the hell do you measure that?'

'You can't, really. You can look at psychological input, but a lot of it is opportunity too. Who presents themselves to which group first? If the rebels can offer to help a lot of people, more are likely to flip on NewGov. But Nanda's application isn't in the university system. Her previous degree scores and records have been duplicated and dumped into an off-campus server, and the trace has been deleted.'

He shows us the screen. 'Carl Wilson's daughter tested at a 147 IQ in high school. He tried to bring her into the company at fifteen, but she rebelled, like a petulant teenager. Moved in with her mum after their divorce and dropped out of college. Worked for him for a year before she moved into town and we met her. Carl Wilson recently granted the local university a million pounds for their computer development course and paid his daughter's re-enrolment fees.'

'Ashley said she worked around the clock in his company. Do you think she might have been working directly on the project?'

'The wonder girl is going to return to the fold. Wonder what the hell she developed for them?' Lara says.

Ollie hands me the tablet; Nanda's matriculation file is onscreen.

'Nanda is this important to the military?' I ask.

'Her brain is. I reckon she not only worked on it, she might have had a hand in its development.'

Mark takes the tablet from me. 'Nanda's going to develop Apostle software.'

'Guess that's why we never heard of her. She went dark.'

'No. Nanda doesn't have a mean bone in her body. We tested her when we got here. She checks out. She scored high. We would've taken her in as one of our own in the future. Why the hell did she cut Ashley out of her life?'

'The girl's a genius. Doesn't take much to fool people,' Mark says.

I grit my teeth. 'Something could have happened to her, or maybe NewGov held her and her family.'

'Either way, what are we going to do about it?' Mark asks.

'She didn't have Cameron last time round. He was dead. Maybe we can use him to keep Nanda working in our direction.' I retrieve my phone and pull up Finley's number. 'I'll see if Finley can get Cameron to return to town. He might connect with Nanda again, and we'll have an in.'

I look at Mark, holding back tears. If only Ashley from our time were here. She could fix everything, tell us what to do with Dylan and Finley. She could help us win everything.

Ollie shows us a black screen filled with red dots on a map of the UK.

'What's that?' Mark asks.

'Places of interest. The Apostle's thermal pin was recording twenty-four hours before his death. These are all the places he went in 2042, before he came through the portal. Looks like he travelled in a southern direction, starting in Skye, near the top of Scotland, and working his way here.'

'How the hell did he cover most of the UK in twenty-four hours?'

231

Ollie shrugs. 'It records by speed and height location. Looks like car, plane, and helicopter. The red dots are locations they stopped, pink indicates they stayed only a few minutes, and deeper red was where they tarried.'

'Is there any way to figure out what they were doing?'

'Cleansing, looks like.'

'Cleansing what?'

'Us. Each place is where we planned to put a bunker in the next three months.'

My heart stops. 'You said you'd be careful, that you had it covered.'

'I did, and I am. This means someone talked. Perhaps not yet, but they will at some point in the future. The Apostles find out our safety plan.'

'This particular soldier didn't enter the bunkers. He might have been part of another team who did, or maybe a soldier whose chip doesn't survive goes in. The chip never goes offline, like he's been underground, and the GPS height doesn't register the difference in terrain height, which you'd expect from someone descending a flight of stairs into the ground or a basement.'

'He might have found the locations but not the actual bunkers?'

'It's a possibility. They also might have dropped a grenade down the hatch, without checking if there were people inside.'

'That's not enough information,' Mark says. 'How are we supposed to know if any of our people have been using the bunkers? What if we just set up a whole load of locations for our people to be slaughtered?'

'What the hell do we do now?' My life is crumbling again. Our reason to survive in the past was to make life easier for those we left behind. Now we might have made them easier to find and destroy.

'There's a plus side,' Mark says. 'The bunkers might have been empty. We have an opportunity to make sure we list these locations as unsafe. Make sure none of our people use them. If they found any of us, they wouldn't have kept travelling south. Maybe our people haven't used the bunkers yet.'

'Well, they can't anymore. The Apostles will have them booby-trapped and surveillance set up. Or maybe they only found one or two people and kept looking for others. Either way, those locations are unusable.'

Lara joins the discussion. 'You said the next three months. What about the bunker we converted when we got here? Was it compromised?'

'Not on this soldier's travels, as far as I can tell. We've some time. We can still try to locate the source and erase everything from history.'

'Unless the person or information has already got to the top.'

'So we take out the top.'

Ollie holds his hands up. 'I don't think that's necessary. We've created a diagram of who's in power now and in the future. There aren't many crossovers. I think the information's been hidden, and we have a chance to clean it up, otherwise—'

'It's one of us.' Mark finishes. 'They got hold of one of us and broke them.'

'Someone could've released faulty information as a decoy. Given the enemy information on bunkers they know are or will be obsolete.' Ollie nudges my elbow. 'You know, like you?'

'You think at some point I'll be captured and spill this? And what, it gets sent to the future?'

'It's a possibility.' Mark slams his phone down on the table, screen up. 'And apparently our security system sucks.'

I squint at the screen. Two police officers are at the door. 'Hide,' I hiss at Mark.

233

Ollie runs up the stairs and shouts for Ashley as I walk to the front of the house and open the door.

'Ashley is on her way down,' I tell the officers, waiting at the door.

Ollie checks out their shoulder numbers from our security feed, and I wait for his signal before I let them inside.

Ashley comes downstairs, and I invite the officers into the front living room and hover at the doorway.

'We want to speak to your boyfriend,' the first officer says. 'Thought he might be here, since we can't find an address for him.'

The panic is all over her face. 'What do you want with Dylan?'

'We want to ask him a few questions. He can come down to the station if he prefers.'

'No need,' I say. 'He's here. I'll go get him.'

I leave Ashley in the living room while I get Dylan. He has a bruise on the side of his face from the altercation with Rian, and it's big enough that the police will notice.

The police ask to be left alone with him, and we oblige; the house is wired for our protection. We'll video everything that happens.

Ollie is in the dining room. I pick up a laptop and take Ashley upstairs with me. Finley is waiting in my bedroom. I raise the screen.

The police ask Dylan about Ashley's attack again and the scarring, and if he knows anything about its significance. They subtly ask after his whereabouts when Lucy was killed and not so subtly about the dates of the other murdered girls.

Luckily, three out of four previous attacks happened while Dylan was on active duty. The police scribble notes.

When they are leaving, Dylan says, 'I had nothing to do with killing those girls.'

'What girls?' they ask.

'The dates you're asking about are when the girls were murdered. It's nothing to do with me, and I certainly had nothing to do with attacking my girlfriend.'

'How do you know the dates the women were murdered?' the first officer asks.

'I watch the news. They carved the same shit into my girlfriend's chest. Doesn't take a genius to figure it out.'

Fuck.

Dylan forgot we hacked that information. It's not in the public domain.

# thirty-three

## Erin

After our security system was compromised, we've resorted to old-fashioned manned stations at the portal. What worries me most is, if Finley saw a portal in Afghanistan, our fear of there being multiple places around the world might be true, and we've no idea how many people from the future could be here already.

I concentrate when I'm on shift at the barn. I don't bring along things that might distract me. I turn off the internet on my phone and only leave access for calls. I'm responsible for Finley's life, and I have to keep things professional.

Ashley taught me better than to worry about something else when I'm on a task. *If I give you a job, I expect you to do it. Don't try to multitask.* She'd give us shit if we were telling too many jokes on lookout.

I lean back in the chair and watch the space in front of me and the monitors that surveil our property, and bask in my ability to be on a stakeout with no distractions. Until Finley's car bloody drives down the road.

Our front gate cameras can record a hundred feet to the end of a road that's not even on our property. I sit up and place my hand over the intercom button, waiting for him to ring the gate buzzer.

'I'm out back,' I tell him and buzz him through.

I don't watch him drive around to the barn and park. His presence is enough to unsettle me, and I resent it. It makes me itch and squirm, knowing if he laid his hands on me, all those uncomfortable feelings would melt away, and I could relax.

'Hey, Emissary, how're things?' He perches on the desk in front of me, and I have to shoo him off.

'There're no more seats. You're going to have to stand.' I keep my gaze on the monitors.

'You know, if you can't stand to be around me, you can always reassign me somewhere far away.'

The panic sets in. I don't want him far away. I want him near me, but that's selfish and wrong and will lead to all sorts of broken friendships. 'I assign jobs based on skill sets, not emotion. Besides, I already have something set up for you. Go get Dylan and Ashley. I want them to see this too.'

I text Ollie to cover my shift and meet Finley and the others on the front driveway.

In the middle of the high street, I open the shop door with the dirty glass to reveal the bare insides of a thousand square-foot retail space to Dylan, Ashley, and Finley.

'Tada. What do you think?' I kick at the concrete floor, and dust follows my feet as I move to the middle of the space.

'What is this?' Finley asks.

'Remember I mentioned the idea of having you help us start a charity for servicemen that have returned home? Well, this is it. Marks's been working with the local councillor, you know, the tall one with the bad hair.'

'Fletcher?' Ashley asks.

'Yes! He said there's a gap in finding employment for soldiers who would rather avoid the usual police and security guard offers they get. Hence *HomeJobs* is born.'

'HomeJobs?'

'Jobs at home that will keep ex-soldiers in one place, so they can be with family and friends.'

'What do you want us to do?' Dylan asks.

'Spread the word. Let people know you can hook them up with employment. We'll hire someone to liaise with employers. Mark is a good interviewer, and Ollie is great with scoring and categorising. We can input details and requirements and job match what's on offer.'

'Sounds like a business, not a charity,' Dylan says.

'Can't it be both? The profits can be circulated between related charities or help fund housing while we've people on the books waiting on jobs. Not everyone saved their salaries, like you guys.'

'I'm leaving in two days,' Dylan says. 'You already know this.'

Ashley's grip on Dylan's arm tightens, but otherwise she says nothing.

'And this will be here for you when you get back. Four months until your contract is up. Keep yourself alive until then.' I try to smile but fail at hiding my fear. A lot can happen in four months.

Ashley tries to sound calm, but we all hear her anxiety. 'You're going to get moved to the training office at Catterick. You said your senior officer and psych would recommend it, right?'

Dylan nods. 'But I go wherever they put me first. It might be a week or more before I officially get moved back here.' Dylan turns to Finley. 'What do you think? You're looking after Ashley while I'm gone. If you want me in on this, I'm okay with that.'

'Might be good,' Finley says. 'We can office share, right? Erin, set up space for the adventure company, and I'll run that. We can do fundraising skydives around the country. That would give us a good reason for why we use all the airfields in the UK and not just the local ones.'

'And will give our potential employees a nice view on what jobs might be on offer?' Dylan's tone is accusatory, and I have to admit, it's a good way for him and Finley to recruit more soldiers.

'I don't need a babysitter twenty-four-seven,' Ashley says. 'I've moved in with Erin and her dad. I'm dealing, and I won't hide for the rest of my life.'

I shudder, knowing that's exactly what she's going to do.

'Mark was right,' I say. 'If someone is trying to frame you for the murder of your ex-girlfriends, it's better you're away with the army and have a solid alibi. If Rian's smart, he'll not target any more girls in case it takes the focus off you as a suspect.'

Dylan looks at me. If the girls who used to be in Dylan's life are no longer targets, it means *he* is. Rian might be crazy enough to try and infiltrate another mission Dylan is on.

'So it's settled. I have to admit, Erin Cooper. It's nice to know there's a job waiting for me when I get discharged.' He smiles at Ashley.

'You're damn lucky, you know that? 'Ain't no way I'd let just any guy leave me twice and expect to come back.'

'I'm returning for good this time. Promise.' He kisses her loudly, making her giggle.

Finley rolls his eyes at me. 'I'm heading out on a job with Mark this afternoon.' He checks the time. 'But I'll be back late tonight. Erin and I have plans for the next two days, okay?'

Dylan nods.

'We do?' I ask.

'Pack a bag, emissary girl, you're going on holiday.'

When Finley pulls up at the house, I'm waiting out front with a small backpack over my shoulder.

239

Mark gets out of the Jeep and gives me a quick nod as he passes me. 'Have fun.'

Finley's smile fades as I cross the driveway to him. 'I could've sworn he was getting on board with us. He only grunted once when I told him about our weekend away.'

I laugh. 'I don't think any father's happy about their kids going on a dirty weekend with a bloke.'

Finley places his thumb on my bottom lip, tipping it open a little, and places a kiss over it. 'This is a "show you how awesome 2019 is" weekend. If you want it to be more, that's completely doable.'

I lean forward a heartbeat as he pulls away and I catch myself from following that thumb and landing on my ass at his feet. I smile when I realise that's not a terrible place to be. I thank him when he opens the door for me and hop inside the warm car.

He pulls up his phone and checks the directions. 'You're going to have to do better than that. Read a map, learn your way around in your head.'

He puts his phone away. 'Okay then, let's do this the old-fashioned way. We drive as much as we can remember, then follow the signs the rest of the way.'

'That's not the old-fashioned way, that's the futuristic way.'

'And if we get lost, we can pull into a service station and ask directions. See? I'm a twentieth-century guy who doesn't have a problem asking for directions.'

'In the future, if you stop to ask for directions, you're dead.' I buckle up my seat belt, and Finley starts the engine.

'You're one big ray of sunshine, Erin.'

I wince at the use of the nickname. *Yeah, I know.*

## thirty-four

*Erin*

We've been driving west for more than an hour and a half when we pull off the M6. Finley slows down, looking for signs.

'I can help you if you tell me where we're going.'

'Top secret,' he drawls and looks at a brown tourist sign.

'The Lake District?'

Finley grins. 'I told you I'd organised a trip for us, and I decided I'd trial run our first skydive here. What time do you want to jump?' Finley asks.

'Jump?'

'What's the matter, Erin? You didn't think I was going to strap someone else onto me for the first business jump, did you?'

My mouth goes dry, and I suddenly realise I might be scared. 'I've never jumped out of a plane before. I've never even been on one.'

This confession takes him by surprise. 'Shit, maybe the first time on a plane should've been a trip to Paris. That's way more romantic than making you jump out of the tail end.

'What's wrong, Emissary?'

'How the hell do you trust the parachute will be okay?'

'Just do. When it's the job, you don't think about it. If you hesitate, you jeopardise the mission. Someone could spot you, or you might be late on your arrival because you delayed

241

the team.' He shakes his head. 'Okay, your chute might not open, but that's not my fault.'

He must recognise the shock on my face.

'Granted, it's scary, but it's the surest thing about our work. It's landing without getting shot out of the sky that frightens me the most. With this gig, it's all about fun. We jump together, with backup chutes. I've done it a hundred times. You've done much scarier things than this, Erin.'

Finley takes my hand. 'I'll train you. You'll be up to speed, I promise. I'm your team leader on this, and when I tell you I've covered the basics, you have to trust me.'

I open the map Finley placed on the dashboard, although I've already memorised it. It's an outdated version of a map I used a hundred times before Ashley made sure Blake and I had the entire national park and beyond memorised.

'What's the plan, Fin?' I push my seat back and stretch my legs.

'There are two airfields in the area we can use for supply runs. One is about twenty minutes south of here'—he points to the location on the map—'but it's small and mostly unused. It might work for the drops we need, without drawing much attention. The one we're using today for the skydive is farther away, but it's better suited. Has facilities on site as well.' He points to Kirkbride; it'll take us more than an hour to drive there.

'What time's the pilot booked for?'

'Seven tonight. Wanted you to see the sunset while we're up there.'

My heart melts.

'What are we going to do with the rest of the day?'

'You're going to show me around. I want to see the place where you grew up. You said you spent a lot of time here?'

'In fairness, I spent a lot of time everywhere and also nowhere.' I lay the map flat on my knees. 'We can drive west around Lake Windermere before heading north. It's a little longer but way nicer to look at. There are about five really good peaks on the way. We can climb a couple if you want to see the training runs Garvey made us do.' I look up. 'You brought decent shoes, right?'

He salutes me. 'Always prepared.'

'Well, we have to stop at St Sunday Crag. The view up there is good. You're fit enough we can do it, no problem.'

'Glad you noticed.' Finley smirks.

'There's Wray Castle too. We can stop there, and I'll show you where I freaked my dad out during the best game of hide and seek with Blake when I was a kid. It took him two hours to find me, and that's saying something.' I laugh. 'And the stone circles at Castle Rigg are only a little off route, but they're nice to see. They're old, like pyramids old. That should take us most of the day, and there are a load of small villages we can stop for food.'

'A plan is hatched,' Finley announces. 'What about Lakeside Railway? It's supposed to be nice, with a very Harry Potter feel when the steam trains are on show.'

I shrug. 'My mum tried to tell me the story of Harry Potter once, but it was long, and we got interrupted so many times I lost interest.'

'Your childhood was robbed.' He tries to make it sound like teasing, but I hear the sadness he feels for me underneath.

'Beatrix Potter, though. That was a place my mum didn't compromise. Her house is here.' I point. 'She loved Peter Rabbit when she was a kid. She made my dad take us to Beatrix Potter's house, and when we walked through the gate, she looked at the house and it was like she started to breathe again.

'I was a kid, but even I could see how happy that place made her. She could remember her parents and her life before the world fell apart and she was filled with fear for her kids.

243

'We stayed there for four days. That was a long stop so early on, before resource stripping was everywhere.'

My mum's childhood memory was also mine. 'I remember pretending it was our home. We didn't have to keep moving around, and we were safe. We had beds and a kitchen, and a garden the four of us sat out in, and Mum told us Beatrix Potter's stories. Rabbits running from the fox. I was too young to see the irony. Afterwards, my dad packed us up and moved us on.'

I swallow tears I didn't know were looming at the back of my throat and whisper the next words, knowing I can't say them out loud. 'I hated him after that. My mum was sad, and I wanted to stay too. I thought it was his fault we left, and I rebelled against everything he told me. I was young, but all the anger over everything that had gone before had built up inside me. But instead of reprimanding me, or scolding me for not listening, he helped me channel that pain and anger into the fight. I must have been about six, maybe seven. We ran circuits and practiced martial arts every day, until we were exhausted. "Use the energy in that anger for something productive", he said.'

'Your childhood was robbed,' Finley says again, and this time, there's nothing funny about it.

After a lunch stop, we're on the road and following the winding roads through valleys and along the lakeside to the destinations we chose this morning. I roll down the window, untie my hair, and let the wind run through it. The strong green fields, scattered with golden hay bales, are a hypnotising view. Scattered trees line the roads between lone cottages and stone walls. We stop at the castle grounds, Beatrix Potter's house, and the stone circles, and share with him parts of my life no one knows about.

'Don't look so scared,' Finley says as we pull onto the airstrip. 'Training first, then taking in a few sights before we jump.' He gathers up his phone and keys. 'I can distract you with something even scarier, if you like. You own a dress?'

'What's going on, Fin?'

'Got a family wedding in a couple of months and thought we could schedule work in Scotland that week and spend some time with the family beforehand.'

'Do you miss being so far away from them?'

'Of course. Cameron and I trained together when we first signed up and quickly discovered we were from the same part of Glasgow. After we made it through Special Forces training, we met Dylan. He didn't have family, so he always went to Scotland with us during downtime.'

My grandparents died when my dad was sixteen. He told us that his older brother couldn't take care of him, so he enlisted in the army to have a place to stay. We never met his brother when we were running. I don't even know if Garvey knows if he is alive or not.

'Scotland became our safe haven,' Finley says. 'Especially after the last tour. At home with our families, seeing everyone rally around to help us while we were in therapy and rehab, really made the difference. Helped get us back in the usual way of thinking. Even Dylan crashed at our families' places, whether we were there or not.

'Dylan was strong for us while we were recovering. I hope he keeps his head in the game, and we find the fucker who's killing these girls. 'Cause he feels responsible for their deaths.'

'Your family used to let Dylan crash on their couch when he was on leave.' I swallow thickly. Garvey's friends in Scotland saved him during his dark time and hundreds of times after that.

'You're going to love them.'

245

My heart skips a beat. I've already met them.

Finley opens the door to the airfield building and points to the coffee machine. 'Let's get a brew in, then we can start training.

'What has you scared, Erin? Jumping out of a plane or meeting the fam? Relax. It's not for another couple of months, and they're always nice to the girls I bring home to meet them, despite knowing I'll be introducing them to a new one in a couple of months. They even have this tradition of how to welcome someone new into the family. It's charming, the trouble they go to, and lord knows they've had enough practise to get it perfect by now.'

I swallow hard, not knowing what to say. *Thank you?* Hell, no.

'I'm fucking with you. The last girl I brought home, I was sixteen. They're going to be as nervous as you are, emissary girl.' He slaps me on the bum and crosses to a row of benches along the back wall. 'And a family wedding no less. You know what that means.' He laughs.

I chase after him. 'What does that mean?'

After the safety and instructional tutorials are complete, we don jumpsuits and goggles. Finley helps me into the plane, and we sit down and strap in for take-off.

When we're in the air, Finley is on his feet, organising something I'm too nervous to pay attention to. When he holds out his hand to me, I shake my head.

'Just strapping you on to me. That's not a scary thought, is it?' I relax a little, knowing that Finley will be wrapped around me, protecting me and in charge of my safety. Within a few minutes, we're sitting on the floor, attached to each other.

When it's time to jump, the pilot gives us a thumbs-up, and the rear of the plane slowly opens. He waits for me to adjust to the wind whipping around us before shouting, 'Ready?'

'I can't do this.'

'Yes, you can. You don't have to do anything. We just walk to the edge, and when you're ready, let me do all the work.'

We take baby steps to the opening. I can't enjoy the view because all I can think about is falling and dying.

'Erin, tell me you're ready.'

'I'm not ready.'

'Baby, you're never ready for the scary stuff in life, but you throw yourself into it and have faith everything is going to be okay.' He runs his hand roughly over my hip bone, and I can feel the pressure through the layers of clothes and gloves he wears. 'You don't need hope to see you through,' he says about the tattoo I have under the clothes. 'I'll see you through.' He kisses me on the cheek, and I close my eyes.

'I'm ready,' I say, and I mean it.

I take a confident step to the edge of the plane, and he counts down quickly. When we jump, *I* jump. I don't hold back. I don't let him take the lead. I confidently jump, and we fall through the air.

Screaming with excitement that I'm not afraid anymore, I push my arms out as he taught me, and the wind rushes through my whole body. Finley at my back helps keep the pressure on me and this is happening and not some weird dream.

The sun has already begun to set, and the orange glow in the sky is the best view I've ever seen. And I've seen them all.

Before I know it, Finley is giving me the signal he's going to pull the cord, and I pray the bloody chute opens, like it's supposed to. When we're jerked sharply up, and the falling turns to floating, I laugh in delight. I look out over miles of parkland and scattered dwellings, golden in the setting sun, and

247

feel free. We survived, and we're still technically falling through the air.

When we land, we run for a few feet to slow our momentum before he drops us into a sitting position on the grass. The parachute falls at our backs and lurches slightly as it deflates. I lean back against him and scream out a laugh.

# thirty-five

*Erin*

The drive around the Lake District is beautiful, even in the dark. Moonlight sparkles on the lakes and rivers, and the trees remind me of driving at night when we were kids.

Another twenty minutes on the west side of the Lake District and we pull into a hotel driveway. On the edge of one of the lakes—Windermere, it looks like—we drive into a car park and stop at the front of the property.

'I know you wanted to camp, but I thought, with everything that's happened recently, a hotel room was more secure. Ollie booked us under a fake name.'

'Wow.' The hotel is forty rooms wide and three floors high. I know this because we were here as kids. Even in the desolate future, we knew this was once a high-class place. Seeing it here in its prime, it's breathtaking. The orange glow of the lights across the grass leads the way to a dock, on which there is plush furniture to sit on so one can look out at the water and the hotel's yacht.

A stone wall leading from the car park to the front door, passing under the arched entrance. Rose bushes tangle around a trellis and frame the front of the building.

The main floor of the hotel—where the restaurant, dining rooms, conservatory, and lobby are—are illuminated, setting the place alight like a diamond against the backdrop of the moonlit sky.

'I've stayed here before,' I tell him. 'But it had already been stripped of resources. The carpets were still down in the bedrooms, though, curtains too, so we used the large ones from the dining rooms, making them into mattresses. My mum never took off the curtain hooks, so we could rehang them before we left. She never left any evidence of our squatting.' I kiss him slowly on the lips. 'I love it here. Thank you. How did you know?'

'Total coincidence. It was the only hotel and spa that had a room left for a late booking. I wanted somewhere nice for you. Plus, the view looked amazing online. I hope it lives up to expectations.'

I unbuckle my seat belt. 'Let's go see, shall we?'

He takes the keys out of the ignition, and the notion that he hasn't traded his Jeep in for a newer model with a start/stop engine button makes me smile inside. That one little piece of tech kept off a computer board can save a life in the future.

Instead of crossing the car park to the hotel, we stroll along the path to the dock and sink into thick cushions on a love seat in front of the water. Finley wraps his arms around me, and I bury myself in his heat, the wind of the evening circling us.

I gaze at the water, remembering all the times I sat here with Blake—though then there was no expensive, plush furniture to sit on—and sometimes Ashley and Garvey would quit working and join us for a while. I breathe in the night air and silence of the resort. 'This feels like home. If I could smash these damn lights and be in darkness, I might sleep tonight.'

He runs his hand over my lower back, and the contact sends shivers up my spine. I'm not sure how much sleep I'll get on a night with Finley.

We eventually wander to reception.

'The roof of the hotel has a great view,' I say.

'Wanna take a peek?'

'Ooh, Finley trespassing his first night. You know how to show a girl a good time, don't you?'

'You've no idea how far my talents stretch. The real problem is fighting me for the master bedroom. Last-minute booking, the only a two-room lodge available, with bunk beds in the second room.' He fetches our two bags from the boot and beeps it locked. 'The last one to the door gets the bunk beds,' he declares and sprints to the lobby entrance.

He forgets I'm as fast as he is; I make it to the bottom of the stairs only a pace behind.

'Shit,' I yell as I land on the first step. Finley turns, and I leap up the last steps. 'Tricked ya,' I shout and open the reception door. The night porter glares at us for yelling. I lower my voice. 'There's no way you thought we were sleeping in separate beds.'

He smirks. 'I wanted you to at least have the option.'

We get a key for the room and head for the lifts. On the fourth floor, I look at the end window and see the fire escape I crawled on so many times. I have to shade my eyes to darken the reflection to get a better look.

'There's a ladder you can access from here, and shit, there's a bloody alarm on the door.'

'I usually like to have some alcohol in me before I resort to breaking and entering.'

'It's easy,' I scoff. 'Blake and I'd jump the side of the ladder. Eventually, we left a stack of crates at the side of the building to get up there. But the ladder stops at that emergency exit.' I point out the window to something neither of us can see. I know it from memory. 'There's no glass in the window in the future. We use the ledge to shimmy our way to the roof.' I turn to Finley. 'Can't very well go kicking in windows this time of night?'

Finley looks crestfallen.

251

'Hey, I'll smash it in for you, but we won't have much time before someone comes to investigate,' I joke.

'It's not that. I wanted to see something you see. Why do you want to go out there?'

I put my hands in my jacket pockets. 'Memories, I guess.' I raise my chin at the ceiling in the west corner. 'Blake and I used to climb up there for hours. We'd hoard snacks or whatever and watch the horizon. You can see for miles up there, and you can jump down and hide in the woods in less than a minute. This was one of the few places our parents relaxed enough to let us roam.'

'You climbed up there when you were a kid?'

'It is a nice view.' I turn quickly. 'Although at night, we didn't see fuck all.' I laugh.

'I remember the last time we looked at the stars together, and it was pretty nice.'

'What do you think the showers are like in our room?'

The hardness in his groin presses into me. A grin is forming at the side of his lips. 'In case you're misunderstanding, Finley, I really want to shower with you.'

'Shit, Erin.'

'I saw it in a movie once, and it looked kind of nice, the hot water and soap suds. I have a kink in my neck, and it might be nice to have you rub it out.' I nearly choke. 'Um, I mean massage it.'

He bends down and nibbles on my neck, then clamps down on the skin and pulls back with a low growl. The symbolic claiming of this primal act makes me tingle between my legs.

'Finley,' I pant.

'Let's go.'

Finley is practically pulling me down the hall to our room. Key card in hand, he opens the heavy door. The first thing I see is a large bed covered in throw pillows and a brown tartan quilt that matches the carpet. I can feel the difference in thickness compared to the thin, shabby one that's here in the future. I've been in this room before—I've been in every room—and I know there are two doors to the right, one of which leads to the small second bedroom he mentioned and the other to a bathroom.

I throw myself on the bed and sink into the thick plush sheets and inhale the fabric and softness that's never here in the future.

'You want that shower now, or do you want to eat first?' Finley asks.

The intense sexual tension in the air a few minutes ago has gone, but the promise of the weekend we are going to have, full of takeout food and time with no worries about the future, offers an intimacy I crave and never knew I would get.

'I need both.' I lean up on my elbows. 'But I want that massage before something else gets in our way.'

Finley bends and pulls me into his arms, and I scream and laugh as he carries me to the bathroom and places me on the counter. He takes our shirts off, kisses me, and then undoes the buttons on my jeans.

I undo his belt and push down his trousers and boxers. He kicks them off, and I jump down from the vanity and let him strip the rest of my clothes off.

He swings me into the shower, and he turns on the spray, shielding me from the water as it heats. I get splashed over the back of my hands as I kiss him and explore his hard backside.

'Do you know how many times I've fantasised about this?' he asks as his kisses move across my neck and down to my breasts. He sucks my nipple into his mouth and bites down as he pulls my ass close, crushing his hard dick between us.

I gasp, and he releases me and reaches behind me for the shower gel. 'Turn around.'

The space is compact, and my bum rubs his dick. He stifles a moan. The hot water falling between us makes every touch and movement smooth and warm, and before I realise it, I'm pushing my ass back, grinding against him. He places his hands on my back, and I arch into his touch.

Christ, with my hands pressed against the wall, I'm grinding against his naked body like a porn star. He rubs my back, and the soap lathers. The slippery feeling of his hands glide over me, slip and pinch my sides as he manoeuvres. Finley kisses my neck from behind, his torso covering mine, the soap lather slipping between us. His hands go to my ass, and he rubs my cheeks and then moves lower to cup my vagina. I spread my legs, and he pushes a finger inside me. I gasp and rest my forehead on the cool tiles.

Working me with one hand, he moves the other to my neck, where he massages the knots.

I'm ready to burst. Finley strokes and rubs my clit, and I tighten and pulse around his finger, and I let the pleasure run through me. I chase the feeling, wanting it to last forever.

I take a deep breath and close my eyes to the peace that flows through me for a few seconds and then I straighten. Finley, hands on my hips, pulls me against him, and devours my mouth. He turns off the shower and slides open the door.

He wraps a hotel towel around me and dries me off while backing me out of the bathroom towards the bed.

When I lie down, I pull my hair out of the bobble and let it fall. Finley dries his hair with the towel; he keeps the sides shaved and the top long. It falls over his eyes sometimes. The bulk of a man, naked in front of me, doing something as domesticated as showering, has my stomach flipping over. I've never been selfish before, but I want to be. I want to forget my responsibilities. I want to stay. There're opportunities for a quiet life as a couple living in a utopian facade.

When Finley covers my body with his and shifts me up the bed, I get lost in his kiss. His dick presses tightly against my opening, and he moves, making it rub over my clit and igniting little sparks deep inside that I thought were only going to explode once tonight.

Soon he has a condom on. 'We're going slow this time.'

I nod, anticipating the pain I felt last time, but when he slides into me, there's only fullness, like there was an emptiness I wasn't aware of until he filled it.

'You okay?' He holds himself above me.

'Yes.'

He pushes deeper and lets out a deep sigh when he's fully seated. He starts slowly but gradually the pace increases. I explore his body, touching him everywhere I can reach. I soak in every detail, I memorize his tattoos, the shading and colours over his chest, and the design imperfections caused by scar tissue.

'Erin,' Finley asks, and I realise he's not moving anymore.

'It's all nice.'

'Nice?' Finley sounds incredulous. 'Oh, baby, you've no idea what you just did.'

Finley grabs the back of my legs and pulls my ass higher towards him. Pushing my knees up to my chest, he moves into me and pushes me into the mattress. The quick movements and the feeling as his dick hits something deep inside me makes me gasp. A gurgling noise builds at the back of my throat, and I don't know what's happening, but I want it to keep building. 'Finley!' I need the reassurance that whatever's happening, he's not going to abandon it.

'You're okay, babe. Just let go.' He twists me to the side, pulls out of me, and turns me onto my front. 'On your knees.'

The order has me tingling. I'd love to have him order me around on a mission. To hear those gravelly words spoken with such authority makes me tighten around his dick the moment he's back inside me.

Fin slams into me, and I never knew it could feel so much deeper like this. He spanks me hard on the ass. I gasp at the shock of what that did inside of me. Before I can process, he fists my hair and twists my head around to meet his mouth. He claims my breath and kisses out every ounce of air I have left in my lungs.

I'm shaking when I come, and when he stills inside me, he lets out a groan of relief and lies on top of me.

'Still nice?' he asks.

'Holy fuck, my legs are shaking.' I giggle.

thirty-six

*Erin*

Three weeks of non-stop work go by, and Dylan is back in service before Ollie and I meet JT in Newcastle. Lara's driven down from Scotland. JT's been in the city for the last month, monitoring Nanda. We don't have enough information to go all out and question her, so JT's only focus has been making sure that Rian doesn't show up and capture or kill her. Nanda is also none the wiser that her dad's company was involved in a time travel population culling in the future.

Lara and I sit in a tourist café half an hour outside the city centre, and I look at the North Sea, waiting for Ollie to finish his briefing with JT.

'Remember when we used to sneak out to the south beach and pretend we were sailing away?' Lara says. The view of the ocean from the coffee shop balcony is stunning. 'Those were the best days, curled under a blanket, hiding behind that pier door.'

'Snuggled up with Blake, you mean,' I tease and regret it when a flash of pain crosses her face.

She tugs at the laces of her beach shoes, which are tied up her calf. Her taut muscles are still prominent, like mine. She's been working out. It feels like a lifetime since we've seen each other in the flesh. She was hiding her broken heart as far away from me as she could.

'Do you think he's still looking for us?' she asks.

257

I nod and try not to think about it too much. 'Every day. Blake's not the sort to let things go.'

'We've been gone eight months, Erin. I hope he's given up. That kind of torture is worse than finding our bodies.'

'You were lucky to have each other while you did. Not many people find their soulmates at fifteen.'

Lara chuckles. 'Like you have now, you mean?'

I snort.

'Your boy's good. He's already got basic weaponry delivered to us. Nivek is installing it tomorrow. Plus, he's working the night shift on the social media presence of the skydiving company. Has his first booking too.'

'He does?' Finley and I have been busy. The two nights we've had together since our weekend away were not wasted with talking.

Ollie's been trying to track down Rian, but he's also spent the last few weeks creating a programme to follow the next ten girls on Dylan's list. Their social media posts are being recorded, along with facial recognition that is pinging on private and public CCTVs. We can't protect them all, but we can gather as much evidence as we can in case Rian attacks. Mark is grudgingly looking after Ashley, who has moved into our house while Dylan is away. The rest of us have been keeping on top of daily jobs and trying to find a safe way to keep an eye on the next girl who might be killed.

'You can have fun in life too,' Lara says. 'We had a shitty upbringing, and if you forget what you're fighting for, you'll forget to live. People need relationships and families. Otherwise, what's the point? You going to keep running until you die?'

'What's it like, the pain of losing him? I know what it's like for me. He's my brother, and he was my best friend, but I never understood what a relationship could be like until Finley. And now I'm terrified. I think I love him more than I love Blake. No, that's not what I mean. It's a different love.' One I don't think I'd be able to survive when I have to leave him or if he dies because of us.' My voice croaks. 'How much does it hurt, knowing that you'll never see Blake again?'

She doesn't cry like she did when we first got here. I wanted to get her to hurt, just to leave me the hell alone.

She raises her cup in a silent toast. 'It's worth every damn second of torture to know we had each other while we did. I'd rather have the memories and my dreams of us than nothing. That's a different kind of pain and torture.' She drinks. 'God have mercy on any girl who might take my place, because I'm going to wait for him. If I've to sit here and wait twenty years, one way or another, I'm going back to him.'

'Ew,' I joke. 'You're going to wait around and show up in your forties to claim him?'

'Sure I will. Someone will have to keep Finley company till you guys are all grown up.'

I knock her knee off the table. 'Shut up. If anything serious happens between Finley and me, we'll have to leave, and I don't think we'd be coming back.'

'Maybe that's what always happened. Or perhaps you guys would get a good twenty years together and then get divorced, like your parents. Or maybe you'll die, or he will, before that becomes an issue. Hell, we all could die. But don't deny yourself the opportunity for something great.'

Ollie walks across the boardwalk bar area and sidesteps a blonde who tries to catch his attention. 'We have trouble, ladies.' He pulls a chair out. 'Thanks for meeting me here. I wanted to speak to you away from Mark, because he's going to flip his lid.'

'What's going on?'

'We fucked up. We were watching the wrong girl.'

'How the hell could Dylan not know which girls he's dated in what order?'

'I think it's something simpler—like the CleanDate app.'

Lara chuckles, and I gag. 'You're kidding, right?'

Ollie says, 'Makes sense. A whole dating and sexual activity history on the internet, disguised as a consumer app and a bit of fun on social media to rate your dates. And therefore NewGov to track and monitor combined sexual DNA changes. All it'd take in the future is a two-minute search for anyone who's ever slept with Garvey to create a CleanDate account. Anyone who reversed the search could get a full list of his sexual partners who have CleanDate accounts. It looks like they're using it to frame him.'

'Dylan gave us a list of his exes. How the hell were you watching the wrong girl if this app is so precise?' Lara asks.

Ollie shrugs. 'Maybe the girls who were next on Dylan's list never created an account with CleanDate. Or maybe they're dead by the time the app came into the public domain. Rian missed seven girls from Dylan's list.'

'What you're telling us, then, is that not everyone on the list of ex-girlfriends is a potential target, but we don't know what names Rian has. Do we have to watch them all at the same time? Just in case?'

'Looks that way.'

'You know how many people that is. We can't watch them all in real-time,' I screech. 'The guy was a fucking man whore.'

Lara's trying to hold back her chuckles at my outrage.

'We can take a guess. Almost four million people created accounts with CleanDate. I spoke to JT. We can watch the next five girls simultaneously. Three of them live in the same town. The other two are not far away. If we take JT off Nanda full time, we have the man hours to watch the girls and keep an eye out for Rian.'

'The girl died, Erin. Dylan is being framed. I'm making this our top priority, regardless of whether or not this leads the police to suspect Dylan. We have to do the right thing here.'

I close my eyes and swallow the bile rising in the throat. An innocent girl was murdered because she once knew the infamous Dylan Garvey.

'The twisted good news is my programme worked. CCTV tracking her was backed up in the cloud, and after her name came up as deceased, the programme pulled all the recordings for the last two weeks and downloaded them to me. I will view the footage now, see if there's anything with Rian in it. Hopefully, we get him on stalking.'

'We don't know where Rian is or who his next target is.' I feel defeated.

Ollie swallows thickly. 'Purchase orders I hid for the bunkers keep popping back up on our server. Normally I'd think it's a glitch and re-hide them, but given everything else, I think someone's trying to bring everything we buried to light.'

'That's our entire lives here in the past,' Lara says.

'That's not even the bad news. I've information from the thermal pin tracker we got off the Apostle soldier. Someone has already hacked it and extracted information.'

'How the hell could they do that? No one here should have known that pin arrived in this timeline,' Lara says.

'A parasite merge was created so if a soldier was ever lost or compromised to the point of death, they could remove their chip and activate an extraction download to a nearby soldier pin. All data would be uploaded to the main server, which can only mean there's another active chip in this timeline. The pins have extracted data from the prototype server already, and we have a copy of everything they have.'

'What information?'

'Dylan, mostly. Ashley too, and the last five years of her life. It looks like someone was trying to cross-reference their lives.'

'Cross-reference for what?' Lara asks.

'To find out when they met,' I say. 'When did this start?'

'About a year before we got here. That's all I have. I don't know who or how many people or even if it was the same location we came through. If it was, we're in deep shit. There are files on all of us. Finley, Cameron, and Nanda too. It looks like whoever was here was searching for information on how to hit Dylan's team. There were a few things that didn't add up. A few military orders were changed on Garvey's last mission via a virus in the system.'

'Dylan's in danger?'

'Who's crazy enough to go on a suicide mission into the past and knows they aren't getting home but sensible enough not to tackle Dylan and his friends head-on?' Lara asks.

'The soldier's scared of fighting with Dylan,' I say.

'He's trying to sabotage him, take him out of the picture without having to kill him,' Ollie tells us.

'Like put him in prison?' Lara asks. 'Right where he would be when the takeover happens and where he would stay until someone in the future released him.'

I say, 'Then they'd have the rebel leader already a prisoner. Job done.'

'Or flip him,' Ollie says. 'There's something I didn't tell you. When I ran the personality check on Finley and Cameron, I also ran it on Dylan. He didn't pass.'

'Excuse me?' I have to keep myself in my seat. 'What do you mean, he didn't pass?'

'Dylan has an agenda-based flip alert on his personality test. Basically, under the right circumstances, the other side could turn him.'

'Circumstances like twenty years incarcerated, no family to speak of?' Lara asks.

'Exactly.' Ollie points at her. 'Dylan is someone who would operate on a personal goals level. If he's offered something enticing, that doesn't insult his moral code, he could work for the other side. In our original timeline, Dylan was as selfish as they came. He kept his family alive. He did things that might be morally questionable to keep us all safe. He built a community because he knew that would keep his family safer and give them some normality in life.'

'He saved people,' I say.

Ollie nods. 'But it can be described as selfish. He wanted to build a life for his family. He didn't necessarily do it for the greater good.'

'It was for moral reasons,' I shout. 'How is that not for the greater good?'

Ollie holds up his hands. 'All I'm saying is if we got this result from someone in the future, Garvey wouldn't let him into the compound.'

'Dylan Garvey's unpredictable,' Lara says.

'Are we acknowledging that a futuristic Apostle soldier is recruiting people here in the past?' Lara asks.

I throw a fiver on the table for the coffees and cross to the edge of the balcony to watch the waves and dream of a time when I wished with all my heart I could swim to France.

Ollie joins me. 'Rian has a full history. I sent Nivek and Eleda to Dublin to check out his hometown. His parents are still at their original address. Neighbours remember him, but he left at a young age. It was right around the time JT says he fell off the grid. Looks like he might have been homeless. A neighbour said his parents weren't happy about him bringing home a boyfriend, and they think he was thrown out.'

I sigh and rest my head on my hands on the railing.

'Nivek even visited his old primary school. There are class photos on the wall. He's legit from 2019, but somehow, someone from the future is grooming him. His apartment in Darligton contains files on Dylan since birth. It's like a bloody Interpol database, what he's pulled.'

'He also had a lot of info on Nanda and Ashley. Looks like he planned to work his way into their lives while Dylan was away. Who his focus was on, I don't know.'

'But then we showed up,' Erin says.

'He must have thought he hit the jackpot when he saw you.' Lara comes to stand on my other side and rests her elbows on the railing.

'That's why he was trying to control me. To get me out of the way,' I say.

'The girl was murdered this morning in Stirling. He could be anywhere by now. But I don't know where he'll pop up. If he's working with the Apostle soldier, like we think he is, he's extracted his thermal pin, and he'll have it close by. That will take me some time.'

'Lara, call Mark. I want him here with you. That way we've a team coming at him from north and south.'

'Mark won't leave Ashley on her own,' Lara says.

'Finley can keep an eye on her. I'll be back home in an hour. Looking for the thermal pin is strictly a recon exercise. If you spot Rian, then, of course, take him out if it's safe to do so. But it's unlikely, so information gathering only.'

'I'll get to work on it right away. If you dispatch Mark now, we can get on the road.'

# thirty-seven

## FINLEY

Erin called Mark after he brought Ashley home from work, and he headed straight out while Ashley took the stairs to wash up. All he told me was to stay here while he took care of something, and I waited like a good soldier for Erin to call me with an update. 'We're assuming Rian was in Stirling, where the girl was killed this morning.'

Adrenaline runs through my veins, and I try to stop myself from shaking with anger that another woman has been murdered by someone I let slip through my fingers.

'I'm on the road,' Erin says. 'I need to see you. It's been one hell of a day.'

An alarm beeps on her side and there is silence while she checks her screen.

'Finley, the barn!' Erin shouts.

The run from the house to the shed takes two-and-a-half minutes.

There's no padlock on the door, and I pull the metal hook up and slide it open. Apart from the clang of metal on metal, there's no resistance. I hear the low thrum of electricity. The portal has already opened.

'Someone's coming through.' I pull my weapon.

265

A throat is cleared behind me. 'I'm already here, asshole.'

I turn slowly until I'm face to face with our intruder. It takes a moment to put it all together, and if I hadn't already known about Erin and the portal, I wouldn't believe it.

The wrinkles around his eyes show years beyond what I'd expect. His skin is darker, like he's spent the last few years outside, and his hair is long and grey and pushed back out of the way. Even his grubby black stubble is speckled with grey. He's covered in grime; what you expect from a soldier who's constantly been on duty in a war zone for years.

'Dylan Garvey,' I say.

'Finley. Why are you not surprised to see me?' Future Garvey asks. He's flanked by a man a few years younger than me. 'My boy,' Garvey says, and the familiarity of the twenty-something man looking back at me is unsettling. 'Where are we?' His hand rests on the machine gun at his side. The future must be as bleak as Erin describes if this is how Garvey walks the streets.

'Darlington, 2019.'

Garvey's son says, 'We've heard NewGov was trying to mess with the past. Invent a time machine of whatever. Whispers while we scavenged for information. Thought it was all theories and wishful thinking.'

'Wishful thinking?' I ask.

'To send a bunch of soldiers here and end the war before it starts,' Garvey says. 'You know about this?'

'Some of your people got here a while ago.'

'Who?' Garvey steps forward. 'Who's here?'

'Erin, Mark, Ollie, and Lara were through first.'

Garvey lets out a breath, and his kid leans against the barn wall and laughs.

'Do you trust him?' the kid asks his father.

He's exactly like Dylan at this age. Full of confidence and has the swagger and threatening stance down.

I say, 'We have our young Dylan Garvey, Old Garvey, and Kid Garvey. How the hell are we going to keep who's who straight?'

Kid Garvey snickers. 'I'm twenty, not a kid, but feel free to call him Old Garvey.' He slaps his dad on the shoulder. 'OG for short.'

Garvey looks me in the eye. 'Are they still alive?'

'They're on their way back right now. Me, Dylan and Ashley have been spending a lot of time with them. I've been helping with the work, and Ashley and Erin have become good friends.'

'Tell me what you know. Do you trust them? Your read on people has always been good. Our people are missing, that's true, but there is every chance NewGov has people here, posing as rebels to flush us out. They've done it before. We survived many times because of your instincts, so do you trust them?'

I hesitate a second too long, and he catches it.

'They're hiding something,' he says.

'Of course they are,' I exclaim. 'They're from an insurgent group of survivors from the future that is fighting a murdering dictatorship government.'

OG shakes his head. 'Maybe, but it's worth checking out.' He gestures to his kid and they turn to leave. 'In my reality you're dead, and here is someone from the future, claiming to be from my inner circle—from my family—and my best friend is alive.' OG looks over his shoulder to see if I'm following him. 'And Erin is doing all she can to get the younger version of me to play in her war and being best friends with the mother of my children. I need to know who this girl and her family are, and make sure they're on the right side of things.'

'They are,' I snarl at OG. 'You watch your mouth about her.' I take a step forward.

Kid Garvey steps between us and places a friendly hand on our shoulders. 'See what's happening? Everyone's starting to lose it, and we need to be a team. Let's get some air. We can search the main house, have a look around. We won't even touch them.' He snaps his fingers. 'You don't have any pictures of them, do you?'

I grit my teeth. 'No.' The Coopers avoid pictures; there are none on their family website or business pages. Every time one of her friends brings out a phone on a night out, Erin hides her face. I know before checking that Ollie will have taken down any online.

'I guess we're breaking in, honey,' OG slaps my arm. 'Where are they now?'

'Looking into the dead girls,' I say.

'What dead girls?' OG asks.

I tell the OG and his son about the serial killer and that we're holding Rian responsible for it.

'You never told me about dead girlfriends in your past.'

'That's 'cause there weren't any,' Garvey tells his son.

'I never got your name, kid,' I say to Kid Garvey as we bring up the rear.

The kid grins at me. 'Garvey, and you're not in position to be calling me a kid. What are you, thirty?'

OG laughs, and I clear my throat. 'Twenty-seven.'

'Ah, well then, you're practically my long-lost uncle.'

OG taps him on the side of the head. 'Show some respect, man. If this lughead had got out of that shithole and survived, like he did this time, he *would* be your uncle. The closest damn thing I ever had to a family. Until I met your mother, anyway.'

'Where are Erin's parents in the future?' I ask. 'Are they safe?'

'Why, your time travel friends want to know?' the kid asks. 'Maybe we should keep personal information to a minimum until we're sure we're all on the same team.'

'You planning on getting in the way if we decide they're a threat?' OG stops to face me. ''Cause from what I see, they are the central factor in this. Also one of them dated this guy Rian and sent you guys off to investigate on your own. She might have been setting you all up.'

I turn to OG, who's an aged echo of my best friend, who just announced I'd have been an uncle to his kid if I'd survived in his world. Hell, I still could be if they stick around. 'Of course I'll get in your way. I believe what she tells me, so you're not meeting her with weapons drawn. We'll talk this out. I'm telling you, she's not a bad guy.'

I tell him about Cameron's theories, but I skip the details pertinent to Erin and stick with the facts.

Garvey tilts his head. 'What's that look?'

'What look?'

He makes a noise at the back of his throat. 'Awe.' He steps back. 'You're not… in love with her or anything, are you?'

Holy shit, where did that come from! 'Jesus, well, I mean. I guess I am. I mean, it's all new and we've not really got to the point of confessing our love and no one's asked me that, but I guess, yeah, I am?' The realisation of my statement hits me and I look up at OG. 'I love her.'

The kid screws up his face. 'Are you fucking my sister?'

For the second time in two days, I don't see the blow coming.

Garvey hits harder that I remember. He doesn't just hit me, he takes me to the ground and punches me in the ribs. Pain resonates through the scar, and I let out a scream.

'What the fuck, Garvey,' I yell as his kid pulls him off me.

Garvey kicks at me as his kid pulls him away.

'Calm down, Dad. Erin's a big girl.'

I get to my knees and stand. 'Erin is—'

'My sister.' The kid steps forward and holds out his hand. 'Blake Garvey. I should have introduced myself properly.'

I turn to Garvey. 'Erin's your daughter?' I feel the blood draw from my face and everything that she's ever told me about her parents being stuck in the future flashes back through my mind.

Garvey shakes his head and the tension from his body as he storms away from me to the patio doors that lead to the kitchen. He stops short when he crosses the threshold. His stiff shoulders are all we have to see to know there's a threat inside. I grab the back of Blake's, and we dart around the side of the house.

I point to the front door, and we scurry towards it. OG is shouting and another man is taunting him. We ease inside without making a sound.

Gunshots go off, echoing across the quiet fields. Blake moves from room to room as efficiently as a soldier at war, just like his sister.

# thirty-eight

## Erin

The side of my head pounds where Rian slammed me with the butt of his gun. There's no blood, but there must be one hell of a bump. I'm not dizzy, but my body vibrates like it's trying to catch up to what's happening, 'cause I swear I can see my dad standing in the doorway. Older, rougher, and more worn looking than Dylan is in 2019, this man looks like Garvey from the future.

Rian has had Mark tied to a chair since we got back here, and despite being conscious, I've been on the floor since I was knocked out.

There's loud banging, something heavy against steel, from the kitchen. The panic room in the basement—someone is trying like hell to break out, and I can't think who it might be.

Rian hasn't taken his gun off me. He knows I'm awake, but he's waiting for something. He became more alert when I looked out the open back door, but he can't be seeing what I'm seeing. Even if he is—he doesn't know who my dad is.

Garvey steps inside the house and holds his arms out to the side. 'You got me.'

His voice. When I hear it, the breath leaves my body and a quiet sob escapes me. I never knew a man's voice could age. Maybe it's only his soul that's old and tired. The Dylan of 2019 is young and full of naivety. My dad's voice is full of resolve and anger and some exhaustion.

271

Rian pulls me off the ground by the hair and when I face my father, all I want to do is collapse in his arms. Dad's here now. He can take the lead and tell us what to do. He can fix our mistakes and make everything right. He can give me a fucking hug.

But I can't go to him because Rian is using me as a human shield. His gun is pressed to the back of my skull, angled upwards so the bullet will travel through my brain and out my crown. He's not messing around.

Mark kicks in his chair, trying to free himself.

'This only ends one way,' Dad drawls in the doorway. He's giving himself up for me, and it's a mistake. Garvey can never surrender. If he's gone, the rebellion will fail.

'I'm sorry,' I say. I got captured, and he's going to have to bargain for me. Except we never bargain. We don't trade one member of the rebellion for another. But my dad will throw out all the rules when it comes to his kids.

'Missing anyone else lately?' Rian taunts.

Dad strides into the house. He knows what Rian is talking about. *Who* Rian is talking about. But that's impossible. How does Rian know anything about the future or us?

'Congratulations,' he tells Rian. 'You got me.'

'My job wasn't to get you. It was to break you.'

'Don't you want to be remembered as the man who took me out, rather than made me snap?' Dad narrows his eyes. His wrinkled old eyes and grey hair are comforting to see in this weird reunion. But those are his mad eyes. It's the way he looks before he snaps someone's neck.

'Are you one of them?' Is Rian an Apostle soldier?

Rian aims at Garvey's chest.

I get ready, knowing the only time someone as calm and apparently well-trained as Rian moves his weapon is to take a shot.

The scream that leaves my throat is a pleading *NO*.

He fires, the shot deafening. My dad falls to the floor as quickly as Rian's body moves from behind me.

I drop to my knees next to him and press my hand against his chest, where blood pours out. People rush into the room, and I'm vaguely aware of them surrounding Rian and taking his gun. I see more blood; Rian's been shot too.

I look up and cry out when I see Blake. I search for the words to explain what has happened, but I don't know where to start. I don't need to start anywhere but the most important place. 'He's dying,' I choke out. I blink heavily to clear my sight and look at my dad.

'Don't you cry, Sunshine.' He lays his hand over mine on his chest.

Someone unties Mark, who says, 'Ashley's locked in the basement.' He runs for the kitchen door. 'There are medical supplies there.'

Finley kneels at my side while Mark returns with a first-aid kit and pulls out bandages. He rolls Dad on his side and looks at the bullet wound on the back. Blood leaks from the exit wound onto the floor, like a thick overflow of displaced water from the ocean.

'Find your mother,' Dad says.

Mark falters with the bandages.

'I'm so sorry, Daddy,' I cry. 'Please don't leave me.'

273

## thirty-nine

### FINLEY

Mark gazes at Garvey and croaks, 'Where is she?'

'Somewhere here.' Garvey nods towards Rian's body on the ground opposite him. 'You need him for information.'

Mark takes OG's hand while Blake moves to the other side of the kitchen and rolls Rian onto his back. Blake pulls at his clothes and throws bandages on the shot Rian took to the shoulder.

'Tell her I'm sorry for every damn thing I did,' OG says.

Mark cuts open OG's shirt and treats him. I already know it's bad.

'He's losing too much blood,' Mark says.

'You did good, kiddo,' OG whispers to Erin, who's by his side. 'I'm so goddamn proud of you two.'

'Daddy, hold on,' Erin says. 'We can't do this without you.'

'You'll be okay, because you're a Garvey... and Garveys don't know... when to bloody... stop fight—'

Erin drops her head on his chest and screams. I swallow the tears choking my throat as the woman I love grieves for her father.

Blake closes his eyes and cries, and he rests his hands on Erin's shoulders, pulling her to her feet and into his embrace.

Mark breaks the spell of shock by assessing Rian's injuries. 'Finley, help me move him.'

'What the hell are you doing?' Erin asks between sobs.

Mark leaves Rian and takes Erin's hand. 'He's still alive, and he has information about Ash. I have to try, Erin. I have to.' He gets back to work.

Blake releases Erin and says to me, 'Do as you're told.' He joins Mark over the unconscious body of the man who murdered his father.

An hour passes before Blake appears upstairs for water and paracetamol. He doesn't look at anyone in the kitchen.

Erin's been pacing between the kitchen and the basement, waiting for information Rian apparently has about her mother.

I helped get Ashley upstairs, and although shaken, she wasn't harmed. She didn't recognise Garvey, who's still lying on the kitchen floor.

I try to urge Erin to leave the kitchen. 'You should go elsewhere. You can't do anything here.'

'I can't leave him yet. If I step out of this room, it'll be like I'm letting him go, and I'm not ready to do that. Mark joins us at the door. 'Where can he go?'

'We'll figure it out, but for now, we can stay right here, okay?'

She wipes away tears. 'It needs to be a cremation. We can't leave his body in the past.' Looking past me at Blake, she says, 'We can stop this from happening. We'll tell young Dylan to avoid the location you came through.'

Blake approaches us. 'Dad just saved your life. There's no way in hell Dylan can change that.'

Erin's chin quivers. 'He's important to the future.'

'No,' Blake says. 'You're important *to him*. To me and Mum.'

275

Erin looks him in the eye. 'She doesn't even love him anymore.' She places a hand over her mouth, holding in the sobs, and goes back to her father's dead body.

## forty

FINLEY

On the back steps, overlooking the sheds where all this started, Mark sits with his head in his hands.

'You guys have some life,' I say, joining him.

'That's not always a good thing. Do you know how many times I wished for this? To be living before the cullings, when we weren't running for our lives?'

'Be careful what you wish for.' I stretch my legs out. 'How are the other survivors in your group going to fare now that OG is—was—here?'

'The entire Garvey family is here now. You'd think that was a good thing, but we have too many people depending on us back home. A hundred people, maybe more, who aren't strong enough to defend themselves. Those left won't be able to hold everything together.' Mark shrugs. 'There are good years when hardly anyone dies. But sometimes the death rips through the camps like a cleansing—sickness or old-fashioned capture and kill.

'We have to bring everyone through. Erin and Ollie mentioned it as a possibility. This time portal is looking more and more like it's something that can be controlled, at least from the other end. We can keep going with the bunkers, and now that Blake is here, we can get more information on what happened after you guys fell through.'

I change the subject. 'You and Ashley? Didn't see that one coming.'

277

'Ashley is missing somewhere here in the past and doesn't have anyone now. Even though she and Dylan were over, he took care of her. She's the mother of his children. It's why I was never too worried. I missed her, but knowing that Blake and Garvey were still with her, I knew she'd be okay.'

'This is a weird position for me to be in. You're in love with my best friend's wife.'

'And you're in love with their daughter.' He sighs. 'You can't ever tell them about me. I posed as Erin's stepfather in 2019, but they have to live their life as normally as they can. If they know there's an expiration date on their relationship, it could drive them apart sooner than before.'

'You're just going to wait around for her?'

'No, I'm going to look for her and take care of her kids for her.'

I glance back at the house. 'You don't want to go in there and have the first twenty years you should've had together? Tell Dylan and Ashley about their eventual divorce and doomed relationship?'

Mark shakes his head. 'They weren't my years. They were hers, and I love her too damn much to take twenty great years away from her. I'm not an idiot. She loved Garvey when they were together. It was only the last few years they shouldn't have been. Regardless, she has to have her kids. They're the most important thing to her, more than Garvey or me.' He lets out a breath. 'I'm confident that when we meet, and the time is right and her marriage is over, we'll get together. Right now I'm worried about her being all alone somewhere.'

I leave Mark outside and go back into the house. I imagine the scene taking place in the basement, where Blake is sewing up Rian and cleaning out his wound.

We need the fucker alive, and without infection or a temperature to answer our questions.

I descend to the basement mini-hospital. Blake is washing his hands, apparently finished with the job.

Rian is stripped to the waist and lying on a trolley bed, hooked up to a machine monitoring his heart rate.

Mark shows up a few minutes later. 'Erin, wake him up, then go upstairs. Everyone else out.'

Blake flinches and even Erin is surprised. 'You're not questioning him on your own.'

Mark swiftly leads her to the door. 'This is the thing your dad loved the best about me: my ability to do what needs to be done. I won't have you think any less of me for it.'

Blake yanks Mark's arm off Erin. 'We can't trust anything this guy says. He tried to kill you and he *did* kill our dad.' Blake shakes his head. 'We need to get rid of him.'

'Let's see what Mark can get from him.' Erin makes for the door. 'You heard him. Everyone out.' She turns around and walks up the steps, the metal of the stairs rattling off the concrete flooring as she moves.

# Chapter

## forty-one

### Erin

I feel numb. I have a hollow hole in my chest, and my throat is closing over, but I still can't *feel*. My dad was everything to everyone in the future, and he just held up his hands and gave up for the feint chance Rian would take his gun off my head.

It's not a worthy way to die. He should've been saving the world, not saving me.

Ollie, JT, and Lara made it back to the farmhouse. Lara and Blake finally had their reunion. They got each other back. It should be a happy day, but instead they held each other and cried. I felt nothing watching them.

Blake's been with me on the patio for the evening. We watched the day turn dark, and the night-time wind has picked up. Finley and Lara hover nearby, bringing us water and food while Mark tortures information out of the man who killed our father.

The night is pitch dark, given the lack of streetlights here in the countryside. There's only the outside light attached to the back wall of the house to illuminate us in the garden.

Ollie clears his throat as he approaches, and when I look around, I realise Finley is sitting next to me, and Lara and Blake are in seats across the wicker table.

'There are things I've been working on today,' Ollie says. 'I swiped Rian's computer and a box of things from his house. Lara's got layered access into Rian's computer, and it looks like he's leaving information for his superiors in the future in multiple places.'

Lara says, 'Leaving secret codes for them to find later on, in places that he knows are controlled by NewGov in the future—social media, police records, bank files. It's like a technology time capsule. I'm bummed we had the same idea, but a psychopath figured it out, and we didn't.'

Mark appears at the back door, leaning on the frame of the house.

'Well?' Ollie asks.

Blake stands before Mark can speak. 'Does it matter? We have to get moving, go somewhere else. This place is too well known.'

Ollie persists. 'Mark, what did you get from Rian?'

He doesn't answer. Blake pulls Lara to her feet. 'We need to regroup somewhere else.'

'Mark?' I ask.

'I can tell when people are lying. I believe what he told me.'

'What did he tell you?' I say.

Mark averts his eyes. 'One of our own made a deal with NewGov in the future. Gave us all up for citizenship in London.'

Blake exhales next to me, and I walk to the end of the patio and scream.

# forty-two

## Erin

Mark's on a break from the basement. He stubs his cigarette out on the porch step. 'There's a problem with Finley.'

'You don't like him, do you? I get it, but I can't deal with this anti-pep talk right now.'

'That's not what it is. I see how you're falling in love, and he'll look after you.'

I chuckle. 'That's not a bad thing.'

'Sometimes it is. He's like your dad. Too damn stubborn and too in love to know when to quit when it's best to let someone go and save himself, save everyone else.'

I squeeze Mark's arm. 'Garvey never made your life difficult to be mean.'

Mark purses his lips. 'It was a tough situation to be in.' He wants to say more, to say it was my dad's own damn fault for pushing my mum away, for screwing up his relationship.

'She loves you. I know it's hard, seeing Dylan and Ashley fall in love in this time. They're perfect for each other, apart from the fact that in twenty years, they won't be married to each other.'

'I love her, and when you love someone, you let them live the life they want.' He kicks at the steps, then leans over and places a quick kiss on my head. 'You and Blake mean more to her than anything in the whole world. Ain't no damn way I'm getting in the way of her being a mother to you two.'

I swallow back the tears, but when I speak, my voice is broken, and I can't control the flow. 'My dad died because of me. If he'd just let me go, let me die here, it'd be better.'

Mark places his hands on my arms. 'If the roles were reversed, you would've done everything in your power to save him and Blake. Don't forget that, because Blake's going to need it. I'm damn glad I'm here with you. I only hope your mother knows I'm with you. Maybe then she can relax a little, 'cause she knows I'll look after you just like you're my own.'

Ever since he married my mother, that's exactly what he's done. Protect any heartache that might have caused my mum if I'd been harmed. And here he is, forty years old, watching the love of his life fall in love with someone else. Damn.

'Finley and I have to leave.'

'Is that what you want?'

'I don't want to split up the unit, but I have to be with him. I never realised how much until today. Everything's fallen apart, and my dad is dead.' I swallow. 'I don't want to lose him, too. I think I love him?'

I look at Mark like he's going to tell me if I do or not.

Mark draws me into a hug and I let him hold me. 'If the timeline keeps accelerating, as Ollie expects it to, Ashley will be pregnant soon. Maybe neither of us should stick around for that. Finley wants to move his family and Cameron's, and prepare for the future.' Mark sits on the bottom step of the deck. 'When we were in Scotland, I followed him to Glasgow. He visited Cameron's family, and I listened with Ollie's extended microphone thingy—'

'Mark,' I scold. 'We don't bug our own people.'

'Finley isn't one of us. Not yet, anyway. I wanted to make sure he wasn't going to say more that he should.'

'Why didn't you tell me sooner?'

'After we got back, so much stuff started happening, it didn't seem important.'

'He passed your little confidentiality test?'

Mark nods. 'He's started something I didn't see coming. From what I heard, Cameron's mum has cancer and his sister is trying to hold the family together while Cameron is away. Finley helped with errands and chores and had dinner with them. They seem close. He dropped the idea about retiring early and living off-grid, maybe moving to an island for a quieter life. He said he and Cameron could fund the move and purchase everything they need.'

'He's trying to relocate his family before the takeovers start.'

'He did save them.'

'What do you mean?'

'Cameron's sister is Heather Swan.'

'*Our* Heather?' I remember our conversation at the lake about Dylan crashing with his family. 'What the hell does this mean?'

'It means that maybe Cameron and Finley aren't dead in the future after all.'

## forty-three

### FINLEY

Mark and Erin have spent most of the night and morning in the command room, discussing a plan the rest of us are excluded from. Everyone is nervous about a traitor being so embedded in the rebel family, especially Blake, who doesn't know any of the people in 2019.

By midmorning, Erin calls me off the watch on Rian's hospital room, trading me out for JT, and asks me to meet them in the dining room.

Lara and Blake have made everyone sandwiches, and I fill the biggest plate I can find and take it to Erin and Mark. I sit next to Erin and move my chair closer to her, wrapping my arm over her shoulder as she eats the first food since her dad died.

'The world's still ending, Finley,' she says between mouthfuls. 'Ollie has a theory about our original time line speeding up, and we might not have as long as we originally thought.'

'What does that mean?'

'Everyone outside of London is going to die.'

I freeze. I knew this was coming, but I thought we'd have enough time to stop it. 'My family and friends are in Scotland. How many of them are going to survive?'

Erin looks at me with sadness. 'A handful, if they're lucky.'

'My family can't fight, Erin. They're not like you. Cameron's mum is sick. She needs doctors and supplies.'

'We know, and we want to help. There are lots of smaller off-grid villages and islands that aren't hooked up to the main water supply. If we get your people off the mainland, they might have a chance to survive the first wave.'

'And the next wave, when people turn on their neighbours and fight for supplies? How will they fare then?'

'We'll keep them safe. Dylan already saved your families. That's why we spent so much time in Scotland when we were growing up. Although they lived on a small island, I never realised it must have been your families,' she says.

'The Isle of Gigha was the first place we sank a bunker. No one knows about it apart from the four of us who were here first. The Apostle soldier who destroys our plan in the future never went near the islands. Gigha has a handful of houses and is still standing in the future. It's not always safe, but it's one place we've always been able to hide and hop from one island to another when things get risky. After Dylan added security and helped his people learn how to fight, we kept moving and only checked in on them a few times.'

'But you think they're our families, mine and Cameron's, in the future?'

'They are,' Mark says. 'Dylan spent a lot of time and resources helping Scotland.' Mark leans forward as he speaks to me across the table. 'And Heather Swan just so happens to be my best friend.'

'You're friends with Cameron's sister?'

'Not yet,' he says. 'We can't save the entire world, and I'm sorry if that seems callous. We'll help as many as we can. Your families are at the top of the list.'

'This move needs to happen now, not later,' Erin says. 'Try not to get emotionally involved. Billions of people will die. I'm assigning JT and you to the Scottish islands with Eleda and Nivek. Your next job is to move your family and friends, and as many others as you can, out there, without giving anything away.'

'You're shipping me off after all?'

Erin smiles tightly. 'There are more important things than a happy ever after, right?'

'And where are you going to be?'

'I'll be here, working on Rian. Psychological warfare.'

'Garvey said we need Rian,' Mark tells me. 'We're going to fuck with his head so badly, he'll have no idea what's right and wrong. We're going to flip him and have a commanding officer in the future that's ours.'

'But that's Plan B,' I tell him.

'What's Plan A?' Finley asks.

'We're going to save the fucking world.'

## THANK YOU FOR READING TIME GLITCH

I really hope you enjoyed the first book in the series and follow along the rest of the gang's journey!

Don't forget to leave a review on your platform of choice. It really does help out readers and Indie authors alike.

If you're not already following me on social media:

www.facebook.com/bronamillsauthor

www.instagram.com/bronamillsauthor

or join up my readers group on facebook: Brona Mills Finding Time for Everything

If you want to keep up to date on news, blogs and releases, head on over to my website bronamills.com and sign up to my newsletter.

# OTHER BOOKS BY THE AUTHOR

## TIME FOR INFINITY SERIES: